Jack the Ripp

Key to Map (

1. **Martha Tabram – George Yard**
In the early hours of Tuesday August ..e 7th Martha was found on
t… High
S… as
d…

2. M…
T… body
w… d no
st… was
sc…

3. A…
C… the
b… ns.
S… e
p…

4. E…
A… ody
w… cut
a… had
b…

5. C…
F… Mitre
s…
b…
M… of

6. M…
Ma…
No…
door and was so savage that fortunately its' like is still very rare indeed

A SECRET STEP

A SECRET STEP

COLLECTOR'S EDITION

Ian Parson

COPPERJOB PUBLISHING

Published in 2013 by Copperjob Ltd

A catalogue record for this book is available from the British Library

ISBN 978-0-9546013-4-8

www.asecretstep.co.uk

Printed and Bound in Great Britain by
CPI Group (UK) CR0 4YY

About the Author

Ian Parson, the author of 'A Secret Step', is a working, qualified horticulturalist, a Member of the Institute of Horticulture and passionate about his work. He prefers to think of himself as a gardener and whilst 'gardening' prepares his thoughts for his other lifetime passion of writing. He has written numerous articles and been published many times in a variety of magazines both in the UK and abroad.

Like many, Ian has a keen interest in Jack the Ripper and the politics of those times. In pursuit of this, Ian is a member of The Whitechapel Society. He attends the East End of London based bi-monthly meetings and regularly contributes to the Society's magazine.

Ian also has a keen interest in the 1940/41 Blitz of the East End of London and is particularly interested in the social history & culture of Victorian/Edwardian life in the East End. He currently divides his time between the South West & London.

These combined interests have led to the writing of 'A Secret Step'. A story based on the facts and events of the times experienced in the East End of London, accompanied by some of the human stories that occurred alongside them.

About the Book

The novel 'A Secret Step' is set in the East End of London and has a feel and backdrop similar to the recent popular TV series 'Ripper Street' and 'Call the Midwife'.

It encompasses the iconic Jack the Ripper times in 1888 and the East End Blitz of 1940. The fact that they are only 50 years apart means some lifetimes will have spanned both eras and the author has used this rarely considered link.

In both of these times, a child born and growing up in the East End of London only ever had two chances, live best you can or die from malnutrition, disease or violence.

This story is told by a character that lived through both times. The life our character was subjected to and what he witnessed around him had lasting effects on his character and his life.

From the horror of murder in Victorian times to the courageous antics of the Dead End kids during the Blitz, if you lived in London's East End your first lesson in life was nobody made it on their own!

About the Story

In 1888 Percy Miller was ten years old, growing up in the slums of Whitechapel, in the East End of London. It was also the year that Jack the Ripper was wreaking havoc in the area. Percy got caught up in the shocking events and ended up traumatised by the murders in a time before 'trauma' had been invented. He lived but could never tell the tale. It was no surprise to anyone that he ended up settling into the life of a career criminal.

It was another fifty years before the East End saw violence on a scale to eclipse the Whitechapel Murders of 1888 and once again Percy was right in the thick of it.

The Blitz of London was truly a terrifying thing to live through. Percy, against all the odds, was now a grandfather of one. Billy Miller, Percy's grandson was ten years old when the Blitz began in September 1940. To Billy the air raids were times of excitement and adventure. Without adult supervision Billy and his friends were free to roam as the bombs rained down. Their criminal instincts were not easy to shake off until Billy turned one daring rescue into a game.

Publisher Comments

Ian signed the Author/Publisher contract at Greenway, Devon, holiday home of Agatha Christie, now looked after for us all by the National Trust.

'A Secret Step' will be launched in London on the 7th August 2013 at The White Hart pub, Whitechapel High Street. This is the 125th anniversary of the first suspected victim of 'Jack the Ripper', a Martha Tabram, who was murdered within yards of this popular public house.

With Ian's horticultural background, it was inevitable that he would feature plants on the book cover. Both featured plants have the ability to colonise bomb sites or burned out & derelict spaces. Each plant is particularly relevant to the East End.

One is Rosebay Willow Herb *(Chamerion angustifolium)* which is otherwise known as Fireweed. It was voted the county Flower of London in 2002. There are many stories of people using the young shoots to mix with other greens to supplement their wartime rationed diet! The mature stems are full of vitamin C and pro-vitamin A, so were picked, peeled and eaten raw. The roots can also be roasted but may taste bitter.

The other, London Pride *(Saxifraga x urbium)*, a garden escape, was chosen as it represents the pride and resilience shown by the people of London in their determination not to be beaten by the Blitz. Indeed, Noël Coward's song of 1941 celebrates both the flower and the City.

COPPERJOB PUBLISHING

Foreword

"The common thief is not distinguished for manual dexterity and accomplishment, like the pickpocket or mobman, nor for courage, ingenuity and skill, like the burglar, but is characterised by low cunning and stealth and hence he is termed the sneak and is despised by the higher classes of thieves"

So wrote Henry Mayhew in his classic study of impoverished London, 'London Labour and the London Poor.'

Ian Parson's novel 'A Secret Step' is a tour-de-force of East London's underclass between 1888 and 1941, and the blighted, twisted lives its characters live.

It is a work in which the main character grows up in a hellish environment and becomes firstly an apprentice mobsman and then a fully fledged one on entering adulthood. In the era of the 1960s he would have been enrolled as a 'face' in the Kray firm.

He is an individual fashioned by the poverty which sears across every page of Ian's book. And lurking in the shadows of this purblind landscape is the East End's criminal of criminals, Jack the Ripper!

Ian strips away the obscene glamour which has built up around this degraded creature and portrays him as the sort of man he undoubtedly was, a low grade criminal who fits Mayhew's criteria as a 'sneak', the underclass of the underclass.

We have to wait until the end of the novel to see him get his just deserts but it is a journey worth making and leaves us with a feeling of satisfaction, the more so because it gives Ian's main character the opportunity to make amends for his own sins.

Enjoy your read

Bill Beadle - Jack the Ripper Author and Vice President of The Whitechapel Society

Acknowledgements

Thanks are due to the following members of
The Whitechapel Society:

Bill Beadle
Sue Parry
Frogg Moody
Liza Hopkinson

As well as thanks to the following people for their assistance:

Janet Farrage – Editor
Simon (Sibs) Sibley – Cover Design & Artwork
Malcolm McGregor – Honorary President The Saxifrage Society
The staff & volunteers at Greenway House – The National Trust

To dead-end kids everywhere

Chapter One

August 1888

I GREW up in the East End. To explain further would be futile, a waste of words. Men, women and children from all corners of the globe know exactly where the East End is, in which country it can be found, which city it is a part of, but none knew it as I knew it.

Back then I lived with my family in a single, musty room just off Commercial Street. We were lucky, we had a room.

I remember that long summer of 1888 very well. August 7th had been my tenth birthday and I had woken early, full of excitement. I had slipped out onto the street before anyone else stirred, expecting great things of the new day. Hoping to find some birthday cheer, hoping for a day to look back on and savour. Unfortunately, the words on everyone's lips were not the greetings I had been hoping for that morning. Not 'Happy Birthday' but an entirely different phrase, a phrase that would turn up the heat in our crowded little corner of London to another level.

'There's been another murder,' was the phrase.

Chapter Two

4pm 7th September 1940

DURING those early years of my life I had been raised on horror stories. Blood soaked tales that were a remarkably accurate reflection of the world I knew. A world where young and old would search side by side through market garbage, thrusting their hands into mounds of rotting fruit or fighting over rancid meat. Desperately seeking nourishment to drip down parched throats into empty, rattling stomachs. It was a cruel world where innocent babies died of hunger and were left to rot where they lay, while families carried on with the crushing struggle around them.

Where old folk made weak by the daily grind, succumbed to infected sores caused by the filth they lived in and the official reports called it 'self-neglect', conveniently sidestepping any obligation to improve our lot. After cold nights, the dead would be found on the streets where they had been forced to lay their heads, finally succumbing to the sleep that never ends.

This was very much life as I knew it, unless you worked for the mob of course, we never went hungry or died alone. We watched each other's backs and went into battle on full stomachs. Of course there were still accidents and injuries and it was true that guns and knives could be pulled out for the slightest of reasons. When they were, it invariably ended badly for somebody, but as I said, casual violence was a daily occurrence for as far back as I could remember.

Personally, I found myself more attracted to organised violence. I loved being part of a baying crowd as two hard men ripped lumps out of each other and I was in my element when reputation enhancing mob battles were arranged. Huge affairs, on a grand scale involving hundreds of participants that took place in Victoria or Regent's Park. Always a wide range of multiple injuries on both sides. Then at the age of ten, I saw things that have haunted me for over 50 years and will surely haunt me to my grave.

I truly thought if anyone knew, then I knew, the very worst depths that mankind was capable of sinking to. However, as I now cowered underground with my ten-year-old grandson, listening to Hitler's bombs pounding London above us, I questioned that sentiment, for the first time in years. I was rapidly realising that as far as 'organised violence' was concerned, we knew nothing. We were less than children playing games compared with this.

"Pops, Pops, I'm scared."

A frightened voice broke my train of thought and I shook off the childhood memories. Disguising my own fear as best I could I forced a smile as I answered.

"Don't be scared little fella, we're safe down 'ere. Those bombers ain't gonna do us just yet." I mustered the bravest smile circumstances would allow.

"You sure?" He looked up at me doubtfully then asked in a frightened voice, "Is it just us Pops? Are the nobs getting bombed up West, Pops?"

"Course it ain't just us!" I grinned more broadly and playfully shook his tiny shoulders. As I moved, a screaming bomb crashed to earth somewhere close by. Thick clouds of dust whooshed downwards from the ceiling and squeaking rodents scurried about in the shadows. Even they were in a panic tonight. So agitated they didn't even care about the noisy humans who had invaded their underground lair.

"Why is there a war, Pops?" he looked up at me, it was a genuine question.

"Because they're idiots," I told him, "but don't worry, we're safe down 'ere."

"I don't feel safe," declared Billy in a trembling voice, clinging to me as tightly as his skinny little arms would allow. I looked down at him. He shouldn't even be here, he should be in the countryside with all the others, but he had refused to go and I'd been too weak to insist.

"Oi! None o' that now, you're a Miller an' us Millers stay calm under fire," I ruffled his matted hair, "that's the truth son, innit?"

He looked up at me trying to instil bravery into his gaze and I thought my heart would burst into a thousand pieces. I had held such hopes for him but here he was in danger for his very life. Some would say I had failed him, but it wasn't just tonight. Danger was an everyday occurrence for him. He spent every waking moment in danger, so I suppose I had failed him. I, however, could not be held responsible for putting him through this.

"Listen to it, son." The boy was straining himself for the deadly whine of falling bombs anyway, so I wasn't making him feel any worse. "Listen to that. It's only a few bombs boy.

"When we get up top, I bet you 'ardly even notice the damage. The Docks will still be there good as new, all that timber from Africa still lined up on the quay." I didn't mention that the plan to steal the timber was off, he had probably worked that one out for himself. "The dome of St. Paul's, the Union Flag flying atop of Big Ben, Westminster Palace, Buck 'ouse, our courtyard, they'll all still be there in the mornin'. It's just a few German bombers, for a few hours. You can 'andle that can't ya?"

I lent in closer and whispered in his ear, "I bet you've been on more scary capers than this, eh?" He tried to force a smile to his face, so at least he was listening to me. I continued talking, "You're a Miller don't forget. Strong under fire, don't forget. Am I right boy? Billy?" I turned his chin slightly, forcing him to look me in the eye. "Right, Billy?" I looked at him sternly now, willing him to believe that everything was going to turn out for the best, as another bomb exploded above our heads and the rats were sent into another blind panic. "So don't worry about it," I raised my voice slightly in mock annoyance, "an' stop strainin' your bleeding ears for bombs. If one's gonna land close to ya, you'll know 'bout it soon enough."

I squeezed the lad tightly. He was such a know-it-all normally, I'd sometimes forget how young he was, but I treasured the fact that tonight I offered some kind of reassurance. Even if it was just to a ten-year-old kid with nobody better to turn to than me. Poor little sod, I was his best chance in life. He was doomed before he'd even begun.

It was as much as I could do to stop the shaking, but tonight I had to be brave. Who would have thought it? Old Hitler starts bombing London and, all of a sudden, for the first time in years, I've got responsibilities. Still the boy had been looking after me, more or less for years now and he rarely asked me to do anything in return. So I guess I owed him one brief night of comfort. I was an old, burned-out alcoholic and for the first time since I could remember, somebody needed me. We clung to each other tightly, utterly powerless as London burned furiously above our heads.

'Poor little fella,' I thought. It wasn't certain, was doubtful even, that he would live to see his next birthday, yet I still thought he was better off than I was at the same age. He might well have to live with terrible sights but he would never have to live with the type of secret I carried around.

I hugged my grandson, my only surviving relative and listened to the Germans droning and buzzing through the skies. I dreaded to think what horrors awaited us when we finally got to venture above ground again. Bloody hell, it sounds absolutely terrible out there, I swear I can hear planes screaming not fifty feet above my head. I guessed some of them must be our boys but it really sounded as though Hitler's Luftwaffe had come to finish us all off. Come to demolish every building in London, bury every secret under tons and tons of rubble that should have been houses full of people.

On another day I would have laughed at the irony of my situation. I have wanted the slums gone all my bleeding life and now, after all that, they were going to be blown up by the Germans. Why was I thinking about that now? It never ceased to amaze me how the human mind worked. Ha, don't kid yourself. I was desperately trying to think about anything as long as it wasn't that rainy night. I could have gone to sea like some of the other boys after all, seen a bit of the world. Come back with a bit o' money in me pocket like some of 'em did. But no. Oh no, not ol' Percy! I stayed in the court, running errands for Mickey Tippings. Then fretted and worried away in Stoke Newington prison for 20 years, terrified. Constantly worried that my secret would be discovered, my stash would be found, ironic that it wasn't even my stuff I was so worried about. Sometimes I thought it was the space itself that I wanted so desperately to preserve.

I remember when I had been released from prison, that scuffed old floorboard had been the first thing I had checked on.

I felt Billy sinking deeper into my arms, the movement dragging me back into the present. His breathing grew louder; incredibly amongst all this noise and turmoil he had actually fallen asleep. Children were so resilient. I hugged him tightly for the first time since I could remember and my mind drifted, as it always did, back to my childhood, back to the last time the East End had been in turmoil as severely as this.

Chapter Three

OUR single room off Commercial Street was where I lived with my Ma, my Pa, when he was home, my two brothers, Davie and Adam and my baby sister, Emma. Back then I didn't know we were poor.

Life in the court for the first few years was, as far as I was concerned, one long holiday. There was always a fire burning in an old oil drum surrounded by well-dressed men who would give me treats and rides on their shoulders or throw me up in the air. In three of the rooms our neighbours were women who all spoilt me rotten and would not hear a cross word said to me. There was always one of them on hand whenever I scraped my knees or fell off something or into something. Then they would clean me up and tell me how brave and strong I was. Tell me what a handsome little man I was and how much they all loved me. The court was my playground and I could not have been happier.

I didn't know I lived amongst whores and thieves. That the men were East End mobsters and this was their clubhouse. I didn't know we only had the room because my Pa was in the gang or that Pa was really in prison when they said he was at sea.

I was far too young to realise that the three women, our neighbours, were selling tricks and using their rooms as brothels, or that Nannie Johns was the madam who kept an eye on the girls. I was young enough to be blissfully unaware that the corner room, the boring room, was where the men planned their crimes, hid their stash, even tortured their enemies from time to time.

By the time I was six I knew all of those things and more. However, one of the most important lessons was that men with drink inside them could turn ugly. My brother told me it was the same everywhere, so we simply learnt to keep out of their way. Then I was seven and things changed again.

One night I was suddenly woken by the bloodcurdling sound of my

Ma wailing and screaming. She had woken the whole courtyard but I had lain still, frozen with fear, suddenly feeling very much like the child I was. I remember shaking, squeezing up next to my brother. We were both clutching the ragged blanket tightly about our ears, desperately trying to block out the terrible sounds she was making. Then we had heard heavy footsteps approach. We held our breath and lay motionless as they came right up to the door. I couldn't bear it, I had to know who was coming. I had opened my eyes and seen the door start to creak open. Seen a floorboard lift slightly then lower itself as the door slowly opened. I was sure it was someone terrible, the police perhaps, come to kill us, I struggled to fight back tears that felt about to burst forth.

"Davie! Percy! Kids! Come quick."

It was Nannie Johns.

Something about the urgency in Nannie's voice had us leaping to our feet. We followed her out the door and hurriedly crossed the moonlit yard to her room.

Almost as soon as we had shut the door behind us loud voices filled the courtyard again, men this time. Big menacing shadows were bouncing off the walls. More torches were coming down the narrow passage into the court. Nannie shoved me hard in the small of my back, "Away from the window, hurry up, get out of sight!"

I was scared, confused, I meekly followed her orders. I glanced across and caught Davie's eye, he smiled nervously. We were used to disturbances at night but we could sense that this was something out of the ordinary. With no time to spare Nannie pushed us farther away from the door. "Sssssh," she kept whispering unnecessarily as men's voices and heavy footsteps seemed to come close then fade away before coming near again. Shouts boomed out again and again from all sides of the yard. I heard something being smashed up but I dared not try and see what was happening.

I lay awake listening to the sounds of men shouting and fighting and smashing things and voices demanding to know where our Pa was. Shortly after dawn it went silent, still I lay awake, my child's mind turning over and over what I had heard. Then my baby sister Emma deemed it safe and began calling out for her Ma. I shot her a glance, she knew immediately she was to be silent a while longer.

The night wore on and I watched the dawn cast shadows across the walls and realised none of us had slept more than a handful of moments.

Finally, Emma climbed onto Nannie's lap and her eyes closed almost immediately. Nannie, her face more wrinkled and lined than usual, announced that she was going to have a nap in the chair. She told us to close our eyes and be quiet and as the night's events had been so traumatic, we actually obeyed her. I awoke to the creak of the door opening and through tired eyes I saw our Ma fill the doorframe. Her eyes were red and swollen and she was fidgety, wouldn't stand still. She wouldn't hold our questioning looks, kept whispering to Nannie in the corner of the room. I had seen her walk in the door and assumed things would start to get better now. I was wrong. She was behaving strangely indeed and it was, if anything, making us even more worried. At one point she crouched down and gathered us around her. She looked as though she might be about to say something; reveal some dreadful secret, when once again the door was suddenly pushed open. Nobody had knocked and the unexpected interruption ensured Ma held her tongue. Then stepping through the door into the gloom dressed in a black suit and a matching black trilby was Mickey Tippings himself. He stood in the doorway, not quite entering the room fully, just stood there for a few moments taking us all in, slowly, one at a time. Then he motioned towards me with a slight tip of his head.

"You boy, follow me," and with that he turned on his heel and headed back outside.

I looked around the room for reassurance and saw Nannie motioning with her arms,

"Go on Percy, don't keep him waitin'," she half whispered.

I followed him through the door and through half-closed eyes glanced around the familiar courtyard. Everything seemed normal, as though last night had never happened, quiet but normal. Mickey was strolling over to the oil drum, his hands thrust deeply into his pockets, clearly expecting me to follow. So I walked across the space acutely aware that the usually bustling area was disturbingly quiet.

As I got within a few yards of him he finally looked up at me. He shuffled a few paces to his left and I moved towards the place at his right shoulder.

I stood there shivering despite the warm flames, looking up in awe at the smartly dressed man beside me.

Finally he turned to face me, he smiled and I felt somehow better, safer.

"Bit of a night, wasn't it?" he said, shaking his head in despair.

I nodded in reply and stood there shivering.

"What did you see?" he asked.

And I shrugged my shoulders.

"What did you hear?" he asked and I shrugged again.

For a while now Mickey had been taking me to one side for this sort of questioning and he knew only too well that I always told him everything I knew.

"Anything you do remember?" he said after rather a pause.

"I found a hidin' place," I ventured.

He crouched down at this revelation, so we were eye-to-eye and I had no option but to meet his steady reassuring gaze.

"Why didn't you hide then?" he asked with, what seemed like, genuine interest.

I was confused, momentarily disorientated by the question. I looked at him, not really understanding, but wanting to say the right thing.

"No, a small space, for stuff, you know."

"Oh I see! A small space, for stuff," he repeated. "What sort of stuff?"

"I don't know, small stuff," I shrugged and my eyes returned to my feet.

"Let's go over there then, see if I can find it shall we?" Mickey rose back up to his full height.

I shrugged again and when he walked towards our room I followed.

We stepped inside and immediately it struck me how cold the room seemed. Not that it was ever warm, but it seemed somehow empty, neglected already.

Mickey let the door close behind us, then he asked me, "Was there anything in this hiding place?"

"I dunno," I replied honestly.

He glanced across at me.

"Alright, let's see if I can find it, shall we?"

I stood quietly whilst he systematically covered every inch of the room without success.

I waited patiently, watching as he ran his hands over the walls and tapped on floorboards and finally stood in the centre of the room with his hands on his hips, an amused smile on his face and a large cobweb stuck to his left shoulder. He pulled out a silver cigarette box and flicked one of the filter tips into his mouth. Looking right at me, still half smiling, he spoke around the cigarette, "Here!" He lobbed the silver case up in an arc and I snatched it from the air as it came close.

He smiled as I did so. "Hide that while I go for a smoke."

I waited until the door closed fully behind him, then alone in the room I stepped on the loose floorboard and using the tips of my fingers managed to create a gap and force it away from its position. I felt behind it to make sure the cigarette case wouldn't disappear into some unseen hole. My fingers poked around thoroughly but made contact with the back of the front step and the dusty soil and nothing else. There was no hole. It was as I suspected, a cavity created by the shoddy workmanship of the step. It was a dry, dark gap running the length of the front step. I slid Mickey's silver case in and strolled out into the yard. Already I was feeling better, the fear of the previous night already beginning to wear off.

I spotted Mickey back by the oil drum smoking and laughing with Bertie and some of his other men as though nothing had happened. I adjusted my bearings and headed across towards them but before I got there, when I was within earshot Mickey called to me,

"Get back over there," he motioned towards Nannie's room with his head, "an' I'll see you about that thing later."

I flicked my head in a brief signal of comprehension and readjusted my path, as instructed, towards Nannie's.

Her room was still silent and it stayed that way as the day slowly dragged itself towards evening. Davie and Adam had made good their escape shortly after I had gone with Mickey, and Emma was still asleep on Nannie's lap. I sat quietly as time seemed to do its utmost to stand still for me. It was a feeling of pure release when finally my brothers returned and Nannie gathered us all at her feet and announced bluntly that Pa was dead and wouldn't be coming back. We sat there dumbfounded, Emma started to cry. We were all so shocked by her words that our sister's tears barely registered. That was how she put it, 'He was dead and he wouldn't be coming back'. It always struck me as odd that the 'won't be coming back' bit had been deemed necessary.

Life for me changed from that day and was never the same again.

The following morning Mickey called me to him, "Good hidin' place that is, does anyone else know about it?"

I shook my head in the negative.

He laughed unexpectedly, "Well I couldn't find it. So let's leave the case there an' I'll let you know when I want it back, alright?"

I nodded again and he dismissed me with a smile.

Not long after, I was taken out on a cart and told to climb up a drainpipe and through a tiny vent. Then make my way on hands and knees along a dusty, dark tunnel until I reached a wooden door. I was to open the huge, heavy wooden door from the inside. I was good at climbing and tunnelling; I had no problem there but the men had threatened me. Told me what they would do to me if I wasn't opening that door as quick as was possible. It was confusing. I was more than willing to do what they asked. Why shouldn't I? They were my friends. So why had the threats been necessary? I had never been threatened like that before.

I asked Mickey about it and he frowned and mumbled that I should let him know if it happened again. It never happened again, but I learnt an important lesson from the episode. That people can change when you least expect them to, when you least want them to.

Soon I was out most nights using my well-honed climbing skills to gain access to some small entrance for them. On more mundane occasions, standing on street corners watching out for the law or causing a distraction for one reason or another. I didn't mind, it was right that I paid my way and the fact that they needed me made me feel like I was becoming a man.

Around this time Ma started drinking more and more and staying out later and later. Then she started bringing strange men back to the room and we kids were sent out to roam the streets, with strict instructions not to return to the court until morning. My two older brothers started hanging out with their friends up Liverpool Street station, leaving me to look after Emma. Sometimes I would guide her through the busy streets and we would go up to Liverpool Street station ourselves. We would sit by the warm vents where we knew the police would leave us alone when we fell asleep. Occasionally, we would spot our brothers but they would always ignore our greetings and after a while we stopped calling their names when they ran past with their boys.

That winter I heard that Adam had died.

I heard the story third hand from the daughter of the grocer in Artillery Passage. She stopped me one morning and managed to provide me with the details before her mother hurried her away from my side. They had, she said, been robbing a warehouse down at St. Katharine Docks when some watchman had spotted them and started blowing his whistle. That would be sure to bring every Bobby in the docks running so they had legged it across the roof. Unfortunately Adam had slipped on a patch of moss and gone tumbling over the side. He had never been registered with the authorities, none of us had. So Davie and the gang had just left him there for the police to find. They would know who he was but they would never be able to prove it. The authorities would have to bury him in a pauper's grave. He stopped being our responsibility the second he slipped off the roof. Years later they learnt how to identify individual people just from the marks of their fingertips. I thought about Adam when I learnt that. The night of Adam's death Davie disappeared. Sometime later I heard he was hanging around in Soho, but I never heard exactly what he was doing there and I never saw him again.

Sometimes, large groups of ladies would gather at Liverpool Street train terminus. They would chant and sing and wave their banners. Then they would smile at Emma and me as we pushed ourselves as far back as we could under the air vents. Other times, when there were a lot of them, they marched right down the middle of Bishopsgate, causing all the carts and buggies to wait in big queues. Emma and I would run down the stationary line of vehicles begging for change and kicking their horses when the drivers or passengers refused to pay up. It was an easy way to get money because we only had to spook one horse and the other drivers would all find some change they could spare. The ladies with the banners saw what we were doing but they seemed to think it was funny. They would point at the nobs in their carriages and laugh at them. "You can't escape the little people now, can you?" they would taunt.

Ma was now drunk practically all the time. Emma and I preferred to sleep at Nannie's when we slept in the court. We had stopped going to the train terminus because the police kept moving us on. For some reason they wouldn't let us sleep by the vents any more. So when Nannie wouldn't have us I would take Emma down to the docks and we would sleep under the solid oak wharfs, whilst above us men worked noisily all through the night. The wood was so thick and solid that I always felt safe. I felt sure nothing on earth would be able to get at us through such sturdy lumps of timber.

With all the noise of the dockers above and the river traffic alongside we would never sleep well and sometimes we would have to share the space with other kids or deserters from the navy. One time however we saw an owl and another time I thought I saw a fox scavenging on the shore line but when I mentioned it to Nannie she scoffed and loudly declared, "You won't never see no fox in London, they're countryside animals. Owls, yes maybe, 'cos they got wings, but foxes, in London, I don't think so!"

Emma and I would normally head home to the court after the workers had taken their morning snack. It was always worth hanging around until then because often they would give us bits of food. After the loud klaxon sounded the 'back to work' and the men returned to the docks we would make our way home to the court in silence, dreading what we might find there. When we arrived I would peek through the window in silence. Ma would normally be asleep, spread right across the bed. When she was, Emma and I could find our own food and go wherever we thought best.

On one particular morning something was amiss. As we approached the alley leading to our court I could see three policemen standing by the entrance. I grabbed Emma's hand and held her tightly, just in case I judged it safest to walk right past and I didn't want her giving away where we were really heading. I slowed down as much as I dared and scanned both sides of the street. Scattered amongst the crowds I spotted brief glimpses of uniform. There were Bobbies all over the place. I had no time to think, I was almost on top of them so quickly. It was all happening so fast. There hadn't been time to warn Emma what was going on or what I was about to do. I had assumed that she was already alert, had noticed the police herself and realised there might be danger. At the very least, the way I had grabbed her should have got her attention but she had been busily skipping a new dance that was the latest craze amongst her friends, concentrating on the steps. She hadn't been paying attention, thought I was squeezing her hand tight because she was wriggling, because she was dancing. When we drew level with the alley she darted from my grip and ran down it. Before I could do anything a big bear of a policeman had grabbed her.

"Where are you off to, missy?" I had heard him say as he whisked her off her feet.

I had no choice but to keep walking, otherwise they would have grabbed me as well and I knew what would happen then. It would be Barnado's home down Bower Street or the workhouse for me, I couldn't take that chance. I was full of regrets over her then and I was full of regrets now. I had not known what to do. I had walked past the court all day on both sides of the street, coming at it from a variety of directions but the police had stayed put into the night. In the end I couldn't risk another pass in case they got suspicious, so I had gone back to the docks. Four days I had stayed away and when I returned everything was different. I had gone to Nannie's and lay on the floor. My eyes red from crying, snot streaming from my nose and I had vowed to go and rescue my baby sister from the evil clutches of her jailers. Nannie had sat with me patiently the whole time, explaining over and over again what life was like in the workhouse, explaining repeatedly how most boys my age didn't see too many more birthdays once they disappeared behind those heavy, iron gates.

As the sun rose in the eastern sky I finally relented and agreed to leave it to her to try and get Emma back home. Nannie had gone for Emma early the next morning. She was gone all day, but whatever she said evidently wasn't enough. I never saw Emma again and as I listened to Hitler's bombs pounding the ground above I knew she was probably long dead. Not many of her age survived the workhouse.

After my four days at the docks, Ma's front tooth was gone. I didn't mention that and we didn't mention Emma. It was just me and Ma now but she would be crying and drinking so much or would be out all night so often, really it was just me. I would never go to bed hungry though, because I had a foolproof plan. I would simply stay out until I had found some food somewhere. When I did rest at night I would go to sleep on the floor as close to the door as I possibly could and make sure I was gone before dawn, before anyone returned. Ma was always crying and her men were always angry, sometimes covered in blood. They all smelt of drink, even Ma was getting louder and her moods hard to predict. I only went back there because I had things belonging to Mickey in my secret place.

I started hanging out on the streets with Stan and the boys. Boys who also had home lives they could live without, boys who had made it past their fifth birthday.

Stan Wilson and I first met in Spitalfields Market when we were both seven. One of the inspectors had chased us away from the south entrance, so we had teamed up and hatched an elaborate plan to smear rotten fish all over the back of his clean, white inspector's uniform. The plan had worked brilliantly and after that we started hanging out together, looking for food and usually also finding ways to get into trouble. We would pretend we were leaving home and walk for miles along Whitechapel High Street just ambling on until we turned into the Mile End Road. It seemed no matter how far we walked there were gangs on every corner. The whole world was divided into those with nothing to eat and nowhere to sleep and mobsters with decent clothes and money in their pockets.

The rest of that year and the next Stan and I would roam further and further from home. One day we went all the way up to Regent's Park for a big fight but someone got stabbed to death and the police had turned up in large numbers. It was as much as we could do to get out of their clutches and safely back to the East End.

The East End in 1888 was noisy, dirty and split into two halves. Whitechapel, Spitalfields and Wapping was our half, Bethnal Green, Shoreditch and Hackney, that was their half.

'We' were Mickey Tippings' boys and 'they' were the Blind Beggar mob.

True enough there was also the Russian Houndsditch mob doing their armed robberies all over London and the Polish Jews that formed the Bessarabian and Odessa mobs who were busy offering protection to their own kind, but in my age group we weren't too bothered about the foreigners; it was the Blind Beggar boys that we didn't like.

Now I was ten years old, Queen Victoria herself deemed me grown up enough to face the gallows. It made me feel like a real man and besides if I wasn't working for Mickey I would probably not have made it to the ripe old age of ten anyway. The odds were certainly stacked heavily against me. No, I was one of the lucky ones, I had survived beyond my fifth birthday. This was rare around here and now, today, I was ten, double figures, a real cause for celebration. I was a man, with my whole adult future ahead of me. Not that this was the start of my working life, oh no! I had been far from idle before now, they made sure of that.

I began as a junior member aged six by mainly picking pockets. Then they discovered I had a skill for climbing and I was taken off dipping and moved to breaking and entering. I prided myself on being able to scale any building in any weather. It was about this time that Mickey Tippings himself started saying 'hello' when he saw me out and about.

Now that I was ten, with my senior rank I would be spotting for the younger kids, as they picked pockets in the markets and at Liverpool Street station. Other times we would meet strangers wanting women or meet kids in smart clothes and lead them down to the river where we would rob them. Only now, I would be the one in charge of the chloroform hankie. We would still round up stray dogs, kill them then filch the fur off. Only now, I would be in charge of selling the furs to the Jewish kids. Then, at night whilst others rested, we would be out on the streets clocking drunks, skilfully garrotting them from behind with their neckties or 'bonneting' them with their own hats, as one of us went through their pockets, swiping their valuables, while their faces were covered. Now, I would be in charge of the tie or hat side of things.

From time to time Mickey's mob would give us ten shillings and send us to the pawn shop to buy guns off Solly, one of the Odessa Jews. Now, that was going to be one of my new chores and I couldn't wait to show my worth and dependability.

But I was really in my element when Mickey's boys would have us climbing to the rooftops. They would arm us with nitric acid which we were ordered to throw down only if the police turned up. Usually nothing happened, but sometimes all hell would break loose and whoever was in charge of the nitro would always come away full of bravado and extra respect, now that would be me.

Mickey and his trusty band were the kings of the armed robbery, with a reputation to surpass even the Russians. They had a warehouse at the back of Whitechapel High Street usually crammed full of crate upon crate of brandy and perfumes or huge rolls of Chinese silk straight from the ship. They had little back alley factories churning out a constant supply of fake coins all over the East End and even south of the river. Coins that we would spend wherever they told us to. Mickey Tippings had hiding places coming out of his ears but occasionally, when he had something small to stash away, he would take me to one side and hand me a nondescript, usually hessian, wrapped package.

"Put that away for me, boy," he would say.

I would nod solemnly and at night slip it under the floorboard where I slept, right near the door. It was odd really, the one place, one secret little space in our cramped room that nobody else knew about, yet they all walked on it many times every day.

Usually I hid leaflets or photos for him, pornography or anarchist literature that he would need to hand a short time later. Occasionally,

I would hide coshes, a knife or pistols and they normally stayed hidden for much longer periods of time.

The police did not dare to come down to our court too often. When they did come charging in all mob-handed and throwing things around there were always huge fights and casualties on both sides. On more than one occasion the police charged into our room and trashed the place, invariably standing directly on top of my secret place as they did so. I found out later from a chaplain in jail that official statistics showed a surge in gun crime and armed robbery in London in 1888 and that on these raids the police were usually looking for guns, after the death of one civilian too many. I just thought it was normal, something that happened to everyone now and again.

But looking back all we kids were basically doing was stealing whatever we could get our sticky little fingers on and taking it all back to the flash house for our elders to divide up. Then we got sent back out on the streets. We were being used perhaps but we considered ourselves far better off than any of our peers.

But today it was August 7th, my birthday, my tenth birthday. I was ready to step up, a man at last, and all people were talking about was another murder. A poor unfortunate, Martha something or other, had been done in the night. She had been stabbed so many times it was the talk of the market.

I listened half-heartedly to the gossip for Mickey's sake. He always wanted to know what they were talking about on the streets, but today was supposed to be my day. It had been a hard summer for me during which the thought of my birthday had been the only thing that had kept me going and now her and her 'stabbed, 'til you couldn't stab no more' murder was ruining my big day.

A voice rose through the chatter, rose above all others. I glanced about me.

"Percy, come 'ere!" Bertie Smalls was calling me.

Bertie was Mickey's second-in-command, so I hurried across to where he stood by the Fruit Exchange. He was rubbing his hands together for warmth. The sun had only just risen and there was still a chill in the foul-smelling air.

He waited until I was right up close to him before asking in a quiet tone, "Do ya know George Yard?"

I nodded. Of course I knew it. I could be there in less than a minute from here.

Bertie Smalls had been staring into the middle distance, his expression, from the side, had been difficult to read. Now he turned to face me and barely whispered, "Get over there and see what's 'appening."

I nodded again, turned on my heels and fled. Partly as a response to his direct order but mainly to get away from the frightening look on his face. Was he scared, angry or in the terminal stages of some horrible illness? I didn't know. All I knew for certain was that the expression he wore had worried the life out of me and I liked to think I wasn't that easily scared.

I ran as fast as my legs would take me to George Yard to see what I could find out.

A few days later, after I had got over the disappointment of my tenth birthday being overshadowed by the death of Martha I began to feel sorry for her. I had gone to George Yard as instructed, but by the time I got there the body had been moved, the blood had been washed away and only a few stragglers and a solitary policeman remained to suggest there had even been a murder, barely three hours previously. The Bobbie was appealing for witnesses from the ever-thinning crowd.

I reported back to Bertie, but once I had established that there were no witnesses he seemed to quickly lose interest. For the next few days I would hear talk of nothing but maniacs and see fear in people's eyes as they talked and talked until they had succeeded in scaring the life out of each other. Mickey blamed the massive interest on the new daily papers like the Daily Star and said how stupid it was that these people wanted to read just so they could frighten themselves half to death.

"Does anyone say why Martha was killed yet?" he asked after about a week.

The question threw me a little. I assumed he wished to know who was in the frame.

"Eh, well, they say it must be a foreigner," I glanced nervously at him.

"And?" he motioned impatiently with his hands for me to continue but that was really all I had.

"A Jew, maybe," I ventured. Not even convincing myself.

He snorted at that one, "Yeah, maybe or a Gentile maybe, eh? But why, Percy my boy, let me know if they start wondering why."

I nodded, still rather confused by it all, but willing to play along.

Then three weeks later I was up early as usual at the market looking for whatever opportunities the day would offer when I heard the news.

"He's struck again," was the first phrase I heard and five minutes later, despite the early hour I left the market and hurried back to tell Mickey news I knew he would be keen to hear as soon as possible.

As I slipped down the alley I saw him standing by the oil drum. In the darkness I could only see his silhouette but I knew it was him, standing close to the heat from the fire. He glanced up as he became aware of my approach and without lifting my eyes I could feel his stare burning into me as I walked towards him. He shuffled up slightly, making room for me next to the warmth.

I glanced up at him unsure where to start, he sensed my hesitation. He must have. Without looking round at me he whispered from the side of his mouth, "What's up, boy?"

"There's been another murder. A girl called Mary, over towards the hospital on the High Street, behind Whitechapel station." I glanced up at him, not certain whether to continue. A heavy silence hung between us.

"Go up there, see what's goin' on." He said it without facing me, practically addressing the words to the flames.

Mickey wore his collar turned high and his hat pulled low, so I could barely see his face, yet still I was reminded of the terrible expression Bertie had worn those few weeks before.

I turned and without another word went to find Stan, so I would not have to be alone.

We ran as fast as we could to Buck's Row, a quiet street behind Whitechapel train station. It wasn't really our patch but we knew it as we had mugged a few rail passengers within its dark shadows. We arrived in Buck's Row just in time to see the doctor's coach pull up alongside a small crowd that had gathered in the shadow of a warehouse. We ran closer and pushed through the legs of the people until we were right at the front. I saw the doctor crouching down and covering the body with a blanket. Then he rose up and turning to a police officer said, "I pronounce this poor unfortunate dead at the scene." The doctor sniffed as though a bad smell was invading his nostrils and then added, "I should not think that she has been dead for more than half an hour and I should think she would be better placed in the mortuary." He glanced around him at the growing numbers of people milling about.

Then the doctor turned smartly on his heel almost bowling me over in his haste to vacate the area and the policeman immediately started telling everybody to get back. We hung around and saw the corpse cart turn up and two men hump her body, as though it were a sack of potatoes, into the shell, then they carted her off to the mortuary. Stan and I watched a neighbour come out and throw a pail of water over the bloodstain and rub at it with a hard bristled brush. We were rapidly losing interest. It was cold waiting around and frankly getting a little boring now the body had been moved. Then a senior police officer turned up in a carriage and my interest was piqued once more, but he took in the scene from the comfort of his carriage, didn't even bother to step outside and he left almost immediately. I knew he was right, that there was nothing more to see here, it was time to report back.

Mickey sat at the table listening quietly as I told him of the events. I concluded by making sure he realised that nobody seemed to know anything on this one either. Which frankly I found strange, but that was the truth of the matter.

When I said as much he snorted and shook his head.

"Is that right, boy? Well if somebody knows, why don't we know?"

Mickey's tone was calm but he was no longer smiling, I shrugged by way of reply.

"Get down the market," he told me, "let me know if anything interesting comes up."

I headed for the door but hesitated as he called out, "Anything, Percy, alright?"

"Course, Mickey," I replied and made my exit.

It was odd though. Stan and I were well known from Spitalfields Market, the length and breadth of Commercial Street and right through Brick Lane. We knew all the alleys and courtyards, all of the rogues and most of the traders and yet nobody was telling us anything as far as suspects were concerned.

Only once before had I come across such a wall of silence. Eighteen months ago, when a girl had been hospitalised and then died of her injuries. It had turned out nobody wanted to talk to me then because they all knew it had been Mickey's boys that had done it to her.

Stan and I grew more edgy with each passing day.

Finally, it had to be discussed.

We were leaning against the clean, white-washed wall of the Fruit and Wool Exchange building, using the vantage point to see who was going in and out of Spitalfields Market. We were eating slices of eel and the time seemed right, so I turned to Stan and asked,

"Who do you think it is?" There was no need for me to explain further. I could have been talking about any number of things, but Stan knew instantly what or rather who, I was referring to.

He glanced up and nervously caught my eye. There was no need for him to be nervous around me. It could only mean he was thinking along the same lines as I was.

I had to speak again to break the awkward silence.

"Remember when that girl got beat an' nobody wanted to talk to us about it?"

"That was different," he shot at me.

I raised an eyebrow in a way that negated the need for the word 'why'.

He glanced up again, and I realised he wasn't nervous, he was scared.

"I've been speaking to Solly, he says it's the same with the Jews. Nobody's blaming anyone because nobody knows anything."

I looked at him suspiciously but his gaze was fixed straight ahead, he wouldn't catch my eye. My God, he was scared. 'Why?' I wondered.

I turned away from him and we carried on eating in silence.

Of course, when Stan said nobody was blaming anyone that wasn't strictly true. Armed mobs were patrolling the streets by night and by day. Strangers in pubs were experiencing the very real need to run for their lives because somehow they resembled a killer no-one had actually set eyes on. Jews, doctors, slaughtermen and any number from the great and the good to the great unwashed, were being accused. Accused by the sensationalist press and being accused if they dared show their curious faces anywhere in Whitechapel, but Stan hadn't been referring to the hysterical masses. He had meant nobody in the underworld knew anything. Those who should have known what was going on around here didn't and that was what scared him the most. Mickey and his friends had a network running into thousands of men, women and children, in just these few streets. Most of them up to their necks in the shady goings on. Collectively they knew more or less everything that happened around here. To Stan's mind such deafening silence could only mean that Mickey's mob was involved and nobody wanted to say so out loud.

I looked across at Stan and this time he held my stare. It was telepathic. He thought it, I knew he thought it and he knew I knew.

Stan, still holding my gaze said, "We gotta tell Mickey. I mean..." he cast his eyes downwards, "You gotta tell Mickey."

I feigned surprise, even toyed with the idea of pretending not to know what he meant, but there was no point, he was absolutely right, I pushed myself off the wall.

"I'll see you back 'ere," I called over my shoulder.

"Yes, alright!" Stan replied in a troubled voice.

I trudged the short distance back to our courtyard and went up to Bertie at the oil drum.

"I need to talk to Mickey," I told him.

They all knew that Mickey would see me whenever I asked these days, so he told me to wait by the fire while he sent one of the others to pass on my message.

I rubbed my hands together over the warmth of the flames and let the heat flicker across my face.

"So 'ow's things down the market then?" Bertie asked me in a friendly enough manner.

"Oh, you know, alright!" I never had been known for my over-talkative nature.

"Alright is it?" He shook his head and chuckled slightly. He made no more attempts at small talk so we stood warming ourselves in companionable silence. I preferred it that way anyway. It gave me time to think straight, to work out the best way of telling Mickey what we suspected. The trouble was he wasn't usually that keen on hearing suspicions.

Almost as soon as the messenger had got to Mickey's door he was making his way back across the yard.

He looked at me and wagged his thumb back the way he had just come, indicating that I should not wait around.

As I opened the door I could see Mickey straight away. He was sitting at a large wooden table in the centre of the room, facing the door, counting money. He looked up and nodded as I entered.

"Alright, Percy, what's on your mind?"

"Well," I began, "well, the thing is," I glanced up and was so impressed at the pile of cash on the table in front of him, it distracted me; I forgot momentarily where I was or what I was here for.

"Well?" Mickey repeated, bringing me back to the present.

"Yeah, well," I mumbled.

"Speak up, Percy."

"Well, maybe it's nothin' but maybe it's somethin'. Could it be one of your boys?" I blurted out.

I stood staring at my feet, Mickey had a soft spot for me, I knew that, but he probably hadn't wanted to hear what I had just said.

"Is that what they're sayin'?" he wanted to know. Quite reasonably I thought and quite calmly asked, I was pleased to note.

"Well, no," and I saw the tension visibly drain from his shoulders as I uttered that vital little word.

He sat back in his seat and offered me to elaborate with a movement of his eyebrows and a gesture of his hand.

"Well, if they think it's any of your boys involved, that's the only time people won't talk to me an' Stan. Remember that girl last year?" He silenced me with a raise of his hand.

"So, nobody is actually saying as we's involved?" he asked, still leaning back in his chair, calmly waiting for me to respond.

"No," I declared with no small degree of certainty.

He leant forward now, his elbows on the table, his fingers clasped together and a huge bundle of bank notes in front of him.

"That's good then, in' it?" He smiled at me. "Good boy for tellin' me though, Percy."

He motioned towards the door with his eyes and I knew I was dismissed.

I wandered back to the market and soon found Stan. I sidled up to him and we both stood with our backs to the wall, so that nobody could approach us unseen, so that we could talk without being overheard.

"Well?" he asked, constantly scanning the crowds as he did so.

"He wasn't that bothered," I replied.

Stan looked across at me, and he looked so confused I couldn't help smiling.

"Yeah, he wasn't that bothered!" I repeated. "Asked if people was actually saying it was his mob, an' when I said 'no' to that he wasn't that bothered." I let the smile leave my face before I added, "So maybe we shouldn't be that bothered either, Stan."

He held my gaze briefly then replied, "I suppose so. After all, it's been a week since poor Mary got done. I expect that's an end to it now, anyhow."

I nodded and pushed myself off the wall, the crowds had grown thicker and it was time to get back to work.

The next morning that dreadful phrase was once again the talk of the market.

"There's been another murder!"

I hung around for a bit listening. It didn't take long before I felt I had enough of the details to report back to Mickey. Once again he was standing by the oil drum as I approached, almost as though he was waiting for me. I shook that thought from my mind before it led anywhere too dark and approached him almost in a trance.

"You're back early," he observed without looking in my direction, transfixed as always by the dancing flames before him.

"There's been another murder." There, straight out with it this time. It's truly amazing how you only have to say something a few times before it trips off your tongue as easily as silk off a blade and its uncanny how terrible news, the most shocking of revelations, repeated just once or twice lose almost all their power and are received by the listener in almost docile boredom.

"Where?" He only had the one word question.

"Just around the corner, Hanbury Street," I told him.

This time he did look in my direction but I was afraid to look at him, afraid of what I might read in his face.

"Get over there," he said quietly and I was gone.

Hanbury Street was very much part of our manor. I knew it well, but not like this. I turned off Commercial Street into Hanbury Street and despite still not being 7am the cobbles around me were like a party town. The crowds were thickest jamming into the area around number 29. A much larger number of people than had gathered a week earlier at Buck's Row after the last one. I elbowed a path through their legs to see with my own eyes whatever there was to be seen.

This crowd was bigger, noisier and to my mind, a lot more likely to do something stupid. They grumbled with bad nature as I pushed my way through, that wasn't normal. I listened as man after man denounced the killer. Some were clearly angry, others visibly shaken. All, whether they knew it or not, were whipping up the mob into more and more of a frenzy.

A man in a loud hounds-tooth jacket and a brown trilby caught my eye through the crowd and before I could blink somehow he was standing right next to me.

"Mornin' little man," he smiled far too broadly for my liking.

"Mornin' to yous," I replied suspiciously.

"Fred Best, reporter, Daily Star," he barked and offered his outstretched hand.

I smiled back, accompanied it with a shake of my head and turned my back on him. Mickey hated reporters and he expected us to treat them with the contempt he thought they deserved.

I spent an hour hanging about, just listening to the gossip and keeping my ears and eyes open, until there were more Bobbies in uniform than I had ever seen in my life. It was so busy; people were starting to work the crowds, selling snacks and trinkets, even selling views of the murder site from the overlooking rooms. I headed back home to tell Mickey.

"Yeah," Mickey said after I had told him all my deductions and observations, "they are draftin' in extra Bobbies from all over London."

His face always went a funny purple shade when he was forced to say any word that referred to the police as though acknowledging their mere existence was a real effort for him.

"It's gettin' so it's bad for business." But, he didn't say it in a concerned or even an angry manner. 'It's bad for business' he had said, as though it was just one of those things.

"Somebody must 'ave seen somethin'." He didn't look happy and I was beginning to think that maybe he wasn't involved after all.

"There's a woman 'oo says she saw somethin'."

He seized on these words far more enthusiastically than I had been expecting him to.

"Good, at last. BERTIE!" he called towards the oil drum. I was already dismissed but I hung back and heard him tell Bertie to find this woman, this witness, and bring her here.

It was late in the afternoon before I saw Bertie pushing a woman down our alley and it was dark before she re-emerged but re-emerge she did and she looked quite pleased with herself. That was a good sign. It meant that Mickey had believed her story and had rewarded her in some way. Money probably, coins I expect. I hoped they were real for her sake.

A few days later I finally saw Mickey alone. He was standing by the oil drum, smoking a cigar. I crossed the yard to approach him and he watched my progress.

"Alright, boy?" he asked as I drew near.

"Yes alright, thanks." I looked up at him. "The other day," the words were out of my mouth before I was even fully in position next to him.

He looked down at me. "What about 'the other day'?"

"Well, it's just like everyone is sayin' that Mrs. Long, that witness, got it wrong, 'cos of the time that the doctor says she breathed her last. It's all over the papers, they say."

Mickey crouched down so that we were eye to eye.

"What 'ave I told you about them?" I knew by 'them' on this occasion he was referring to the police, the doctor and the papers.

"That they ain't got a clue?" I replied.

"That's right. Mrs. Long saw what she saw an' that Albert somethin' or other, the carpenter from next door, 'e 'eard what 'e 'eard an' they don't believe 'em because some doctor says the times is wrong. Well, that doctor is an ass, I'm tellin' yous."

I nodded with enthusiastic agreement, "Alright, Mickey." I made to leave.

"'Old on," he commanded, pulling a pile of photographs from his jacket. He shoved them at me. I glanced down at the picture on the top of the pile. It showed a naked woman lying on her stomach, with her arms and legs tied up behind her.

"Look after these for me, boy," he commanded and I grabbed them and headed away.

I knew Ma would be out somewhere drinking and Stan was still in the market. Our room was empty, so I crossed the yard to deposit the pictures in my secret place. Photographs of naked ladies. I was sorely tempted to take a slow look through them, but my fear of what Mickey might do was stronger than any pre-pubescent urges. I stashed them and ran back to the market, back to Stan, back to the daily distractions that stopped me dwelling on the fact that there was undoubtedly a maniac on the prowl in my playground.

Three weeks later it was the early hours of the morning when Stan and I found ourselves in a little side street just behind Whitechapel High Street as it started to rain. We decided to take shelter under some carts in a yard belonging to Mr. Dutfield. We had hidden from the rain in the yard many times before and it was as good a place as any around here. Sometimes we could hear the music coming from the working men's club, which always helped while-away the hours.

Chapter Four

THE increasing volume of droning engines shook me from my memories. Ever more German bombers must be coming across the London sky. I glanced about the gloomy shelter hoping to see a spare bottle of something, anything really, going around. All I saw were little huddles of frightened families, an ARP warden standing halfway up the staircase and a couple of WVS girls standing at the end of the platform guarding a huge urn of scalding tea. I shook my head in despair. Tea, who wants tea? I couldn't believe these people sometimes. Nobody had a bottle on show it seemed. I would need to force the issue.

"Jesus, I could use a drink. There hadn't been time to grab for nothin' tonight," I announced loudly, adding a loud tut, "What a dilemma." I tutted again more loudly and glanced around. Either I had gone invisible or these good people were ignoring me.

"Who really believed they would actually dare to attack?" I mused more loudly, looking around for a response. Nothing. I shook my head in bewildered amusement.

There had been rumours down the Docks and around the pubs for weeks of course, saying that Hitler was planning an invasion of England but I didn't think anyone was taking it seriously. Invade England? Are you sure? Anyway, that's what I thought. So you can imagine the shock on my face when the boy was waking me up, shouting right in my face,

"THE BOMBERS, THE GERMAN BOMBERS IS COMING!"

I opened my eyes to focus and he was right in front of my face, talking at me ten to the dozen and Mrs. Smith had told him that he was to wake me up and take me to the tube station and if I was too drunk to wake he had been ordered to put me on a cart and wheel me there, or die trying, and not dare to come back alone.

Mrs. Smith had also told him to say, "Pops, the whole of London is on fire and that, like as not, we are all gonna die 'cos of some wicked things that she had done as a child and you too, Pops. Wicked things apparently and even me, Pops, I have been an evil child in God's eyes and it occurs to her that it was probably all my fault, as a matter of fact." He sniffed loudly and rubbed his nose against his sleeve.

"Then she had started whipping my legs with her broom and screaming that I should come and wake you, an' the planes would be here any second and if I wasn't quick you would die in your sleep and that would be my fault as well."

"Betty Smith is crazy," I interrupted his flow; I leant in closer and added in a softer tone, "she always 'as been."

The flow of words stopped as he searched my face for a grain of truth, something to pin his hopes on.

Betty had shaken him up pretty bad, a bit too much as always, that bloody woman. I know he acts tough but he's only a boy, Betty, no need to go round making things worse.

The engines of hundreds of German bomber planes thundered above our heads.

"Jesus, Hitler's lot 'ave got it in for us, eh boy?" I attempted humour in the face of adversity but he was having none of it. I didn't really blame him, the noise was thunderous, it was incredible.

"Come on Pops, let's go!" he had screamed in my face again. I allowed him to swing me into a sitting position, then, as I tried to rub my eyes, he pulled me impatiently to my feet. Fortunately I slept in my clothes. I was ready. I had let the boy guide me by the hand.

"'E's always been a good boy this one, bit wild, but a good boy beneath it all,' I thought as he had led me to heaven-knew-what and squadrons of bombers had passed so close over our heads as to make conversation impossible.

And the boy had done good. We were safe now, that much I had to admit. A hundred feet below ground like bleeding moles maybe, but safe at least, down here with thousands of other people, our friends and colleagues, our neighbours. True enough there was no privy and it was a bit whiffy but at least it was calm now. Not like earlier. What a scene. Who could believe those tin hat Bobbies telling us the underground station was closed? By order of the government, if you please. It was designated for 'troops only' they had said. Of course the bombers were so thick in the sky at that point that only those few right up close to him could actually hear what he was saying. Meanwhile, frightened people were pushing forward whilst more and more joined the back of the crowd adding to a growing throng.

I smirked at the thought of the actual moment when the floodgates had opened.

"This station is closed!" the tin hat had barked with as much authority as he could muster.

"Not tonight it ain't mate," replied a high pitched voice and a scruffy little urchin had whipped past his legs and, of course, the dam was burst. We had all pushed along in his wake, brushed aside the few officials and occupied St. Mary's tube station. Streaming down the winding staircase, all with our brave faces on, disguising the fact that each and every one of us was only a few seconds away from utter panic. That had been nearly three hours ago. It was a lot quieter now, we had been below ground so long most were bedding down, having decided to stay put until morning.

I saw a figure picking his way carefully through the sleeping forms. It was a small figure. Perhaps an old man, a woman, or a lad. When they came close enough for me to see more clearly, I saw it was a boy. A kid of about the same age as my Billy. He looked familiar. I squinted in the gloom, trying to catch his face.

"Alright, Billy?" the lad called in a normal tone of voice, with total disregard for those trying to sleep.

"Alright, Jack?" Billy replied at a slightly more respectful level, but not much quieter and mainly because his pal was already those few paces closer.

Now, with a name to put to the face, I recognised him. Of course, how could I not. Jack was another ten year old from the same streets as us. I remember the day he had been born. How there was a bit of a fuss when his mother had insisted on calling him Jack. Some of us had bad memories associated with that name, some of us still do. Not the boy's fault though, his mother had made many poor choices, including the name she had chosen for him and none of those choices were the boy's fault. Jack glanced towards me and I nodded a greeting back at him. He was absolutely filthy as usual, I mean he was grubby at the best of times, but tonight he was blacker than a sweep's lad. My Billy perked up in an instant though, now he was face to face with a peer his mask was on, they were both wearing their brave faces and I knew that they were actually, literally, physically, feeling better, now that they each had an ally, someone of their own age to garner strength from.

Jack looked Billy up and down, "You're scared," he declared.

"No, I ain't scared, you are!" and the accusations helped alleviate their fear further.

"I ain't scared, neither!"

'Oh, you're scared!"

That was the uniform round here, put your brave face on in company, so nobody knows that you're scared. If they know you're scared they will eat you alive. They might still be children but they had learnt that particular lesson some years ago.

Jack was made of the same stern stock as my Billy. I've known him since he was a baby and I've seen him cry only once. He must have been about six years old then, when his mother had whacked him so hard he wore the bruises for a month.

"'ow's your mother, Jack?" I asked.

He shrugged in reply. As well he might. His mother was drunk somewhere, probably with a strange man, and we both knew it.

"On the ups now is she?" He shrugged again and glanced uncomfortably at my Billy.

"Leave 'im alone, Pops. Tell us a story, why don't you?"

Jack's ears pricked up at that. All kids love a story but I wasn't really in the mood. I needed a drink inside me to really do justice to my legendary story-telling skills.

"Maybe some other night."

Neither had the decency to disguise their disappointment, "Nah, not some other night, we could do with one now!" groaned Jack.

"Yes, I'm bored," moaned Billy.

A voice piped up from the gloom behind me.

"Go on Percy, tell the lads a story."

Nancy bleedin' Barlow. I had known Nancy since we were children and she had eaves-dropped her whole life.

"Mind your nose, Nancy," I called back to her.

"Go on, you bore, tell 'em about when we was kids. Tell 'em about Dutfield's yard."

The boys knew that tale. They wriggled excitedly and grinned at each other.

"Dunno what you're on about." I called back but I was lying. When I was Billy and Jack's age there had only been one Dutfield's yard and there had only been one topic of conversation on the streets of Whitechapel.

"What was it like Pops?" offered up Billy in mock innocence.

"Did you live round 'ere as a kid?" asked Jack, wide-eyed, knowing the answer full well.

They knew. They knew exactly what it was like round here when I was a nipper. It was awful and then, in the autumn of 1888, it got much worse.

There were a quarter of a million of us living in Whitechapel back then. Queen Victoria was on the throne and London was the heart of the biggest empire mankind had ever seen. The streets, they said, were paved with gold and all the residents lived a happy, blissful existence. Their lives were full of the latest gadgets and they were all educated to a higher standard than had ever been achieved before, but that was up West. In the East End we lived more like wild natives in the remotest corners of Africa. We struggled from day to day through the filthy, stinking streets, having to use whatever means we possessed, just for the privilege of going through the whole sorry performance again on waking the following day. The slums we lived in had been condemned by successive governments but the promised rebuilding never materialised and nothing was ever done to improve the hygiene. If anyone had asked me what plumbers or plasterers were I wouldn't have had a clue. Ask me about dockers, them I know about. They were big, strong men who could be found queuing up at the dock gates before first light and fighting on the streets at last light. A lucky few would get into the heavy gates and work themselves to exhaustion on any given day. The rest would have the whole of the day to do nothing but visit gin shops and try to block out just how terrible their lives really were. Some formed workers groups or anarchist societies, and tried to fight the system. Others were forced by their lack of work into more criminal enterprises. None of their enterprising ventures made any difference to us. In the evil quarter mile either side of Commercial Street, dockers' wives, daughters and sisters walked the cobbles in desperation. Able to earn in one night what their men would earn in a week. Most of the women around here had families to feed and limited options on how best to go about it. There were public houses everywhere you looked and everybody drank. They drank in order to soften the grubby reality of their everyday struggle from the cradle to the grave.

Childhood did not last long in these streets and the end of my own childhood can be pinpointed with absolute accuracy to the day after Pa died when I was seven, but that was for another time.

Once again a voice brought me back to the present, back to the tube station.

"What was it really like round 'ere when you was our age Mr. Miller?" Jack wanted to know. He had heard all about the old days of course, but children never tired of hearing about the bogeyman who once stalked the very streets they now called home.

"It was worse than now, worse even than tonight, I can tell you that much." I winked at him to take the menace out of my words. "You think this is bad?" I shot at him theatrically as bombs blasted away above us.

The boys actually grinned at that one, sarcasm was our local currency but they had me now and they knew it.

"Very bad?" ventured Billy.

"When I was your age," I began, "things were much worse. We never 'ad no food, nor street lamps, nor privies an' such. Rubbish would pile up in the courtyards for weeks at a time. Nobody 'ad a radio and the Bobbies never came down our street. We was left to fend for ourselves and everyone pitched in, neighbourly, not like today."

"Yeah, for a while," opined nosey Nancy, "tell 'em about the night you saw the Ripper. That's the story they's after an' you knows it."

"They don't wanna 'ear about that."

"Yeah, yeah, we do!" they piped up together.

I suppose if you're going to tell a ghost story, it may as well be in a scary place and true stories grab the attention so much more when told in the perfect location.

"You sure, you wanna hear that ol' tale again?" I gave them one last chance.

"Yeah, yeah! Tell us. It might make being stuck down 'ere less borin'" Jack muttered, and they grinned at each other, almost forgetting the bombardment overhead in anticipation of the story they expected me to tell.

I settled back against the cold wall and sighed. 'Here we go again,' came the familiar voice in the back of my head.

"Well, it was a long time ago, half a century ago, back in 1888. On this particular night, Saturday the 29th of September, it was rainin' and so me and my mate Stan was sheltering in the yard of old Mr. Dutfield, down Berner Street. We were sheltering from the rain, lying under an empty cart and listening to the music comin' out of the club. We knew that sometimes the working girls would bring their punters down into the dark yard. We would keep quiet as mice an' spy on 'em."

Nancy Barlow tutted disapprovingly from the shadows but the boys sniggered deliciously. They didn't yet know the full meaning of what it was to catch a glimpse of female flesh but they knew it was rude and manly. I winked conspiratorially. They stared back with wide excited eyes, wore the expressions of boys on the cusp of discovering the pleasures of the flesh. They were delighted to be in on a man's joke, on some primeval level they knew they would soon be in on the joke completely.

I began to speak but my words were competing with the scream of a falling bomb. Suddenly the walls shook from another blast somewhere above us, yet the boys no longer shivered with dread. Hitler's planes were forgotten to them momentarily. A scary story trumps a scary reality it would seem.

"So, anyway," I smiled, beginning my narrative again, "it was past midnight an' there we was 'iding under the cart, when this girl comes into the yard leading 'er John by the 'and. Me an' Stan pinches ourselves to stop the laughs coming up into our mouths 'oping to get an eyeful of tit or somethin'."

All around me I could feel eyes in the darkness burning into me. Nancy sighed loudly, desperate to appear as though she disapproved. All my neighbours knew this story well but they could never hear it enough times. Even Nancy was in no hurry to vacate the immediate story-telling area. Still, I had learnt to use it sparingly. A good tale was currency; you never knew when funds might be low. The regaling of a memory, good or bad, might be needed to get a free drink or two. Who knew when I might need a good horror yarn to distract a couple of kids whose world was literally falling apart around them?

"So we's 'iding under the boards of this old cart watching real close, like. You know, all excited an' that. Well, this Geezer 'e gives 'er some coins into 'er 'and an' he's smilin' an' talking to 'er real soft, like. Well, as 'e's talkin' 'e's walking round 'er in a circle. Then,"

I paused for effect, and wiped my lips.

"Thirsty work this, you know," I stated, matter of factly, just loud enough to carry into the shadows. Old habits die hard and besides it was true, I was thirsty. Well, I wanted a drink and that amounts to the same thing in my book. Anyway, I waited and not for too long either, they always loved hearing about old Jack.

I took a long pull on the proffered bottle of stout before wiping my lips with gusto.

"Just what the doctor ordered. I'm much obliged to you." I doffed my cap to someone back there in the shadows. Not really interested in whose ale I was supping, but manners never hurt no-one. Anyway, as I didn't intend to return the bottle then the least I could do was say thank you.

"Now where was I? Oh yeah, I remember. So, we're watching 'im do this slow walk round 'er, thinkin' 'e's gonna lift 'er dress up an' give us an eyeful of bloomers." I raised an eyebrow at my young audience and they smiled nervously back at me. They had both heard the story before. Both knew what was coming next but still willed me to carry on.

"But no, that may 'ave been what we thought was going to 'appen. But instead, he grabs 'er real sudden like, round her throat. She struggles and starts screaming but he grabs her scarf an' pulls it real tight. So, naturally, she can't scream out an' he steps in and shakes her a bit. Then keepin' hold of her, he slams 'er against the ground an' straightens up, like he's been distracted or summat. Then his 'ead swivels around, he stares down Berner Street, curses 'Lipski', at some passing Jew I supposed. Not loud like, but threatenin' enough for the Jew it seemed. Me and Stan was just keeping still and hardly daring to breathe, you know. Well, the Jew must have ran off because the next thing we know, real sudden like, he grabs her again with the other hand, round the throat, to stop 'er screaming out, you know. Pins 'er down an' 'e's strangling the very life outta 'er and me an' Stan's just frozen to the spot.

"We can't scream, nor move, nor nothin'. All I can do is watch as 'e pressed 'er down on the cobbles. Then 'e pulled this knife out. Long it was, long and sharp looking. Anyway, before I could even properly take it all in 'e slashed 'er throat. 'E pulled that blade right across 'er neck an' I knew she was dead. I could feel Stan shakin' an' whimpering an' I was really afraid. Afraid he was gonna give us away an' we was gonna get our throats ripped open.

"I wanted to shush Stan, but that would have been far too risky. This killer, this throat Ripper was only ten feet away. We had to stay still, stay quiet. So what was Stan doin'? He knew we was in danger but 'e's bent over makin' this daft noise. An' then I could 'ear a cart comin'.

Well, this mad man 'e 'ad been kind of crouched over that poor girl with his back to us but now 'e jumps up, real unexpected like an' presses himself against the wall right across from us. I'm staring right at 'im. I feels sure 'e can see me an' I'm just about to make a dash for it when the cart turns the corner into the yard an' o' course the pony rears up an' don't wanna go. 'Cos ponies, well all animals as a matter of fact, they can see in the dark when they 'ave to. So, the pony rears up an' as it does I sees the killer crouch down in the shadows. Then me and Stan watched the carman jump down from the coach and light a match to inspect the bundle that made his pony shy up. I swear he was only two feet from the killer when that match flared up but, of course, he's focusing so much on the girl he misses the killer standing over his shoulder. Well, that carman didn't hang about once he realised what he was looking at. He went running into that club practically frothing at the mouth and squealing something over and over in some funny foreign tongue. An' as soon as he disappeared into the club doors that Ripper was sneaking out into Berner Street an' 'e was gone. It was safe to breathe again. My heart was burstin' I swear an' right then Stan started snottin' and blubbin' like a baby, so I slapped 'im, grabbed 'is collar an' we legged it back 'ome as fast as we could."

"What did 'e look like?" Jack shot the question at me the instant I paused for breath.

It was always the first question they asked. Fair enough, really. They didn't know it hit me like a slap in the face every single time. How many times I had been asked that question over the years, I don't know? I lost count long ago. The numbers are unimportant really as it still slaps me hard just like the first time. It's as though I'm being accused of missing something out, of holding something back. Not telling the story in its entirety.

I can't even remember how long ago it was that I began to realise it was too late to tell the truth and it's been too late now for a whole lot of years. But they never have stopped asking, and the asking never has stopped hurting.

Outside the world has gone completely mad. Tonight London was being reduced to rubble. This was, without question, a night out of the ordinary, it seemed only fair that these poor people wanted some extra distraction.

However, things weren't quite so bad that I should tell the whole truth. I wasn't about to finally admit that from the first glimpse of the killer's face I had recognised him. Had known exactly who he was, recognised him without question. Instead, I said what I had always said. "Well, 'e was dressed in black. Long black coat, black 'at, like the one Sherlock 'olmes wears, black trousers an' pointy black boots. He looked foreign."

Before me both boys visibly shivered. Nobody knew, I hid it far too well, but I also shivered internally, and that was all it took. In truth, it sometimes took far less and I was transported right back to that rainy night. I knew that unless I could take my medicine, drink myself to sleep I would see that demon's face every time I tried to close my eyes tonight and the next. If I did manage to doze off I would wake up in a cold sweaty panic, claustrophobic and disorientated. It was best for me to stay in the streets for the next few nights, just until the claustrophobic effect of darkness eased. Never mind the bombs. I would rather take my chances with them than wake up panicking, trapped underground in a bloody train station. It would only be a couple of nights and winter hasn't really started yet, so it would be no bother.

But I could keep these demons at bay as long as I kept talking. As long as I kept awake the nightmares couldn't get me.

So there we had been, two kids innocently lying beneath an old wooden cart just trying to keep out of the rain, just listening to some music. That was it. That was all we were doing, when our lives changed, suddenly and forever. We weren't choirboys, not by a long stretch, we had seen our fair share of blood, seen some pretty nasty beatings dished out, one or two literally kicked to death before our very eyes, but that killer, that Ripper as they called him, he was something different. What I saw that night was no robbery gone wrong or a man under the influence, whose temper had got the better of him. This was killing for the sole purpose of totally controlling another human being. When he jumped up and pressed himself tight against the opposite wall he was barely ten feet away, I was looking right at him. I could see him smiling to himself, his eyes darting everywhere. I froze as he seemed to look right at me, then his black-eyed stare moved on. I knew what he was thinking, could almost hear the cogs turning in his mind. We could both hear the horse hooves on the cobbles, the creak of the cart coming up Berner Street and he knew it was going to turn the corner, I don't know how, he just knew. I was so sure because I knew it as well. The cart rumbled ever closer, he seemed to glance at me again, that evil smile still fixed across his thin lips. I knew and he knew that the pony would not cross a dead body. It would rear up as soon as it was steered into the yard, and when it did he would use that split second of chaos as cover to crouch down, slide smoothly along the wall and out into the street. I swear I knew exactly what he was going to do. I don't know how, maybe 'cos it was the only way out of the yard. Who knew how any of us know anything? Maybe it was because we thought in the same way. I had glanced down at Stan. He was still bent double, eyes covered, he couldn't see anything. He wasn't rationally assessing the escape. Only I was doing that, me and the Ripper, but the fact is its irrelevant how I knew what would happen next. I just did and that poor girl was lying in the mud and I should have jumped up waving my arms and shouting for attention. Me and Stan should have jumped up and then maybe they would have caught him, but we didn't. I had stared into his face for enough seconds to recognise him, to never forget him. I know I should have tried to help her, but that wasn't how we used to do things. Secrets like that you took to the grave and if that meant a lifetime of panic attacks, so be it. Back then, taking secrets to your grave usually meant keeping them for a few years at most. It was unthinkable at the time that I would still be around five decades later.

"What about his face, Pops, what did his face look like?"

Why did they always insist on asking that?

I had drifted again, already preparing mentally for the nightmares that would soon come to haunt me if I let them, if I allowed sleep to come calling.

"Pops, Pops!" Billy's voice forced me back to the present.

I continued talking as the bombs rained down.

"Well, like I say, 'e 'ad an 'at on, the peak pulled down low, like. An' I would say 'e 'ad a moustache, not thick 'n bushy, more like a fair wispy one. An' 'e 'ad black eyes like nuggets of coal an' a smooth shaved chin an' not much in the way of eyebrows or lips." It was complete nonsense of course, but it was the story I stuck to religiously every time, without fail.

I talked for hours. I wasn't going to sleep in so public a place and let them all see how the nightmares still affected me. I didn't want their pity as I rolled and groaned and sweated the night away. No doubt topping off my performance with a bloodcurdling 'NO!' as I suddenly sat bolt upright. No, I would keep talking rubbish and stay awake 'til morning. I had taught myself to stay awake out of necessity. That night of madness had shaped my sleep patterns for the past fifty years.

However, as the years rolled on, I had come to believe that London would never again witness such horror, that I would never again witness such horror. I dared to hope that things might even get better with the passing of time. Evidently, I had been wrong. As the bombs rained down I knew once again the promised better times had not quite materialised, but it was more than that now. This was undeniably much worse. We as a human race had regressed dramatically, some were saying that we had failed completely. Tonight London was more unsafe than it had ever been.

It was absolutely typical of my luck that such a period comes along just as my grandson turns ten. I hugged the lad tighter to me, afraid of the past, but now equally afraid of the days that lay ahead. 'It's the leaders that have failed, not us,' I thought to myself.

"Don't squeeze me so tight." Billy wriggled and I released my grip on him. I hadn't realised he was awake.

What more could I do, he was practically a young man now. Poor little fella. I squeezed him one last time and bit down hard on my lip, this was not the place for a grown man to start blubbing. A night of muttering incoherently was enough of a show for this particular audience.

"Don't squeeze me so!" Billy wriggled out of my lap. "Can't we go now?" he pleaded.

"Yeah, let's go up top now," added Jack's high pitched voice.

"No!" I was horrified at their enthusiasm. "It's too dangerous. Be good lads. If you want something to do go and find someone with a spare ale for me."

"Alright, Pops, we will." They glanced at each other conspiratorially.

I watched them fade into the gloom and pulled the blanket I had been given tighter around my neck. 'Please God; don't let 'em turn out like me.'

I watched them picking their way through the sleeping shapes. They were whispering to each other, watching and waiting for the old man to lose sight of them, no doubt. I didn't blame them, they were bored and they had been down here since 4pm.

Over four hours had passed and the sound of angry planes overhead and the whine of dropping bombs seemed finally to be losing momentum. They were boys, they wanted to get back in the open air and see for themselves what damage all those explosions had caused. Oddly, the sense of anticipatory excitement they both felt was barely tinged with worry or the fear of danger.

I watched as the gloom swallowed them up. I knew they would disobey me and head outside if they could. They had stopped listening to my advice years ago, and that wasn't about to change now. My mind gave in to my inner demons. My thoughts returned unbidden to that morning after the terrible incident at Dutfield's Yard.

I had wandered the streets for ages but eventually I had returned home and there was the killer, as I'd dreaded he would be. Bold as brass, sitting on my Ma's bed, just as he had every day since moving in. Her new boyfriend was the maniac everybody was looking for and now I knew it. He looked up as I walked through the door and gave me a sneer that made my blood run cold. He knew. That little look was all it took to make sure I was aware he had seen me.

"Been anywhere nice 'ave you?" he sneered again as he asked me and I muttered something meaningless and tried to back out of the door, but he had been expecting that. He leapt from the bed, easily blocking my exit, grabbing me by the throat as he did so. Grabbing me with the same hand, that had not so long ago been around the throat of the girl in the yard.

"Where you off to in such a 'urry? Sit down an' we can wait for your Ma to get back," he had insisted.

We sat there for what felt like hours. Me on the floor in front of the cold fire place, he on the bed running a long-bladed knife up and down the strop used for sharpening blades. Every time I tried to turn away from the wall his eyes burned into mine and the rhythmic sound of the blade sliding up and down the strop filled the tiny room.

After an eternity the sound stopped. I continued my scrutiny of the fireplace, defeated already by his psychological superiority, too afraid to turn and face him. I heard the bed groan as he shifted his weight on it, then felt a stinging slap to the back of my head that sent me sprawling across the floor.

I lay still with my hands over my face and peeked up at him towering over me. He motioned as though he was going to kick out at me and I flinched, causing him to laugh, far too loudly.

"Yeah, that's right little rat. You better bleedin' flinch every time you sees me or…" suddenly he had a handful of my hair and his sour breath was right in my face. "Or that dirty whore you call your mother ain't goin' to see another sunrise."

He raised his foot again and this time he did kick out, catching me squarely in the stomach. I gasped for air as he lent in close again.

"Understand?"

He whispered the word and I nodded rapidly, not able to breathe, not daring to catch his eye. He was enjoying this, loving the control he had over me.

"Good." He spat on me and turned on his heel.

I heard the little click as he pressed the catch down on the door. I lay still, willing him to leave.

"Oi!" He was still there, hovering over me, milking every last drop of pleasure out of it. He hadn't taken the steps outside, just pretended to. He was still standing over me, one hand on the door latch, the other clutching the knife.

"Oi!" he repeated, slightly louder and with menace added to the word.

I looked up at him and managed to whimper, "Yes!"

"One word…" he wagged a finger at me then slowly drew it across his own throat, "Got it?"

I nodded again just as rapidly and he put the knife in his pocket and headed out through the door.

I lay frozen to the spot, trying to make sense of it all. Outside I could hear the sounds of the people going about their usual business, as though it was just another day.

Finally, in the middle of the afternoon Ma returned.

"What are you doin' lyin' 'ere?" she demanded.

"Nothin' I..."

"Nothin' is it? Well nothin' ain't goin' to put no food in your belly, is it?" she whacked me half-heartedly across the shoulders, "Get out there an' make yourself useful. Go find somethin' to eat. You think I'm goin' to feed you again, do you?" she protested. "Get out with you, an' don't 'urry back, I got some company this night."

There was nothing else for it. I rose to my feet and without a backwards glance headed out through the door.

It was odd, but for the first time since I could remember, I didn't feel hungry. I just wanted to block out what had happened the night before. There was no chance of that.

Newspaper boys were screaming at the top of their lungs, "RIPPER STRIKES AGAIN. DOUBLE EVENT IN WHITECHAPEL. READ ALL ABOUT IT, READ ALL ABOUT IT!"

I tried to block out their cries, but they weren't the only ones. Small groups of people huddled together outside public houses and on street corners, snippets of their conversations working their way into my ears.

"Yeah, two last night. Two unfortunates."

"They say 'e's a doctor you know."

I saw some of my friends sniggering at the corner, but when I went to join them, hoping for a distraction from my troublesome mind, I was disappointed.

"Look, Percy, we got some chalk." They were barely containing their squeals. "Look what Archie's wrote on the wall."

I looked at the chalk writing, a blur of jumbled shapes to my eyes.

"What does it say?" I demanded of Archie.

"Jack the Ripper lives 'ere", he proudly recited.

"You think you're so smart cos' you can write a bit, don't you?" I blurted out angrily.

Archie saw me making a fist and quickly backed away from me slightly, "Alright, Percy, it's just a joke."

I snorted at him and stormed away from them.

I headed down towards the river, trying to find somewhere where there would be fewer people. I needed time to think. I didn't want him to kill Ma. I would have to tell Mickey. Would that be best? I wasn't sure.

Chapter Five

"COME on Billy, the bombs 'ave stopped, let's go an' see what damage there is," whispered Jack.

"You sure it's stopped?" Billy half expected to hear the drone of the engines returning.

"Oh, don't be so chicken," Jack snorted.

"I ain't no bleedin' chicken," Billy shot back at him.

"Right then, let's go," Jack challenged him.

The two ten year olds made their way carefully through the sleeping bodies, taking detours around any that appeared to be still awake. They made it to the spiral staircase that led out of St. Mary's underground station and climbed as quietly and slowly as their youthful exuberance would allow. They had never been in an air-raid before, never listened as bombs exploded above them. They were ten years old and this was all new to them. Naturally, they were curious; they wanted to check it out with their own eyes.

Reaching ground level, at the top of the staircase, the boys stood open-mouthed. They had expected there to be damage to correspond with the noises they had heard from below. They had expected things to perhaps look a bit different, but not like this.

Thick pink smoke filled the air, angry deep red fires raged in all directions, huge gaps had appeared in the rows of housing familiar to them their whole lives. Men with hosepipes were running around, shouting to each other. London, their London, was burning in all directions. It was horrific, yet beautiful and absolutely awesome.

A fireman shouted something at them.

Billy tried to make out his words, but all he could hear was the angry scream of more planes approaching and they were moving at speed.

"They're comin' back Jack, leg it!"

Billy turned his head left but Jack was no longer there. Then he caught sight of him rummaging in a pile of rags on the opposite side of Whitechapel High Street.

"Jack! Jack!" He started running towards his friend as the engines in the sky screamed louder and louder.

He saw Jack glance skywards then return to his frantic rummaging. Billy stepped up a gear and within a few more strides was kneeling at his friend's side.

"What the 'ell are you doin'? Can't you 'ear 'em? They're comin' back, let's go. Let's go!"

"'Elp me, this cat is trapped." Jack ignored his warning.

"Never mind the cat, let's go." Billy's words were drowned out by the scream of a falling bomb. They may have no experience of air-raids, but that was the unmistakable sound of a bomb about to land somewhere very close and they both knew it.

"In 'ere, in 'ere, quick!" Billy jumped into the closest doorway, closely followed by Jack. He had forsaken the cat's welfare in the sudden need for self-preservation. They looked into each other's eyes, grins starting to spread in celebration at still being alive. In such situations it is down to one or the other to comment 'that was close' or words to that effect, but the bomb exploded before either could verbalise any such utterance. The blast was crystal clear; neither of them would forget it or mistake that sound for something else ever again.

After a few seconds Billy shook his head, his ears were ringing, but incredibly he seemed to be in working order. There was a blanket of shattered glass from fifty shop fronts spread the length and breadth of the High Street but it seemed Billy did not have a scratch on him.

His brain registered smaller incendiary bombs falling all around, the ringing in his ears meant he could no longer make out the grinding noise of the planes or the scream of the falling bombs, but he could see quite clearly that the Germans were having a second bash at bombing his city off the map. Despite his near death, despite the high pitched ringing in his ears he was not afraid, he was excited.

He felt a tug on his sleeve and turned to face his pal.

Jack was offering the thumbs-up, enquiring if he was all right. Billy nodded his head, raising a quizzical eyebrow, asking the question in reverse. Jack nodded back. Realisation dawned that they were both, miraculously, unscathed, and they laughed harder and harder. Loud roars that shook their little bodies, laughter that said, 'we are alive, I don't know how, but we are definitely still alive'.

"Bloody 'ell." Jack's gaze swept the street and he could barely believe his eyes. Huge mounds of rubble, bricks, dust, oh, so much dust, glass everywhere, and that insistent ringing seemed to be getting louder.

Jack realised fires were surrounding them on all sides. Suddenly, just a few feet away a blazing shop started spitting out globs of burning something...

"Get back, Billy!" Jack screamed, "It's going to blow."

The shop was one of the very few in sight that still retained glass in its windows. Billy and Jack huddled low together in the doorway as the front exploded and glass and wood flew outwards, adding even more debris to the odd piles all around.

Billy peered out on the devastation and laughed again. He was having great difficulty taking in the scene around him. He had known this area all his short life, but he had never been able to see the docks from here. It was incredible, there was a big hole where tall buildings had stood only a few hours ago. He could see the warehouses from here and they were totally ablaze. Massive walls of bright red flames towering upwards, where they lent a pink tone to the smoke blowing away up the river.

"Bloody 'ell Billy, the docks are on fire!" Jack's voice broke into his thoughts. There was no need for Jack to have said so, they could both see it, but it was almost as though he needed to confirm in words what his eyes were showing him. 'The docks are on fire.'

Alongside them another blazing shop started to pop alarmingly.

"What we gonna do Billy, 'ead back to the underground?"

Billy didn't answer immediately. Incendiary bombs scattered all around them, hundreds of them, each one causing a new fire to start burning wherever it landed.

"Billy!" Jack screamed, "What are we going to do?"

Their familiar childhood backdrop had been totally demolished and suddenly Jack was not taking it too well.

"Don't be a chicken Jack, pull yourself together!"

"I ain't no chicken, you're the chicken!" screamed Jack, falling to his knees.

Billy grabbed Jack by his grubby collar and pulled him back to his feet.

"Let's go, Jack!" he screamed and headed at high speed down the High

Street. Jack followed, tripping through the rubble in his wake. Billy stumbled a few times on the dangerous footing, but he was determined to get to the river. He had grown up on stories of the docks, how they were the lifeblood of the British Empire, solid, re-affirming, ever dependable. Only, was that true? Billy had to see it with his own eyes. An incendiary fizzed into white hot flames in the road before them, Billy swerved left to avoid it.

"Jack, look out!" He shouted the command in the way a sergeant major issues an order, pushing his friend away from a large chunk of wall that was collapsing across the street in front of them. As it came crashing to earth huge red flames leapt into the gap where the wall had stood seconds before. Incendiary bombs began fizzing all around them. Yesterday, neither boy had even heard of incendiary bombs, now they could recognise the sound of one in all its stages at 20 paces with other noises all around.

"Jeezus talk about growing up quick." Billy laughed as he ran. 'Oh,' he realised, 'my ears have popped, I can hear again,' and he laughed once more at the sheer joy of being alive.

He ran more confidently with every pace, skipping across hazards, leaping onto burning objects and instantly off again, scanning the ground for obstacles as it raced towards him, scanning the horizon and the surrounding buildings. Totally alert and running on pure adrenaline, Billy was breathing easily and taking everything in. He was being extremely cool under fire; for the first time he realised now what that really meant. He was a Miller, Billy Miller, from a long line of East Enders. When death and destruction were closing in on all sides, when all of London was on the very brink of annihilation, Billy, it seemed, stayed calm. He had never felt so alive, his feet barely made contact with solid surfaces, his every sense was heightened to the maximum and he wanted more. In his wake Jack was calmer, more his normal self. Now that Billy had assumed command, now that Jack knew his place in the scheme of things, all was well. After the early hiccup, the two children had taken to warfare effortlessly. Incredibly, whilst grown men were hugging the subterranean walls of Whitechapel tube station, crying in terror, a pair of mere boys were taking it all literally in their stride. Several steps ahead of the authorities, Billy was on his way to check the damage to the docks. He knew they were the gateway to London, to England, knew they were the source of the Empire's great wealth, not to mention the source of Reggie Lawson's wealth. He knew they all relied heavily on the docks for everything. He knew it, the scruffy urchin running alongside him knew it, Winston Churchill knew it, hell, everyone knew it, but the difference here was that this kid was already on his way to check things out. His mind was working clearly and totally logically as he ran.

'If the docks is bad, I'm gonna need a plan B,' he mused.

"Where we going, Billy?" Jack shouted into his ear.

"Wapping," Billy called over his shoulder.

"Wha' do we wanna go there for? That ain't really our Manor is it?"

"I know, but I wanna 'ave a look at what damage the bombs 'ave done to the docks. The whole of London is on fire tonight Jackie Boy, we ain't never goin' to see nothin' like this ever again."

Billy realised that the planes were using the burning buildings to guide their bombs down, they didn't need anything else, 'just aim at the spots burning most fiercely and that…,' he thought.

They rounded the corner and there ahead of them lay the heart of London, Jack gasped.

'. . .that will be the docks.'

Billy stood open-mouthed. The whole of Limehouse was burning ferociously. He had never seen nor even heard of anything remotely like it. The giant warehouses absolutely engulfed in white hot balls of fire. Huge red flames leaping hundreds of feet into the sky. Billy and Jack had never seen anything higher than Nelson's Column in Trafalgar Square; their eyes literally did not believe what they were seeing. Below them on the river's edge a fire crew was spraying one warehouse with a woefully inadequate hosepipe. Their efforts seemed futile in the extreme. Those warehouses had been a feature here since before Billy's granddad had been a kid, since before Jack the Ripper prowled in this beat-up old part of London.

'Well, they sure as 'ell won't be there tomorrow,' thought Billy sullenly.

The pink smoke was much thicker here, but not thick enough to hide the vast fires burning across the river.

"Bloody 'ell Billy, look. The whole of Bermondsey's on fire!" Jack exclaimed.

Billy's eyes looked south of the mighty Thames and saw for himself that the whole of Bermondsey, Rotherhithe, the Surrey Quays, even

Greenwich was indeed burning in all quarters. It truly was an awesome sight. Jack and Billy should have feared for their very lives in the face of such awful danger. They were far from afraid, they were, in fact, mightily impressed by the firepower of the enemy air force.

A cluster of incendiary bombs broke rudely into Billy's thoughts. Without warning, dozens began flashing and whizzing all around his feet. Billy casually jumped a few then he started moving. From a sociological viewpoint it would have frightened the life out of any social worker worth their salt, just how quickly this kid had adapted to finding himself thrust into the worst war in human history. He was dealing with incendiary bombs in the same way he did with every terrible hand that this brutal life dealt him, simply taking things in his stride.

Any military men watching this drama unfold would have concluded that Billy was a natural-born soldier. They would have embraced him into their ranks and taught him all the techniques he would need to kill or be killed. Not thinking for one moment that it's a huge leap from self-preservation to full-blooded warrior and if they hadn't started this madness, this kid, natural soldier or not, could maybe have matured into something far more worthy.

Billy was heading down to the water's edge. Something was pulling him forwards, to Watson's Wharf. He thought they might be safe there, down low, underneath that solid oak wharf and whilst they waited they would have an excellent view of Southwark and Surrey across the river. The sight of the far bank burning so brightly truly fascinated him. Billy had observed the great sheets of fire running along, what appeared to him, the whole of Southwark. He was drawn helplessly to it, a lure more powerful than a moth would feel for such bright flames.

Jack was content to bring up the rear. His pal had a plan, which was good enough for him. He'd had enough of thinking and once again what he really needed was an adult to take control of the situation. He was caught up in this against his will; this was, in absolutely no way, any of his doing. Jack had given up on expecting much from adults long ago. As always he would have to muddle through on a mixture of luck and bravado, making it up as he went along. Fortunately, he had Billy to take the lead.

Those tin hat wardens had tried to stop Jack entering St. Mary's station but he was more afraid of the bombers screaming above his head than he was of some part-time Bobby. He had easily slipped past their grasping hands and legged it down the spiral staircase, blissfully unaware that he had been the catalyst for the angry mob behind him to burst through the ranks of officialdom, determined to shelter in the underground station regardless of whether the authorities wanted them to or not. Like the lad before them they hadn't time to wait for a seal of approval from some office worker in Whitehall. The sudden emergence of 600 German bomber planes in the skies above had lent the situation rather more urgency than bureaucracy would generally allow for.

Now as Jack raced behind Billy through these once familiar streets, he was totally composed. In a few short hours the East End had become like a foreign country to him, but he had more pressing thoughts than worrying about absent landmarks. Survival was the name of the game for now. Well, that was pretty much the name of the game permanently for Jack. These boys were born survivors. They didn't spare any time worrying about things, they just lived in the moment. Coincidently, the perfect mind-set to have in a war zone. Though they only thought like that because it made things slightly more bearable. When the past was crushingly difficult and the future offers nothing at all, living in the present moment is going to be your best option, it had to be. East End kids throughout the ages have also needed to be quick-witted. They are born onto the lowest rung of the most ruthless city ladder anywhere in the world. In a city that respects only greed and self-interest, life is always going to be tough, so to compensate, these kids are loud, disrespectful, over-confident, sharp, alert and, most of all, adaptable to new situations. Situations that come at them thick and fast in a place moving at the pace of London, the busiest port in the world, the biggest docks in the world, the dirtiest slum in the whole of England. That was where these kids were from.

Dockside ports in the poorest parts of any city are never a place where life lends one an easy ride. So Jack may not have been certain of much, as he raced through the streets trying to keep up with Billy, but he was certain of one thing, it would probably be wise to keep his wits about him now.

An hour ago he had been on the verge of terror, that moment was forgotten, already well behind him.

To all intents and purposes Jack lived alone. His father had been dead for many years, or so he was told. He had limited access to a one-roomed hovel he shared with his mother, but he rarely went there. There were too many strange men for his liking, always forcing him to wait outside. Mother was always drunk, always falling on hard times it seemed to him. Besides, there was never any food there. He thought she ate at the pub but he wasn't certain. When he really needed to Jack was able to find her. She would turn up in the Ten Bells on Commercial Street, if he waited outside long enough. Sometimes they would let him in and tell him where he could find her, but more recently he hadn't seen her for days and, actually, it was easier that way. He was still hungry practically round the clock, it just meant he wasn't being screamed at and beaten for trivial things his mother couldn't even remember the following day. Jack appreciated his mate not expecting any help in getting them out of this mess. When the chips were down he was better at following than leading.

'If only we had stayed in the tube station,' Jack considered silently, 'Billy's granddad would have got us some food when he woke up. He was always a friendly old geezer, who didn't get punchy half as much as some round here when they've been drinking.'

'Yes,' another voice inside his head interrupted the first internal monologue, 'then we would have missed all this.'

He had to admit, it was kind of exciting and tomorrow it would all be over. So, in a way, he was glad not to be missing out.

Their laughter dried up as the two boys ran on. The docks as they had never seen them before were spellbinding. An eerie, unrecognisable, sinister landscape had replaced what they had been familiar with all their lives. They were surrounded by fire and debris in all directions; this was too serious for laughter. All around scattered groups of firemen worked frantically at a seemingly impossible task. The few other people outdoors huddled in doorways or stood transfixed, facing skywards. The same handful of locals who would otherwise be shuffling along their daily routes, fixated on picking up cigarette ends or edible scraps off the roads and pavements. Blissfully safe in their private hells, barely aware that a bigger hell was developing around them, unaware but transfixed by the noise and lights in the sky.

Billy found himself at the water's edge more quickly than he had anticipated; short cuts were easy when whole swathes of buildings have gone. All the fires and missing buildings were throwing out his sense of direction. He was determined to have a good look around tomorrow, to re-acquaint himself with his now unfamiliar home turf.

He reached the metal ladder that dropped down the stone wall to the little patch of beach below. Both boys shot down it and slid through the wet sand to get underneath the solid wooden jetty. Now they were finally at their destination it looked far less of a protective force than it had been in Billy's mind's eye, but they were here now and it was a good enough place to catch their breath and work out what their next move should be.

"Who's that?" a voice called to them from the dark shadows. Billy was not stopping here in the middle of the open space. He ignored the shout and kept walking, Jack following closely at his heels.

"Who goes there?" This time the voice asking the question came across with a squeakier, higher pitch. Whoever it was, there was no need for Billy to panic.

"It's me, Billy Miller," he declared, "why, who are you?"

And with two more paces he was into the shadows, safely under the wharf. Well, as safely as it was possible to be in the shelter of a wooden structure in the middle of a raging inferno.

Billy could see the shape of a boy standing in front of him.

"Who are you? I said," he was going to brazen this one out.

"I'm Ronnie, an' this is my wharf."

The boy looked about fourteen to Billy, but he didn't seem to want trouble, so Billy dropped his aggressive posture slightly. The two sized each other up as Jack lurked behind Billy, waiting to see which way the wind was going to blow.

"Get caught out in it as well, did you?" asked Ronnie, as though he was discussing a particularly nasty rain shower.

Billy adopted the same irreverent tone, "Yeah, you know, just wanted to 'ave a look 'cos well, we'll never see nothin' like tonight again, will we?"

Ronnie chuckled. It was amazing how quickly children will bond when the mood takes them.

"Oh, no boys, you're wrong there! This war ain't all going to be over and done with in one night. There's goin' to be at least a couple of weeks of this so we 'ave got to make the most of it, eh?"

"What do you mean 'make the most of it'?" Billy asked.

Ronnie became more serious, "Get what we can 'afore they burn it all down, is what."

The boys settled down and began to discuss the endless possibilities of where and what they could plunder as soon as the bombing stopped, whilst civilisation burned all around them.

Hours later the bombers began drifting back in the direction of mainland Europe.

Jack cocked an ear skywards, "They're goin'," he declared.

Billy nodded in agreement.

The bombardment was easing as they headed up the rusty metal steps and started to walk towards the remnants of what used to be London. They had decided to head west into the City where Ronnie and Jack confidently expected to see the Bank of England with its doors hanging off and not a policeman, soldier or warden within sight of the place. Billy was a little less sure but had agreed to head west with them, just in case. He was, however, taking a more 'wait and see what unfolds' attitude.

Away in the distance somewhere they could still hear bombs falling, but that wasn't here, that was somewhere else. Another part of the capital perhaps, but it was no longer overhead. There was very little else to say on the subject as far as they were concerned. Yesterday, such an event was completely beyond their realms of comprehension. Today, it was just another experience in life's rich tapestry.

"Oi! What are you kids doin'?" A pair of wardens had appeared through the smoke. Fresh reinforcements from somewhere, smartly dressed in blue tunics and tin hats. They were crossing the road towards the three boys. These were the first people they had come across since leaving the docks behind.

"What do you mean 'what are we doin'?' We ain't doin' nothin'," Jack answered, playing for extra seconds to come up with something plausible. "Why, what are you doin'?" he added, causing Ronnie to snigger slightly behind his grimy hand.

"Oi! Don't be cheeky," The elder of the two tin hats gripped his younger colleague's shoulder.

"Don't be too hard on 'em son, they're just a group of dead-end kids." He lowered his voice slightly as the bombing had stopped in those few moments. All was eerily silent again and the boys clearly picked up every word he spoke.

"There's a lot of these East End kids you'll see roaming around. They ain't all bad. It's the families, too much gin, not enough work. So, don't be too harsh with 'em, they are just dead-end kids, forced to fend for themselves."

Jack's voice carried across the smoky street to the two men, "I ain't trying to be cheeky, it's just that Pat 'ere 'as lost his Granny. What with all the bombs an' that. So, when it started easing off a bit we said we would come out with him and look for her." The answer was actually quite plausible, until Billy butted in, "'Cos we're just Dead-End, East End Kids."

The boys all burst out laughing and ran away from the authority figures, who could do little except watch them go.

They had barely covered any ground when Jack stopped dead in his tracks.

"Ssssh," he ordered. "Listen, what's that noise?"

He seemed so serious, so suddenly, that the wardens also fell silent, and now they could all hear what he heard. A voice, a female voice, calling for help.

"It's coming from down 'ere," the younger of the two wardens said, as he started to climb over a pile of rubble blocking what used to be the entrance to a tenement block. It was the only way in or out to the little hovels, which yesterday were home to over a hundred people.

"Help!" There it was again.

By now both wardens were blowing frantically on their whistles then scrabbling rubble away with their bare hands, trying to get to the source of the voice as soon as they possibly could.

"Oi, Billy, Jack, come on, let's go!" Ronnie had correctly identified this as the opportune time to re-focus on the real reason they were wandering ever closer to the banking district.

"Come on," he said, "let's go. Remember?"

"Nah, you go, we're gonna see who that is shouting." Billy gave a half-wave of goodbye.

"Let the tin hats deal with her. Come on, 'else in a couple of weeks when this is all over you won't half kick yourself."

"Nah, you're alright." Billy rarely changed his mind.

"Suit yourself. More for me." He glanced across at Jack, "You comin'?"

Jack shook his head firmly. He liked Ronnie but he liked Billy better. He was staying.

Ronnie shrugged and turned on his heel. He couldn't care less; he could only afford to consider himself, anyway. Other people usually ended up being extra baggage. He wandered off, leaving them to their new found situation.

Cautiously, the two remaining boys edged closer to the pile of rubble, closer to the shouts.

It was pretty obvious what the two wardens were hoping to achieve. The cries for help were coming from the rubble-filled courtyard, so they were removing broken bricks and rubble from the pile, as fast as they could, until there was a gap big enough to permit access.

"D'you see what they're trying to do?" Jack asked.

"Yes," Billy replied doubtfully.

"Yes, the ol' lady will probably die of 'unger before that works."

Billy sniggered at his friend's wicked joke. He understood that Jack was really saying even if they did manage to create a gap large enough to be any use they would also loosen the cracked and dangerously tilted section of wall above. Loosen it to such an extent that it would probably engulf the courtyard totally, inevitably that would include wherever the pleas for help emanated from.

The two pals surveyed the scene as Billy snorted a small laugh and glancing sideways said, "Dead-End Kids."

Jack caught his eye, "Yeah, I kind of like the sound of it though, don't you?" They smiled at each other, nodding in unison as more wardens approached at speed. An unwilling pony harnessed to a cart loaded with rescue gear was being pulled along.

"I tell you somethin'," Billy offered up as a topic of conversation.

"What?" came the standard, ever curious reply.

"I bet you, I could climb up that pub there." He pointed to a four-storey building, which still had about half its frontage intact. A building that they had both passed enough times to know it was, until very recently, a pub.

"Yeah," Jack opined doubtfully.

"No. Not up the front, stupid. There up the side, up that drainpipe."

That, as an option, looked slightly more plausible to Jack. "Go on," he said, "then what?"

"Then, across the roof there and from that edge," he pointed, "lower a rope down to the court. Then the old lady could tie herself on." He paused for questions but Jack had none at this stage. He knew climbing skills ran deep in Billy. If he had wanted to be pedantic Jack could have pointed out that she wasn't necessarily an 'old lady', nor did they have a rope to hand but otherwise, to him, for someone as agile as Billy Miller, it was possible.

Billy explained the rest of his plan to Jack. He was seriously considering scaling a metal drainpipe on the side of a four-storey building whose front was being greedily licked by white hot flames. That bit was easy; scaling drainpipes was second nature to these kids.

Then he would have to jump across a missing section of roof to the adjoining property. A dangerous jump of several feet that would see him land on a high narrow ledge, but a pretty straightforward jump in Billy's eyes. Then he would move at speed along the narrow ledge, the length of two houses. Half way along that ledge, with smoke and heat no doubt hampering every move, he would have to loop his rope through the eye of a pulley before continuing to the corner of the ledge, where he would drop one end down to the helpless woman before returning to safety, the way he had come. Here he could give the other end of the rope to the fire wardens and their pony could pull her to safety.

To a couple of ten-year-old urchins on their very first day in a war zone it was a very cunning plan indeed, and it just might work.

"So, go on then," Billy muttered, "get over to that warden's cart and grab me the longest piece of rope they got on board."

Jack glanced across at the truck. A small group of people had gathered there now, but all were totally preoccupied with shifting rubble. For Jack this would be a doddle. He was well known for his 'sticky fingers', his ability to make desirable objects that weren't necessarily his, stick to the inside of his pockets. He sauntered nonchalantly across to the cart and was back at Billy's side within a few short minutes.

"This was the longest one," he handed across a big, thick, heavy coil of rope, "but I didn't know if it would be long enough, so I got this as well." He handed other another heavy coil.

"Nicely done, Jack." Billy dropped to his knees and swiftly, with confident movements, knotted the two pieces together and looped the extended length of rope across his shoulder.

"Right, Jacky boy, when you see me waving, get them blokes ready to pull all together on the rope, got it?"

Jack nodded. He had his orders and he knew what to do. He was silently thrilled to be on the team. He wasn't going to be letting the side down.

The two boys circled in a loop so as to approach the passage with Billy nearer to it, Jack shielding him from what was, by now, a small crowd.

When they drew level with the narrow gap Jack paused, stretched and made a show of looking about him, while Billy slipped quietly into the shadowy passageway and was gone. Instantly, he was shinning up the old metal drainpipe with confidence, speed and great agility.

Only when he saw his pal was halfway up the pub did Jack continue with his leisurely pace towards the cluster of helpful citizens.

"That wall'll collapse if you keep taking bricks away," he observed, raising his voice to carry above the confused chatter and pointing at the section of wall in question.

People turned to stare at this scruffy little urchin who seemed to have appeared out of the depths of the smoke. Surely, he was far too young to be out alone on such a dangerous night as this and, surely, he was way too poor to have any legitimate business around here.

"Excuse me young fellow, nobody was addressing you," a man told him with a sneer.

"Maybe so, Mister, but you are now, ain't you?" He smiled purposefully to really infuriate him before adding, "Anyway, my mate up there…" he pointed skywards and, of course, they all followed his finger with their eyes.

"My mate is..." but they had stopped listening; Billy was sixty feet above them, crossing a ledge only inches wide, arms outstretched and flames licking at his legs. Jack raised his voice,

"Oi! Listen! My mate is going to lower the rope down to her. The other end 'e'll wrap round that pulley." He pointed to an old lifting pulley on the side of the building next door to the pub. It was a relic from when the place had been a working Victorian warehouse and large crates had been unloaded from the back of horse-drawn carts into the store rooms on the top floors. The men could see what the kid was planning to do and if they used the pony they might even be able to hoist the trapped woman to safety.

"Go on kid!" someone shouted. The crowd began muttering encouraging snippets that grew louder and more voracious as Billy worked closer and closer to his intended destination. Finally, he had looped the rope through the pulley and was leaning right out over the courtyard. From up there he should be able to see whoever it was calling for help.

Up on the rooftop Billy could hear the woman still calling out, but the smoke drifting across was obscuring his vision. He couldn't spot her on the ground and didn't know where to aim, where to drop the rope.

Then he thought he caught a brief movement but he wasn't sure. It might have just been flames dancing in the light. He wiped his eyes and looked again. There it was again and there she was, waving a red handkerchief up at him. He waved back, silently satisfied with his guess work. All he had to do was edge maybe ten feet to his left and he would be directly above her. He shuffled along as close to the edge as gravity would allow, while flames lapped at his feet and the smoke billowed in circles around him.

He shouted at the top of his voice, "I'm goin' to throw down a rope. Tie yourself on, alright?"

He didn't wait for a response; he had removed the rope from around his waist in a flash. Now he hurled one end far out over the edge. The rope's own weight forced it to fall at quite a speed. Billy held on tightly to his end and edged backwards on the slippery roof tiles until his back struck against the chimney stack. He gripped hard and braced himself. He wasn't expecting a sudden jolt as the rope should be much too long, but he wasn't taking unnecessary chances. At least, in his mind he wasn't taking unnecessary chances. Those watching him from below thought he was taking a massive chance.

Chapter Six

DAWN was breaking over London as people stirred in the make-shift air raid shelter that was St. Mary's tube station. Over ten thousand people had used it on the first night of the Blitz and over the next few hours, as morning came and went, they would all venture back above ground. Some as single figures, others in pathetic little family groups and all would do precisely the same thing on reaching ground level. Stand blinking in the daylight, scanning from left to right and right to left, trying to establish that their eyes were not deceiving them, just standing in the middle of the road, gawping in absolute shock, at the devastation surrounding them. Fires may not carry the same gravitas in the daytime, but piles of rubble where tall buildings had stood only yesterday and dead bodies lying uncovered in the streets brought home the seriousness of the night to each and everyone who surfaced, young and old, rich and poor. Right across the sprawling city, people were re-assessing what they held dear and when the chickens really had come home to roost, finding themselves coming up with completely different answers than they would have expected to.

Midday came and went and still so much was burning that smoke from all corners of the capital was mingling together and blowing across the river, creating a dense, threatening cloud. A cacophony of noise filled the streets, against the steady backdrop of the endless ringing of church bells. Shouts echoed everywhere, mostly calls for those still missing, mostly unintelligible. Confusion reigned supreme. People were trying to return home, but in many cases their homes no longer existed. Elderly citizens sat alone here and there on piles of dusty house bricks, their progress blocked by huge craters stretching from one side of the road to the other and taking in both pavements. From some of these huge craters the tails of unexploded bombs could be clearly seen facing skywards. These attracted excited groups of local children, craning their necks to look down in the hole, trying to spot real, live bombs with their own eyes. Creeping ever closer, daring each other to actually reach out and touch a real, live, German bomb. Wardens in white tin hats scurried around the area, entrusted to keep the children from harm's way as best they could.

I shuffled out of the tube station like everybody else, blinking and rubbing my eyes. I took in the scene of horror with no more than a sweeping glance, I had my own problems. Somebody pushed me aside to get past, and I shot them an angry look.

"Don't push me, just 'cos I'm old. 'ave some respect, you."

But the shape had already moved on. I shuffled along, knowing I should have probably kept the boy with me, but what can you do? I wondered if I should return home to see if Billy turned up.

'Sod it, he'll be alright.' I took a left turn instead, swinging open the door of the nearest public house. The nightmares were returning with a vengeance, the beginnings of bad thoughts creeping into my tired mind. I needed a drink.

I was who I was because of that night. Oh, that night. If only we hadn't gone into Dutfield's Yard. If only it hadn't started raining. If only, if only. 'You baby!' I admonished my weakness, but I had talked about the old days all night. I had let the genie out of the bottle again. The memories came flooding back as I remembered that night. I had to fight it, couldn't let sleep take hold of me. I was exhausted, but I had to keep moving. They hadn't let me sit in the pub for very long. They had a rule about old tramps who sit talking to themselves with no money to spend. So I had started walking. Within two streets I saw a hole in an off-licence shop with shelves full of Scotch whisky. I climbed across the small mound of rubble and helped myself. It was that easy. I was beginning to like the war a lot more now the bombing had stopped.

I had kept on walking until I had come to the bank of the River Thames. Then I had simply turned right and followed the Embankment all the way to Westminster Palace and the clock of Big Ben. I found a park just past the famous gothic building, where I crawled into a flower bed. Night had fallen now and I reasoned that I would be safe enough here. I could see the shiny Westminster Bridge stretching magnificently across the mighty river. I knew that the far bank was south. I wished that I was heading south or west or even to the cold, bitter north. I wished I had anywhere to go except east, but life didn't work like that. I pulled my rags tighter around my neck and gratefully fell asleep, too drunk to dream.

In the morning I was woken by the toe of a man gently poking me in the small of my back. I opened my eyes, instantly remembering the events of the previous day, grimacing at the thought of what today may bring. Unaware I had slept through a second night of bombing. I rolled over to face my tormentor, oblivious to the look of panic etched deeply into my face.

"What are you doin? Don't panic, it's alright." The stranger, on catching a glimpse of my worried countenance, had been startled. He had certainly not intended to frighten the poor vagabond that I am.

I had looked up into the stranger's eyes. Even in my half-awake state I could see he looked just as worried as I was. I had imagined it was the Ripper kicking me again. So the relief at being kicked by someone I had never set eyes on was more of a blessing than he would ever know.

"You hungry?" asked the smartly dressed young man, fishing into his pocket.

I nodded, and he smiled.

"Here." He flicked a shiny sixpence in the manner of someone tossing a coin. It spun through the air towards me and in one fluid motion I plucked it cleanly out of the sky and secreted it deep within my pocket. We briefly locked eyes and allowed smiles to pass over our mouths.

"Good catch," he offered, still smiling.

"Thanks," I mumbled.

The benevolent stranger tipped his hat in reply and continued his amble through the little park, heading towards Westminster Palace. I watched him go, genuinely amazed at the act of random kindness that had just fallen into my lap. 'Maybe war did that to people,' I mused.

Years before, back when I was ten, a similar act of random kindness had befallen me, just when I had needed it most

That day, I had roamed the streets of the West End. I had bought a toffee apple in Trafalgar Square, wandered down to Fleet Street and purchased a piece of pork from a street vendor.

I had spent hours amusing myself by watching the toffs strutting up and down Regent Street, but as the afternoon grew colder and more and more people kept pouring out of the offices and shops it began to get too crowded. People were staring. I became more conscious of the rags I called my clothes. I made the mistake of comparing myself with those passing me in the street dressed in posh clothing. Subconsciously, at that point I started heading east and then, suddenly, I could see the Tower of London. I wasn't that far from home. I didn't try and fight it. Oddly, I wanted to go home; it had been a long day. I was ready; I just hoped there was nobody in when I got there.

I had been walking for hours. There were very few places to sit and rest up West, I had decided. Wearily, with a heavy heart, I had trudged past the Aldgate Pump and was instantly back in the East End. I dragged my heels and tried to talk myself off this chosen path, but deep in my heart of hearts, even at ten years old, I knew that this was where I truly belonged.

As I had entered Whitechapel the very atmosphere changed. Groups of people were gathered in doorways and outside shops, heads bowed close, their voices kept to whispers. I picked up the odd word as I passed them. 'Ripper' and 'Unfortunates' floated through the air alongside me. I kept my head down and at the speed of a chief mourner continued picking my way through the crowds, back to the squalid little room I knew as home.

Taking a deep breath to try and stay calm I slipped into the narrow alley that gave access to the courtyard where I lived and who should be the first person to come into view? It was Ma's boyfriend. He was standing with Mickey and Alf at the oil drum. They all looked up as I exited the alleyway.

Mickey called out sharply, "Come 'ere boy!"

I crossed the courtyard and stood at the oil drum across from them, with my head bowed.

"Where've you been?" Mickey wanted to know.

I glanced up at the killer. He smiled back, enjoying me being on the spot, interested in what I would give as an answer.

"I... I got a bit lost," I replied.

I felt my cheeks starting to burn. I hesitated; strongly tempted to turn on my heel and run for it, but then Ma appeared behind me at the door of our room. She called out, "Percy! Where the bloody 'ell 'ave you been?"

Without saying a word I turned and ran towards her.

I had a clear line to her. I ran for Ma as fast as I could, burying myself in her swirling green skirts.

She was all ready to chastise me for disappearing for so long, but the unexpected display of affection had caught her somewhat off-guard.

She had ruffled the top of my dirty head in the manner of one not accustomed to displays of tenderness. She dragged me inside and the laughter of Mickey and his men followed us through the door.

"Where the bloody 'ell 'ave you been, Percy? They've been askin' about you." She knuckled the top of my head. As I didn't answer the silence hung briefly in the air, punctuated only by the sound of the men laughing and crowds on the streets in the background.

"Well you're 'ere now, I suppose," she mumbled less harshly and the knuckles pressed into my head turned to the more gentle palms of her hands. I held on to her tightly, genuinely pleased that she was still alive.

Displays of emotion were rare around here and within a few short moments I began to release my grip. Ma was all right and he was quiet, he didn't seem drunk or in a bad mood. That was enough for me. That was about as good as it got. I released Ma's legs and attempted to slip into the back of the room I called home. She, however, had other ideas.

"Where do you think you're goin'?" she shrieked at me in the tone of voice I was much more used to. We were mother and son again, back on old familiar territory.

"Jus' goin' in 'ere is all, to lie down."

"No you ain't, it's getting dark. I don't need you in the corner cluttering up the place now. Go see if Nannie Johns will let you stay with 'er if you're so bleedin' tired."

I turned and looked her in the eye. I was tired and it had been a long day. I was prepared to argue the point even if she was my mother, but the defeated expression she wore would have made stinging accusations too easy to land home. I understood she didn't want me out of the way, but she had no choice because of them. Crossing the yard I glanced towards the oil drum where the men always gathered. Bertie Smalls nodded at me and I nodded reverentially back, then turned quickly away. I didn't want to risk catching the eye of Ma's boyfriend, that maniac. The throat Ripper. I looked back to Ma standing in the doorway and nodded at her, trying to tell her with my eyes that I understood. Then giving her boyfriend and his mates a wide berth I trudged through the mud to the far end of the court.

Access to the courtyard in which we lived could only be achieved by way of the alley. This alley was our first line of defence. It may open straight onto the High Street but very few ventured down here that didn't belong.

Our alley was the length of the two houses it ran between. Mickey liked it kept unlit and two people meeting in it would have to turn side on to each other in order to pass simultaneously. The alley opened up onto a square, muddy yard. The first thing you saw in the middle of the yard was a water trough and an old oil drum with a fire in it. For as far back as I can remember there was usually at least two or three men sitting or standing around. Sometimes they were playing cards and drinking. Sometimes arguing and drinking and sometimes just drinking. To the right of the alley was our room, number 1. It was the back room of a High Street shop really but someone had blocked it off from the rest of the shop and made a door at the back and it had become part of the court. Next to our room there was another door but that led into the shop passage and out to the High Street. Only the men ever used that door and they only used it late at night. I knew 'cos their crates scraping against the other side of the wall and their nervous horses would wake me up and I would lie dead still, listening as they unloaded crates and boxes containing all manner of things. Following those occasions the next day would be like a holiday as me and Stan would be sent out to the markets and the pubs, spreading the word on what was for sale. We always managed to cream off a little for ourselves and I'd lie there counting how many loads they carried through and imagining what might be in those loads.

Straight ahead, opposite the alley opening, there were three more rooms, numbers 2, 3 and 4. These were where the women would bring the sailors, dockers and even foreign fellows who wanted sex.

On the left hand side and around the corner were numbers 5 and 6. Nannie Johns lived in the far corner in number 6. She wasn't really my nan but she had known me since I was a baby. She was older than my Ma and all the other women so she didn't have to walk the streets at night anymore. She generally stayed home, minding things, like an old nannie would. She had always been a favourite of mine and I still had a piece of pork left that she would, no doubt, be most grateful to share with me. Nannie Johns' it would be then. It was as good a place as any when I wanted to be left alone for a while.

One afternoon a few days later I was helping Nannie polish some pocket watches she was minding for Mickey, when the door creaked open unexpectedly and there was Ma, bold as brass. She came straight over to where I was sitting on the floor and ruffled my hair.

"Alright Percy are you?"

I looked up at her, scanning her face for bruises, as I always did. She was in surprisingly good condition. She carried the remnants of a scratch on her left ear, but that was an old injury and it was healing. No new markings, that was good.

"I'm alright Ma, I like it 'ere." I glanced across the room. Nannie was collecting up the watches into a box, acting as though we weren't there. I jabbed a thumb towards her. "With 'er," I added.

She looked up now and smiled at me, but didn't say anything.

Nannie had collected all the watches now, except the one I was polishing. She snatched it out of my hand, snatched the cloth from my other hand and placed the watch in the box with the others, covering them all over with the cloth.

"I'm just gonna nip these over to Mickey," she announced over her shoulder and we were alone. Outside I could hear a paper boy calling out the headlines, trying to sell his papers. I couldn't hear the words, but then I didn't really have to. There was only one headline round here these days.

When we were alone Ma came closer and hugged the top of my head again.

"So you're alright, really?"

"Yeah, I'm fine," I looked up at her. "What about you?" I couldn't help adding.

"Oh, listen to you. Proper little gent, askin' 'ow the lady is. You are growin' up ain't you?"

But there was something in her tone that betrayed her too casual manner. I had touched a nerve and we both knew it. Maybe something in my tone had given away that I perhaps knew more than she had originally realised.

My raised eyebrow left the question hanging in the air. Finally she could bear it no longer.

"Yeah, I'm alright," she said, "you ain't gotta worry none about me."

But she was protesting too hard and we both knew it.

"Ma, what about your fella. He ain't..."

She interrupted me with a sneer.

"He ain't my fella," she could see I was unconvinced. So she tried another tack.

"No, you got it all wrong, 'e's just a friend is all. 'E lent me some money a while back you see an' 'e's just gonna be around for a while 'til I pays 'im back is all." She stared into my eyes defying me to doubt her story. "That's all," she added with finality.

So that was that. She had given me her version of events and I could take it or leave it. I was brought up to know that when my Ma told a lie she was going to stick to it, no matter what.

"So 'e won't be around for long?" I said doubtfully

"Nah, dearie, 'e'll be gone soon." She sounded genuine.

"That's good, 'cos I don't like 'im," I said.

She smiled and ruffled my hair.

"That's fine. Cos you don't 'ave to like 'im," she slipped her arm around my waist. "You still like me though, right?"

I smiled up at her, "Course, you're my Ma, ain't you."

She hugged me tight and for a split second the maniac went completely out of my head.

The next day I stayed in Nannie's window spying on the comings and goings in the courtyard, but I didn't see Ma's 'friend', not even once. A few more days passed and still there was no sign of him. I saw Ma hanging out the washing and went to see her, but she only wanted to talk about me staying indoors too much and wanted to know what was troubling me. So I made an excuse that Nannie needed me and ran back to my surveillance spot at the window. I didn't like being asked what was wrong. Where would I start? It was impossible to tell Ma, or anybody, what was troubling me. But I had to admit I hadn't seen him for, well five whole days and nights. Maybe Ma was telling the truth, maybe he was gone and that would be the end of it.

After witnessing the murder in the yard Stan had also been laying low. Part of me wanted to see him, to discuss with somebody else what had happened that night. Yet only when a full week had passed did he venture out again. I saw him with a couple of other boys and they all had toffee apples, but I resisted the temptation to call out to them, just kept up my surveillance.

Then fate took a hand and I had to go outside. One of our gang had taken a beating from the Blind Beggar boys, so everyone moved around in groups whilst the tit-for-tat beatings were ongoing. I was needed to set an ambush on the Ratcliffe Highway with Stan. Then a week became a fortnight. There had been no more murders and the Blind Beggar Gang wanted to call a truce; I started to relax slightly on both fronts.

Three weeks after the event Stan and I finally found ourselves alone together. We both felt awkward. But now that we finally had an opportunity to discuss that night I no longer felt the need. Odd we were such good friends before, told each other everything. Now we couldn't even look each other in the eye.

"'Ave you told anyone?" I finally asked, looking at him from the side.

Stan shook his head vehemently in denial. He knew exactly what I was talking about. "'Ave you?" he shot back, still looking straight ahead.

"Nah," I mumbled, just loud enough for him to hear.

"Did you see 'is face?" I managed to ask without tripping over the words, terrified that he might say yes. Not really enjoying this conversation one little bit.

"I didn't look," he paused then added, "did you?" Now he was looking at me.

I shook my head in the negative and shrugged my shoulders. Inside I experienced conflicting emotions. Part of me was glad that Stan still had no idea as to the killer's identity yet, at the same time, part of me hated the idea of bearing such a piece of information on my own.

"We won't be going to Dutfield's Yard again anytime soon, eh!" I managed to spit out.

Stan jumped down from the wall as though he had not a care in the world and scooped up a news sheet that was blowing down the road and had gotten trapped by his expertly timed jump…

"Not bloody likely," he answered.

He smoothed out the crumpled-up sheet and instantly we were staring at the picture of a shadowy ghoul clutching a long knife. We couldn't read the words around the image, but we didn't really have to. Stan dropped the sheet as his face returned to the ashen shade he had been sporting for the past three weeks.

"Come on," he said, whilst screwing the news sheet into a ball and kicking it down the road, where the wind caught it and sent it flying back past us. "Let's go!"

If only we could get rid of our thoughts so easily, I mused.

I jumped from the wall as well and side by side we headed down Whitechapel High Street, darting unnoticed through the trams, horses and crowds of people. I followed Stan.

"Anyway," he called to me over his shoulder, "in a few weeks we will probably 'ave forgotten all about it."

"Yeah," I agreed as enthusiastically as I could. I was still blissfully unaware that the murder would haunt me forever. We were young, we didn't realise that was how the world worked. Get caught up in something beyond your control as a child and regret your actions for the rest of your days.

I managed to stay with Nannie for a bit longer than expected. She didn't ask why, which I appreciated, just said she would clear it with my Ma. So I stopped staying indoors, made a point of managing to avoid the boyfriend. But we were living in such close proximity it was a meeting that could only be postponed for so long.

One morning I was trying to sneak out of the courtyard unseen. I had made it as far as the street end of the alley, thought I was home and dry in fact, when I spotted a familiar shape, one foot up on the wall, blocking my exit.

"'Ello little fella. Where you off to in such an 'urry then?" He attempted a smile and my heart sank.

"Nowhere," I replied noncommittally.

"Good, 'cos I need you to come with me."

He grabbed me firmly by the wrist and began to march me down the High Street. Resistance was pointless and besides if I complied he might loosen his grip, might stop hurting me. I complied, scurrying along behind him, trying to keep pace with his huge steps. Wondering if this was it, today I was going to die. We walked for many minutes, were almost at the river before he finally loosened his grip. But, although my wrist throbbed, this was not the end of it. Not the signal I had hoped for. He had released me with one hand right enough, but with the other he had slammed me up against a wall. He caught me off-guard, the suddenness of his moves pushing the air out of my lungs. I tried to catch a breath as he leant in close and whispered menacingly.

"When we get to these warehouses I'm goin' to lift you up to a little window." He grabbed me more firmly, wringing the neck of my shirt so tight I could barely breathe. He saw the pain in my eyes and smiling with pleasure he leant in closer, satisfied that he had my full attention, "An' you are goin' to drop in an' come runnin' as fast as you can to open the door an' let me in. Got it?"

I nodded my head in agreement, with as much conviction as I could muster.

Without another word he released his grip on my throat and in a fluid movement grabbed me once again by the wrist. With him pulling and me following we continued on our way.

I could see the masts of the giant ships now over the roofs of the warehouses. We were practically at the river and I couldn't understand why there were not men all over the place. I didn't bother commenting on the lack of people, just counted my lucky stars and assumed he had arranged it that way.

"'Ere we are, down this alley, boy. This one, 'ere, 'ere," he was hissing at me.

There really had been no need. I had heard him, had understood, it was just that normally on these sort of jobs we were told not to speak unless it was absolutely essential.

His amateur ways would be his undoing I told myself.

"This door, right," he tapped his knuckles on an old wooden side door as we walked past it.

I glanced at it, not quite catching his eye, but close enough, and nodded that I understood.

Twenty paces ahead of us was a little window, probably a staff cloakroom I guessed. That window was the only jot on an otherwise solid brick wall. Obviously that would be my way in.

He shoved me roughly towards it and cupped his hands together for me to use as a step.

"That side door, got it?" he hissed as I put my arms around his neck and my foot on his hands. I actually felt his breath on my cheek as I lifted myself up, but I was too scared to look into his eyes. Not scared of the job, I had done this hundreds of times. Not even scared of him being a murderer. I knew lots of killers. No, I was scared because I had never met anyone before who would go out killing in their free time, for fun. I was scared for my Ma.

Inside I padded down the cold warehouse. Crates were piled everywhere, blocking my way. I walked forwards with my hands outstretched in front of me, manoeuvring around the crates. Running on instinct I headed in the general direction of the door. After what felt like long minutes, but was probably only a matter of seconds, I finally saw the side door. Gratefully, I hurried to open it for him. As he squeezed in I attempted to slip past him out into the light, but he grabbed the back of my jacket and pushed me back inside, sending me sprawling up the passage.

"No you bloody don't. Get up there, there, left," he pointed and I went the way of his finger. Then he closed the door and using a metal spike he began frantically to pierce the boxes, seemingly at random, obviously looking for something in particular.

It didn't take long and he found it. He began ripping at the opening and hissing at me to come closer.

"Here," he shoved a paper envelope into my hands and began filling it with tea. In no time at all we were both carrying large amounts of loose tea about our persons and he hissed at me to get out of there.

"We're goin' back to the flash 'ouse and I don't wanna 'ear a word out o' you 'til we get there." He kicked me on the rear to emphasise the point.

By 'the flash 'ouse' I knew he meant number 5, next to Nannie Johns. This was the place where they organised robberies and stashed their weapons. This was the place where we were trained in stealing watches and handkerchiefs. The place where money was divided up and they said the tunnels beneath your feet contained more gold than the Bank of England.

We made it back without any mishaps and he told me to sit by the fireplace while Nannie Johns weighed up the tea and put it into packets that would be small enough to sell in the market and the pubs.

I lay with my eyes closed in front of the fire, knowing that tomorrow I would be selling tea. I fell asleep and dreamt of my Ma laying on the cobbles somewhere, with her throat cut open.

The next day was the 10th of October and I was up bright and early down the market, my pockets filled with packets of tea. Through the whole month he had me with him every day, there were no murders in October, because we were selling tea during the day and at night he was busy working for Mickey.

That whole month Mickey was unbearable, he wanted everyone out working their fingers to the bone. Then he said, come Friday the 9th of November, the Lord Mayor's Day Procession, we could all take the day off and spend it with our pockets full. We could see the sense in this and we obligingly focused on the carrot being offered.

We talked about the coming festivities and it gave us something else to discuss other than the murders. I still had my nightmares, but not every night now.

On the day of the Lord Mayor's parade I was up early as usual, I headed down to the market, looking forward to the Punch and Judy show in particular.

Without thinking about it I was eavesdropping as I walked. Then I heard a snippet and my heart skipped a beat. My worst fear had come true, and on today of all days.

The Ripper has struck again. I had dared to hope that was an end to it, now that he knew I had seen him, he would stop. I had been very wrong; he had stopped because Mickey hadn't given him any free time that was all. As soon as he had been given a night off he was straight back at it. Unusually for such an early hour the commotion was of the angry sort. A communal buzz, the noise of a group of scared people getting angry. The sound of a crowd not satisfied with the answers to their questions.

I exited the market and saw immediately where the noise was emanating from. I could see a man standing on a crate outside the Fruit and Wool Exchange, addressing a crowd so large they were spilling off the pavements right out into the street. I shuffled closer and heard him clearly say.

"People of Whitechapel 'ave we not 'ad enough?"

A loud cheer went up from the crowd. Discreetly I scanned their faces, recognising most of them as neighbours, men and women who lived in the courts. Courts that spread the length and breadth of Whitechapel and covering all parts of the East End.

The man on the crate said something about the Chief of Police, old Warren, how he was calling us dangerous people 'cos we think for ourselves, and the crowd booed Warren's name then cheered again at the comment that quickly followed.

I focused my attention back on the speaker just in time to hear him say, "And that is why we formed the Whitechapel Vigilance Committee an' we need you," he jabbed a finger at the crowd again and again, emphasising the fact that he needed them all to assist.

"Yes, we need you, 'cos the police ain't doin' nothin' to catch this maniac," he raised his voice in order to make himself heard over the cacophony of 'boos' that had started once again at the mere mention of the police.

"Last night, just down there," he motioned to his right, "another poor unfortunate was done to death. This time in 'er own bed."

Cries of shock and horror emanated from the ever-growing band assembled before him.

"So there will be a meetin' at my yard in the Mile End Road at 7 o'clock this evening."

I had heard enough. I turned on my heel and slunk back towards Nannie Johns. The phrase 'He has struck again' was ringing in my ears. Tears began to well up in my eyes. I bowed my head and hurried back inside as fast as I could, before anyone saw me crying.

Chapter Seven

As I got older I realised the best way to keep the demons at bay was to drink myself into a stupor. Mainly I drink to forget the Ripper, only now I also drink to forget the German bombers. Oh well, that's the beauty of drinking to oblivion, any old excuse will do. If you want to add excuses to the list as you go along, that's fine too. Drinking hard was definitely my plan today and I intended to get on with it as soon as possible.

The bar-room door had barely stopped swinging when it came flying open again. I re-appeared shouting over my shoulder, "I fought in the last war for you lot."

"No you never, Percy Miller, you went AWOL I seem to remember," the taunts followed me down the street, followed by laughter.

That particular day for no particular reason I headed west. I passed large numbers of people all nervously scanning the sky for more bombers. I kept my eyes glued to the ground. Somewhere around here lay something that would enable me to get absolutely blotto, I just had to find it, whatever it might be. And whatever it was, I certainly wouldn't find it up in the clouds. I really came into my own playing the opportunist while they were all distracted by warplanes. It really was like taking sweeties from a baby.

I didn't have to wait very long before I hit the jackpot. A few streets further on a brewery had taken a direct hit. A 5000lb bomb had skidded through one of its perimeter walls, but the device had not exploded. Merely crashed all the way through to the offices and it looked like the place was unsafe because nobody was around. I could see crates and crates of ale stacked up in piles, clearly visible through the hole in the wall.

I slowed my movements to a crawl. Slower and slower until with mock exhaustion I slumped to a sitting position on the kerb right by the gaping hole. I scratched my itchy scalp and picked at a scab on my neck, all the time surreptitiously scanning the surrounding area. There were people on the street, but none that could be mistaken for authority figures, and absolutely nobody paying any attention to me. My elaborate pretence of an old man sitting on a random pile of bricks had been totally unnecessary. I abandoned all attempts at discretion and rising to my feet peered through the hole.

By mid-afternoon I was three sheets to the wind and slumped on a kerb along Whitechapel High Street. I had been sleeping soundly, totally devoid of the usual nightmares when I was rudely awakened by the high pitched whine of the air-raid warning system. That was the trouble with ale, those sirens would never have been able to penetrate through a decent whisky black out.

The ear splitting noise had woken me with a start, disorientating me completely. That horrible split second of dread that hit me immediately upon waking. I didn't know where I was. I looked left, then right, taking in my surroundings and although it had changed dramatically I realised that I was on the High Street. It was all right, I began to breathe more easily. People were hurrying about me in all directions. All desperate to get underground as quickly as they possibly could, all except me. I liked the empty streets, the easy pickings. It had been exactly the same yesterday with this palpable tension in the air. Not quite a collective fear, but definitely making everyone very nervous. Definitely stopping them worrying about me. I heard the sound of approaching engines, it looked like the Germans were coming back to give us another going over, coming back for so many consecutive nights I had lost count. No wonder that people were starting to look a bit more edgy than usual. I grabbed for the beer bottle that I hadn't quite drained and took a long pull. A woman tripped over my legs in her haste to get to a shelter no doubt, she hadn't noticed me there, with her eyes turned skywards, trying to make out the shape of the approaching aeroplanes.

"Oi! Watch it!" I called after her.

She didn't slow her pace, probably had a cute little family shelter that she was rushing to, sod 'er, sod them all. I took another swig, I wasn't moving. I had run away underground on the first night and it had caused me all end of trouble.

'What with the boy an' everything. An' the dreams back again, sod 'em, I ain't moving.'

I was unaware I was drooling and mumbling incoherently. I noticed people were passing me with a wide berth, rushing to get to the last port of the desperate. Into the underground station before the bombs started dropping again. But I was used to being ignored, would have found it strange if they had not behaved in such a way. I knew I wasn't really appreciated by the general public. Knew only too well that people had their own worries, their own concerns, and now on top of everything else, there was a war to worry about.

Anti-aircraft guns suddenly opened up, firing long arcs high into the sky. They were followed almost instantly by the droning of engines above our heads.

"Sod you!" I raised my bottle skywards as the bombers passed so low their shadows danced across the rooftops.

"Sod you and all who sail in you," I toasted them and started giggling, absent-mindedly I scratched again at my itchy scalp. Reaching behind me to locate the exact source of the irritation was a reach too far. Even in a sitting position I was too wobbly to remain upright. I fell backwards still laughing and the back of my head hit the kerb with a resounding crack.

Chapter Eight

ONE rainy night, a week after the non-event of the Lord Mayor's day, I was sleeping in front of the cold fireplace at Nannie Johns. I had found a puppy that day and it was curled up with me. Taking the place of the cold fire and keeping me warm with his thick fur. I was probably having my best night's sleep in months. Like all good things it came to a sudden, unwanted end.

I was woken by the sound of the door being kicked open.

The mutt scurried away at my thrashing arms, my warmth cruelly vanished with him.

I had roused slightly in the manner of one who thinks they are still asleep. Now, without the dog for warmth, I was most certainly wide awake.

I woke up and it was just a dream. A week had passed now since poor Mary Kelly got it and I was having the same nightmares every night again. It was no good, despite his threats to my Ma, I had to do something. I had to tell Mickey. I slipped through the door and saw Bertie standing at the oil drum, I sidled up to him, scanning the yard for Ma's boyfriend, but luckily he was nowhere to be seen.

"Alright, Kid?" He could see by my expression that I wasn't all right.

"I need to speak to Mickey," I told him.

"Alright, wait 'ere, I'll go tell 'im."

The next thing I remember I was standing in front of Mickey's table, blurting out the whole story, stressing over and over how he had threatened to kill Ma if I had said anything to anyone.

"Alright Percy, you done the right thing, leave it with me, go back to your room. Percy!"

I turned to face him.

"Not a word now."

So I had gone back to the empty room and hidden behind the door, hoping to see them frogmarching him to his execution. But I fell asleep and when I woke up the sun was in the sky and the street hustle was at full volume. I ignored the hunger pains and stayed put.

Only when it was dark did Mickey finally call me. I dutifully stood at the end of his table and he gave me a hunk of bread and told me not to worry about that problem anymore. Then he gave me a hessian package and dismissed me with the phrase, "Look after that for me boy."

It was shortly after this that Stan got killed in a knife fight in Bethnal Green. Still I carried on. In some ways I envied him his release from the day-to-day torment of knowing what we knew. Now it was my secret, and Mickey's. But Stan was gone and I had gin to help me sleep.

One morning a few days after Stan's death I woke up with a real hankering for a warm, fresh hunk of bread. So I pulled my jacket over my nightshirt and padded down to the market in the High Street. It was only when I went to pay for the bread that I realised I had come out without any money. But no problem, I bought bread here every day, he knew me. At least that's what you would think. But, unfortunately for me, we had beaten his son the week before and he had a real problem with me about it. So he starts shouting and screaming and going on and on so naturally I just took the loaf.

"Ain't you goin' to pay for that?" he shouted after me.

"Screw you!" I had shouted back.

It was sheer bad luck that was the precise moment when two Bobbies turned the corner and witnessed our little exchange. Well, these two policemen didn't particularly like me that much anyway and they had been dying to pin something on me for ages. So you can just imagine how excited they got, handcuffing me in front of everyone and making a real song and dance about taking me in. They got me for receiving bread under false pretences and gave me three months hard labour in the clink.

On my release I headed back to the courtyard with trepidation. I had been away for three months, which had felt like a lifetime to me serving my sentence. But I stepped from the High Street into the alley and nothing had changed. It was as though I had never even been away. I swear there were even the same hoods standing around the fire. It was then that I realised nothing ever changed around here. I went to the room I shared with Ma. Fortunately for me the room was empty. That was a pleasant surprise, I had been expecting, well I don't know what I had been expecting, but a quiet, empty space wasn't it. I slid down on the floor and raising the floorboard touched on that familiar scrap of hessian cloth. There it was exactly where I had left it, I pulled the bag out, I needed to be absolutely certain. Heart racing I could feel something cool. I was curious as to what I had been hiding all this time and I squeezed the shape through the sack. It felt very much like a dagger to me.

I loosened the drawstring opening of the sack and worried the object out. There it was, a long, narrow, razor-sharp knife. As used, I had no doubt, by Ma's crazy boyfriend, the man they were all calling 'Jack the Ripper'. Mickey must have killed him and kept the knife as some kind of weird memento. I slid it hurriedly into the sack and stashed it back where it had lain for the past three months.

I had only a few moments to myself when there was a knock on the door.

"Hello," I heard a man's voice call.

I opened the door to be confronted by Bertie Smalls himself. He smiled his menacing grin when he saw me. I took in the smart clothes at a glance and realised that the mob must be doing well for themselves these days.

"Ma ain't 'ere," I offered as an opening gambit. Clearly he wanted to see her.

"Yeah," he sniffed, "It's you Mickey wants to 'ave a word with."

I followed Bertie across the yard to the flash house. The men around the fire smiled at me and called out pleasantries. I had done my time; I was one of them now, brothers in arms welcoming me back. I felt like a man.

Bertie pushed open the door without knocking and there was Mickey. He was sitting in a plush armchair whilst a young girl shaved him. He motioned for her to leave and wiping the foam off his face with a towel, he looked up and smiling, said to me.

"So you're back 'ome eh?"

I nodded by way of reply.

"An' I 'eard nothin' but good things about you in there. You've done well boy." He carefully folded the towel and standing up, hung it over the back of his chair.

I stood still, not thinking he really expected a response.

Mickey pulled a wad of notes from his pocket and came towards me peeling off a few from the pile. He pressed them into my hand and almost whispered at me.

"Still got that thing, boy?" he spoke quietly, but I caught the words.

I nodded again.

"Good boy, 'ere, take this, get some new clothes, go out an' 'ave a bit of fun." He still had hold of my hand and he squeezed it tightly, causing me to look up at his face. He held my gaze with his cold, black eyes adding, "Ready to join the mob proper are you?"

I was ready. I wanted the security that came with belonging to the gang and I wanted the money, but most of all I wanted to be taken seriously, to be a man.

"I'm ready," I declared.

Mickey released my hand, still smiling, still holding my eyes he added, "Bertie will be in touch."

I nodded my thanks and headed out of the door as fast as good grace would allow. As I crossed the yard I couldn't resist pulling the money out of my pocket and counting how much I had been given. Notes, banknotes, my banknotes, I liked the feeling, a lot.

Over the next two or three years I made a good living. Mainly we would bribe dock workers or threaten to hurt their families. Whatever it took, as long as it ended with us getting our hands on a cut of the valuables they brought ashore.

Then I was caught carrying a pistol and it was one arrest too far. The police wanted me behind bars and this time it seemed they would get their way. Ironically when they pinched me I hadn't done anything wrong. I had literally just bought a pistol in a pawn shop off the Tottenham Court Road. I had managed to barter the 'Uncle' down to nine shillings and so walked out of the shop feeling a little too pleased with myself and wasn't really paying attention to those around me on the street as I normally would. That was when the police grabbed me and, of course, they found the gun in my pocket. It wasn't long before they've traced this gun as being one that was used to kill a Polish Jew a few months previously. Obviously they wanted to pin his murder on me and as the pawn broker had no licence to sell firearms I couldn't really tell them exactly how it had gotten into my possession.

I kept my mouth shut and stood in the dock with my head held high. The murder charge didn't stick but the judge still sentenced me to 20 years, hard labour.

I did my years and on my release returned straight back to the courtyard I knew as home.

Mickey Tipping was long dead, as was Bertie. Nannie was gone and my Ma, the consumption had got them both the same winter apparently. The faces of all the players had changed but fundamentally everything remained the same.

Reggie Lawson was the boss now. Lads my age were the inner circle. Boys I had grown up with were the ones loitering around the oil drum. They had progressed from stealing watches and handkerchiefs. They had moved onto wagons full of goods and safes full of money. As the old guard had died or gone to prison, my pals had stepped up and filled their shoes. Such was the way in which the world worked.

Our courtyard had been condemned as unfit to live in for 30 years now, but it was still the same and we still lived there. Never saw any signs of improvement from one year to the next. They had put in some gas street lamps down Commercial Street and along the Whitechapel Road after the Ripper murders but it made no overall difference. The authorities remorselessly refused to fulfil their endless promises.

I drank the gin the boys pushed on me and forced myself on the girl they had picked out for me. All the while listening to their tales with mock interest and finally when they had all drunk their fill and exhausted their vast supplies of anecdotes, I managed to excuse myself and check on my secret hiding place. It was 1913 now, it had been nearly 25 years since I had first placed it there. I had worried constantly about it behind bars, but never said a word to a living soul. I lifted the floorboard and slipped my hand into the dark space, not really knowing whether I wanted anything to still be there or not. But my fingers touched the hessian sack and for some reason my heart soared.

Then I heard footsteps and I quickly jumped away as the door was pushed open. Reggie Lawson himself stood there in silhouette.

"Been a long time eh, Percy!" he opened the conversation.

"Yeah, but you know, it's only time," he was backlit so I couldn't read his expression.

"Good to 'ear it Percy, good to 'ear," he made as if to leave, then stopped and added over his shoulder, "welcome back."

I wasn't sure to what I owed the honour of his visit.

I stood there momentarily confused, then dismissed the moment and went to have sex again, glad to be home.

The next couple of months had been a whirlwind of activity. Reggie Lawson had pubs all over London and with the threat of war looming, business was booming. There was nothing quite like imminent disaster to whet people's whistles.

When it turned out that the whore was pregnant and that I was going to be a father far later in life than would be considered healthy the teasing and the ribbing was a constant, merciless barrage. It didn't bother me in the slightest; I was going to be a Pa. I tried to make the girl settle down with me, told her I would provide for them, but she didn't love me and didn't need no gangster who was going to get himself shot and leave her to bring up a baby alone anyway. It hurt to hear her words. So I went back to my old friend the bottle and carried on taking foolish risks trying to prove what a tough guy I was. I watched my daughter grow up surrounded by whores who smothered her with love and spoilt her like a princess and I didn't feel it was my place to try and interfere, even if I had thought for one second that they might have let me.

She survived into infancy, then into childhood and then she went to work.

I knew I was from good stock, not only had I sired a child late in life, my daughter gave birth practically nine months after she began working.

When she began to show as pregnant I took over the rent on her room. It was ironic; I was right back where I had started, responsible for the room where the dagger lay hidden. Then when the boy was still only two years old, she was stabbed to death in a brawl over money and the boy, my grandson, had nobody to look after him.

I moved back into the room and let the girls do most of the raising of the baby. I'd lost my edge in the world of robbery anyway by now and wanted to ease things up a bit before I got caught again or killed. It was strongly argued that I had brought my bad luck on myself with my constant drinking and babysitting like an old washer woman.

But Reggie made allowances owing to my years of good service and the silence I had maintained in my prison years. In the end he decided that I would keep on the room my daughter had died in and the boy could stay with me. I may not be much use in a fight any more but I could fence and mind and provide alibis and when the boy, Billy, was a few years older he too could start pulling his weight and earning his keep within the mob.

I allowed myself to accept this new role, for the boy's sake. To embrace the hand fate had dealt me. Besides it wasn't as though I was raising him alone. The working girls kept the boy clean and fed to the best of my ability. But from the very beginning he had the temperament of a caged animal and in just a few short years he didn't need me anymore. By the age of seven he was running boys much older than himself and already catching the attention of Reggie and the men at the top. He might be no more than a dirty little street urchin to society at large, but I knew he would go far in our world and my heart filled with pride every time I looked at him.

At the age of eight he no longer needed me. He had moved two of his pals into our room and they were earning a lot of money for the gang. He had outgrown whatever care I was capable of providing. I was effectively unemployed from that day on.

A few more years passed in a drunken haze, and Jack the Ripper's knife stayed put, right in the heart of his old stomping ground.

Maybe the Germans would bomb the court tonight and the knife would be forever lost or taken up by somebody with no regard for what they held. Would either outcome really be such a bad thing? Why should I care, but oddly enough, even after all these years I did care, I cared too much. I needed that knife to be where I had left it. It was the one thing I had done right in my whole life. 'Look after that for me, boy', he had said, and I had done so. In over 60 years that was the single thing I had managed to achieve. I had successfully kept a murder weapon hidden from view. It wasn't much of an achievement perhaps, but it was all I had. I needed its closeness, just to remind myself that no matter how worthless I might be in other areas here was something I had managed to do right. I listened to the bombs crashing into unseen parts of London above me and hoped Billy was safely underground somewhere.

Chapter Nine

BILLY had successfully retraced his steps back across three burning buildings. Now he stood directly above the ever growing crowd below. He took a deep breath and threw the rope down to them. He watched as eager hands grabbed at it and it was hurriedly looped a couple of times around the axle of the fire cart and tied tightly.

"Walk on, Walk on!" He heard a voice order the beast.

The pony was led at a gentle pace taking up the slack with each step. It wasn't long before the rope stood taut. The way Billy had rigged it up, if they carried on pulling, the trapped woman should soon appear on top of the pile of rubble. Billy realised the crowd had been wasting time trying to clear a way. From his vantage point he could make out the rubble was acting as a support on the two walls either side of it, holding it firmly enough that someone light should be able to guide her across the bricks and broken debris and safely down onto firm ground right amongst them.

"Walk on," he heard again and the pony set off at its usual steady pace. Shouts of encouragement came rising up to Billy's ears from the crowd.

By now Billy had reached the roof ladder on the last leg of his journey back to terra firma. One old lady was still watching him intently, but for everyone else the woman on the rope was the new focus of attention. She was just becoming visible, swinging upwards. Every time the pony took a step she rose, in a jerky manner, a few more inches. Then suddenly, as the top of her head came into view a cheer went up from the gathered onlookers. Next, her face appeared, then one jerk at a time, a few inches at a time, the rest of her rose up. She was using her feet to stop herself slamming against the wall with every jerk and in her arms she was tightly holding a screaming bundle of rags.

"I say, she's holding a child," exclaimed a male voice in the crowd.

"Yes, listen, it's a baby crying."

"Three cheers for Mother and baby, hip hip … HOORAY!" the excited response went up the customary three times.

"What drama, that's two lucky souls right there," declared one of the wardens.

There were no dead here this time. Perhaps next time, who knew, but for now, this was a tremendous victory. 'Thank the Lord for those quick-witted little urchins.' The warden swivelled three hundred and sixty degrees trying to pick out the brave little boy and his cheeky colleague. They should be thanked for their part in the event at the very least, but he couldn't spot them anywhere. He scanned the crowd once more to no avail. The hero of the hour, it would seem, had vanished into thin air. The warden started moving through the crowd making absolutely certain that the young hero was gone, because, if that was the case, he mused, this incident would require a new hero. Somebody was needed who would be available to take the accolades and explain how he had commanded the whole operation, practically single-handedly.

Two streets away, in a narrow gloomy passage, the two boys were resting on their heels.

"I'm tellin' you Jacky boy, you should o' seen it from up there. I swear to you there was a ring of fire right around me, flames 50 feet into the sky. It was bloody marvellous is what it was."

"Wasn't you a bit scared, like?" Jack asked as diplomatically as he knew how.

"Nah, not at all, it was brilliant, Jack. I can't wait for the next time." He glanced sideways at his friend. "Though I suppose, technically, it's your turn next time," he glanced sideways again, "unless you're scared o' course."

"Huh, I ain't scared o' that. It looked bloody easy to me. I've 'ad walks in the park that 'ave been more dangerous than that."

"Huh!" Billy mocked the comparison.

"Anyway," Jack continued, "look what else I found on that fire cart." He pulled a wax paper parcel from his pocket. Both knew full well it could only contain one thing.

Billy laughed, "You 'alf-inched the warden's sandwich." He laughed again and tried to grab it from his friend's hand. Jack was too quick for him, he closed his hand but felt the need to rise up from his haunches and race away with Billy, shouting "I 'ope it's ham, I 'ope it's ham."

"You'll be bloody lucky," Billy taunted, "it'll be spam not ham, spam not ham!"

They didn't really care what filling was inside the warden's snack, no doubt provided by his loving wife. They were just glad to be eating so early in the day. It wasn't very often that happened. Jack unwrapped the food as he ran, dividing it equally and slowing down to give half to his friend.

Billy took the first large mouthful. "Mmmm, what is it?" he asked through swallows.

Jack shrugged with his mouth too full to answer straightaway.

"Dunno," he managed at last, "tasty though."

"Mmmm."

The boys slowed to a walking pace, taking in the devastation as they strolled. The panic and fear of all around seemed not to affect them. These kids were not like everyone else. They did not have solid, comfortable lives that had suddenly been ripped apart. They lived a day-to-day, hand-to-mouth struggle. True, London looked a bit different this morning but to Billy and Jack this was just another day, like any other.

Their little, undernourished stomachs were full after half a sandwich. They would not feel the need to eat for many hours. The usual business of their day was not normally taken care of so early in the morning.

"We could head back to mine," offered Billy.

Jack nodded his head enthusiastically, so they carried on through the craters, the fires and the piles of rubble, already comfortable in the new surroundings that had been forced upon them. Left and right, in front and behind, people were dazed and confused, struggling to accept this new reality. The two dead-end kids were totally unfazed. Like domesticated cats released into the wild, they had adapted immediately. They were an example of how to cope in such situations to all and sundry, but they were too insignificant for anyone to seriously seek their direction or instruction.

"'Ere we are." Billy pushed open the door to the dark little room he shared with his grandfather. A single mattress lay tight up against two walls behind the door and a tatty old armchair, with its back to the door, faced a fire grate that had not been cleaned for many a day. Billy slumped down on the mattress and exhaled deeply.

"Phew! What a night. I might grab a bit o' kip. You tired?"

Jack was tired. Yes, it would be nice to get some sleep but he thought he was being told to leave.

"Nah, I ain't tired."

Billy laughed, "Well, you look it. I'm goin' to sleep. You can take the chair if you like, I doubt me Pops will be back any time soon."

That of course changed things.

"All right. I'll take the chair then." Jack didn't ask if there was a spare blanket. People like them didn't possess such luxuries. They had a roof over their heads and a door to close. The door may not have a lock on it and the chair may stink like an old brewery, but to Jack this was on a par with a room at the Ritz. He settled into the chair and was asleep almost immediately.

The boys slept soundly for hours. It was early afternoon before the noise of war woke them.

Billy laid still, one arm under his head. He was listening to the warning sound of the air-raid sirens and was waiting for it to be interspersed with the intermittent boom boom of the anti-aircraft guns he had heard the previous night. The guns would confirm when the bombers were close.

'Boom! Boom!' there they were.

"Did you 'ear that, Jack?"

"I 'ear it. The guns 'ave started up an' the bombers will be close now."

"Yes," Billy replied. Then the boys settled back into silence. Billy working out in his mind what would be the best thing to do, while Jack waited patiently to be let in on what they should do next.

"Want to go back down the tube station?" Billy asked casually. The bombs had started falling now, the sound of explosions easily distinguishable over the cacophony of sound assaulting their ears.

"I ain't bothered," Jack replied. "What do you want to do?"

"Dunno. I might just stay put."

"What about the bombs?"

"What about 'em?"

Jack sniggered, "You don't think we're missin' out, do you?"

"Let's leave it 'til it's dark. Maybe go out then."

"Goin' to rescue another ol' lady are you?"

Billy snorted, "Maybe. It was a real nice feelin'."

"An' a real nice sandwich," added Jack.

"Yeah." Billy rolled over and nodded off again re-living the taste of the stolen sandwich. Overhead bombers did their best to kill him.

Chapter Ten

A POLICE constable was standing over a comatose tramp outside Whitechapel tube station.

"Oi! You! Wake up!" He resisted poking the sleeping form with his boot.

I recall rolling my eyes and immediately clocking the large, hob-nailed boots before me. I hurriedly closed my eyes tightly shut again but he had been looking out for such a movement.

"Oi! You!" the constable thundered far too loudly for a man in my condition. "Come on, wake up! You can't lie 'ere. Can't you 'ear the bombs?"

One screamed overhead, as if to emphasise his point. It just missed the ornate chimney tops on the roof of the tube station. It slammed into the very next street with a massive explosion that caused the Bobby standing over me to jump so high his boots left the ground. Glass flew hundreds of feet up into the air; I could see it above the rooftops that separated us from the bomb. A pungent cloud of dark smoke began drifting towards us. Something had caught fire. I wondered if it might be worth investigating. The smoke drifted upwards and mingled with other smoke. Another dark cloud was gathering.

"Bleedin' 'ell. It's worse than last night," I muttered, trying to illicit his sympathy.

"Ah, you're awake. Good. Come on old timer, you can't stay 'ere. Let's get you down underground and get some food inside you, eh?" He was smiling nervously, far more desperate to vacate the area than I was.

The young policeman pulled me to my feet and led me towards the station.

"What are you doin' to my city?" I demanded to know as he dragged me towards the shelter.

"What? I ain't doin' nothin'." He seemed indignant.

"Yes you are. You lot are supposed to be in charge. Look at the mess you are makin' of it all." I attempted a sweeping gesture and very nearly pulled him over.

"It ain't me, its bloody Hitler," he tried to defend himself.

"Hitler, Churchill, you, you're all the bloody same." I was trying to be serious and he started to chuckle. He started to laugh in my face. I abruptly stopped moving and shook myself free of his grasp. I put my fists up in the classic boxer pose and angrily blurted out, "Come on then, if I'm such a joke."

I was still a bit drunk from the night before, so I was wobbling a bit and kept losing sight of him behind my fists, but when he came close I was going to be ready for the cheeky, young sod. I didn't mind that successive governments had lied to us repeatedly about improving our lives, about giving us a slice of their pie, but now look, they weren't satisfied with that. Now they have to bomb us relentlessly as well. It didn't matter if 'they' were Churchill, Stalin, Roosevelt or Hitler himself. They are supposed to be in charge and all they are doing is destroying everything and this young pup thinks that's funny, he thinks I'm a joke. If he would only stand still I was furious enough to knock his head off.

"All right, that's enough now. You're 'ere now. Mind 'ow you go." Then he called over my head as though I wasn't there, "Got another one for you, Joe!"

A warden, who was presumably called Joe, called something I didn't catch in reply and the policeman was gone.

The warden eyed me nervously and left me leaning unsteadily against the doorframe. He seemed to be controlling who was allowed in or out of the shelter. That was something new from yesterday. Things were developing much too fast for a man of my age and befuddled state of mind to keep up with. Still, I had to admit, all this destruction certainly stopped me thinking constantly about the Ripper. Now he came into mind more as a comparison for this current state of death and terror.

He was bad enough, leaving a trail of devastation in his wake that affected many of us for years afterwards, but Jeesus, he had nothing on this. He at least selected single victims. This was killing on an industrial scale and despite the newsreels I felt sure we were probably doing exactly the same to the poor sods in Germany.

"You 'ungry? Want summat to eat?" The warden was addressing me now. He seemed pleasant enough and I was feeling hungry, I supposed.

"Food, you say, what sort o' food would that be then?" I asked gruffly.

"That would be whatever food you're lucky enough to get," he replied, half smiling.

"I'll take it," I told him.

"Miss! Miss!" The warden was now addressing a young woman standing at the top of the spiral staircase. He was going to pass on the responsibility. He had already grown weary of having this old tramp in his life, no matter how tenuously or for how brief a period of time.

The woman, dressed in the uniform of the great Sally Army, realising she was being addressed by the smartly uniformed warden, blushed and straightened down the sides of her dress.

"Yes, Joe, how can I help you?" she enquired brightly.

"Well, see this ol' tr... ol' man 'ere? I want you to sort him out with something to eat. He's 'ad a bit of a time of it an' he just needs a bit of a sit down, you know, then 'e'll be fine again."

The officer of Jesus gave me an untrusting glance, first up and then down.

"Oh, I see!" she answered.

I clearly wasn't quite the sort she had been hoping for, but we were all God's children deep down I suppose, if you looked deep enough beneath the grime.

"Soup?" She shot the question at me without warning.

"That'll be lovely, Miss," I replied, lowering myself down into the chair she had just vacated.

She stopped in her tracks, clearly not altogether happy that I was taking over her chair.

"I got a bit of trouble with me back, see Miss. All they bombs an' that yesterday an' 'aving to kip down in the tube station an' now I've gone and lost my boy. Well, he ain't my boy, 'e's my grandson but 'e's like my own boy, you know. Oooh, is that my soup? Lovely. Looks lovely, that does."

I stretched out my hands to take it before she changed her mind. She handed it over still trying to make sense of the old tramp and my inane jabbering. They didn't really come across folk like me wherever she came from. She had thought the East End would be a thrilling adventure, but it was developing into a constant stream of human misery. She was sure this wretched place was the cause of her recent bout of migraine. No, enough was enough. Daddy was just going to have to get her moved.

"Miss! Miss, got any bread 'ave you?"

She handed me the plate as she had been taught. This old tramp threw two slices into his soup where it soaked up most of the watery gruel she was trying to pass off as nourishing soup. Scooping up the remaining slices in my grubby hand I very quickly tucked in, gulping without really chewing and flashing my uneven, blackened teeth at her.

"Much obliged, Miss. Very good of you indeed," I ate as I spoke as usual. I had been much hungrier than I had realised.

'What on Earth is he saying?' wondered Amy. She smiled as politely as she could, expertly, she thought, concealing her distaste at having to deal with him on such a personal level.

'Snooty cow, she don't like me,' I realised. But she was providing me with hot nourishment and I was sitting in her chair. I pretended not to notice her lack of empathy; just decided that she would not be getting her seat back any time soon.

Chapter Eleven

BILLY and Jack were walking down the very centre of Commercial Street, heading towards the docks, back to Watson's Wharf. They had decided nowhere was really safe, and the wharf seemed as good a place as any to get a bit of privacy. Incendiary bombs were landing all around, exploding on impact and sending lethal fires in all directions. Some fizzed into silence, others disappearing harmlessly into craters in the road, but most were burning merrily and giving at least a little light in the blackout. Every time they came to a place with no raging fires, it was impossible to see where they were walking.

"I prefer it when there's fires," Jack moaned as he slipped into another massive bomb crater, grazing himself, as he slid out of view.

"Yes, at least we can see then." Billy chuckled at his own, perfectly timed joke.

Jack's head popped back into sight, "Hey, what's that?"

Billy strained his eyes. It looked like a ball of fire moving towards them and then he saw it was somebody carrying a flaming torch.

As the flame came closer a child's voice called out to them.

"All right, Billy?"

"Who's that?" Billy shot back.

"It's me, Tommy Barker!"

"All right, Tommy." Billy had always liked Tommy; they had shared some pranks together in the back of the classroom and shared some corporal punishments together at the front of the class.

He altered his voice to imitate the teacher they had both shared. That seemed a lifetime ago now. All the local schools had closed their doors in 1939 and they had remained closed ever since. Not that Billy or Jack, for that matter, would have still been attending, but some of the local kids would have shown up if there had been any schools to show up at. When the evacuated children started missing London, they returned at a rate of two or three thousand a week, nobody thought about re-opening the schools to accommodate them. East End kids were all supposed to be safely out in the countryside, but in reality thousands of them were operating in a twilight world that involved no adult supervision at all. Most got up to no good. Billy had done that already, now he wanted to be a hero.

"What you up to Tommy?" he asked.

"Oh, you know, not much. Got a crate of apples last night when it was Bedlam everywhere."

"Looks like it's goin' to be more Bedlam tonight an' all, eh?" Billy replied.

"Yeah, looks that way."

The three ten-year-old kids surveyed the skies above, offering their expert opinions.

"Did you 'ear 'ow many bombers came last night?" Tommy asked them.

They hadn't but didn't want to admit it.

"How many did you 'ear?" Billy asked him.

"I 'eard eight hundred German bombers, just in the East End," Tommy blurted out.

"Well, it was a thousand actually, weren't it Jack?"

"Yeah, it was a thousand. A Bobby down Threadneedle Street told us. A thousand bombers 'e said. The most there 'as ever been in the sky at once, ever."

"Yeah?" Tommy wasn't sure and his voice gave him away. It didn't sound correct and it wasn't correct. The number of German bombers over London on the first night of the Blitz was around 350 but Tommy didn't know that and he was outnumbered, two to one, anyway.

"It's bloody true enough," Billy confirmed, and Tommy knew he had to concede.

"What was you doin' down Threadneedle Street anyhow?" He changed the topic.

The boys looked at each other, instinctively wary about revealing too much about anything to anyone, but it was only Tommy. He was one of them and it was a good story.

"Billy climbed a burning building down in the City and saved an old lady's life," Jack revealed. "That's what we done last night."

"You climbed a burnin' building?" Tommy looked up at Billy's face, "Really?"

"Yeah, really. It was easy." Billy told him about the plan and how they had executed it, embellishing some parts slightly but making his role that of the undoubted hero of the piece.

"Good, innit?" Jack asked him, once the tale was told.

"I suppose."

"You suppose?" Billy was slightly put out. "I'd like to 'ave seen you do it."

Tommy snorted his contempt. "What, climb a drainpipe and throw a rope to someone? Easy. I can do much better than that."

"Oh, can you now? I'd like to see it."

"Come on then, an' you will see it."

"I bet I'm braver than you," Billy shot at his new opponent.

"'Ow much do you wanna bet then?" Tommy wanted to know.

Very shortly the bet was on. They had sent Jack out to scour the surrounding area with a wish list of items they needed. Jack was soon back with all their requirements, So, armed with a handcart, a length of rope, a bucket of sand and a rusty old shovel they set off. They were searching for somebody who needed rescuing. Ideally, it would be somebody elderly and preferably female but most importantly they would have to be trapped in a burning building or caught up in some such predicament which would entail their rescuers putting themselves in extreme danger. This was a game of boyish bravado. It was a game being played out in the epicentre of the worst war of the 20th century without a second of concern for the danger they were planning to put themselves in. It was at this point that some much needed adult supervision was called for, but that sort of help simply was not available. So our half-sized heroes would just have to go it alone. With Jack pulling the cart the three children set off, blissfully unaware that the odds of making it through to dawn were heavily stacked against them. This was a new game; they would have to make up the rules as they went along, just as mankind has been doing since the dawn of creation.

Once they started moving the first thing that became obvious was the sheer abundance of opportunities for carrying out a rescue. Last night had been bad but tonight they felt as though a city of death and fire was what faced them.

"Bloody 'ell," Tommy exclaimed, "this is just madness!"

He was, of course, absolutely correct. How could the whim of one bitter man decide the fate of so many souls?

But that hadn't been what Tommy had meant.

"How are we goin' to choose one? There's so many needs 'elp!"

Tommy certainly had a point; the number of humans in distress was almost overwhelming. Billy scanned left, up a side road. It looked like an old lady had somehow lost her ceiling, her wall and her privacy. She was two storeys up, still in her bed, clutching a cat and screaming hysterically. Below her the whole ground floor was ablaze and they could see flames had already started licking the top of her interior staircase.

"That one," Billy declared pointing at it, "that ol' lady there. Look. That beam 'as fallen across from the 'ouse over the street. Reckon you can cross it do you?" He looked across at Tommy.

Tommy really had no choice but to accept the challenge.

"Easy," he declared.

"An' 'ow are you goin' to get her out safely?" Billy wanted to know.

"Tie the rope round 'er and drop 'er over the side, like you done with your one."

"Not this one you can't," Billy offered up.

"Nah, she's too big," Jack piped in.

"Exactly," Billy continued, "so, we're both going to go and get 'er. We'll roll 'er in the blanket an' with me at the 'ead an' you at the feet we can run 'er back along the beam. Unless you're chicken."

"I ain't no chicken. Let's go." Tommy was fired up and ready.

"Race you to the top," he called, already running, trying to get an unfair advantage.

Billy flew past him. "Yeah, see you up there, slow boy. Don't forget this." Billy threw the rope at, rather than to him, causing Tommy to lose a bit of the momentum he had built up. This was Billy's game and he wasn't going to have newcomers waltzing in taking over.

Billy didn't slow down as he neared the burning building. He leapt at the yard wall and over it without breaking pace, then he was shinning his way up the metal drainpipe at a speed that would have put a chimpanzee to shame. He felt the pipe shudder and guessed Tommy had just landed on it, a little behind him.

A few people had noticed the two kids suddenly race into action and were watching them in half interest, but it was such a busy night they were just another crazy moment in a long montage of crazy moments.

Halfway up the old Victorian pipe the boys became obscured from ground level. Their eyes were being affected by the acrid smoke that seemed to be emanating from a million different sources. By the time they had reached the very top of the drainpipe they were completely hidden from view by smoke. First Billy, then Tommy, raced, unseen and forever unreported, along a burning roof beam, 16 feet long, only four inches wide, and 30 feet above the ground. They edged their way along half a crumbling wall, their fingers clawing for some kind of grip. They held their breath when a thick cloud of steam blasted them without warning, engulfing them in a cloud of vapour from a broken gas water heater. Tommy slipped momentarily, but managed to keep his grip. They scrambled across bricks that moved like a wave of water, slowing every movement they made, tearing at their hands and knees. Then they were alongside the bed. They wrapped the old lady, kicking and screaming, in her own blanket, tied her tight with the rope and, much against her wishes, carried her back through the flames safely down to street level, where they unrolled her with a flourish.

By the time she had regained her composure, her house was destroyed and she was sipping tea in the back of an ambulance. She had wanted to thank those boys personally but the dead-end kids had long vanished into the treacherous, crater filled darkness beyond civilised society. They weren't interested in hanging around to collect kind words. They were always going to leave the scene in a hurry, before someone confiscated the food Jack had commandeered whilst they had been busily showing off to each other.

"That was a real thrill," Tommy kept saying as they headed back to Billy's room to devour their evening meal of five sausages, an apple and one piece of bread. The boys were in high spirits. None of them could recall the last time they had enjoyed two good days in a row like this. They were innocents caught up in the Blitz of London, it was only in its second day but already these kids had adapted and embraced this new reality. The way they saw it, running errands for Reggie Lawson just got you a spell in Bedlam or prison. This was fun and this was really living.

The boys brought Tommy back to their courtyard. He had nowhere better to be and they felt like comrades now. So they were heading for a de-briefing in Billy's room when Tommy spotted a large figure hanging back in the shadows. He motioned with his hand and they slowed their pace. Danger was ever present around here.

"Who's that?" Jack called out.

The figure tried to shift further back, pressing more tightly against the dark wall.

"We can see you," Jack added, "come out." The boys all braced themselves for trouble.

"'Arry bloody Perkins, as I live and breathe."

Harry Perkins was a giant for his age. Not a kid to be messed with,but not somebody who would mess with others purely because he was bigger and stronger than most. He was fortunate enough to have been born the youngest of seven siblings. His four older brothers were already contributing to the family coffers by the time Harry was born. There was enough food to satisfy the growing infant, ensuring he was able to develop physically and normally.

"What are you doin' over this way 'Arry?" Billy asked as he skipped down the alley.

Billy opened the door and his little band filed in. He kept the door ajar, signifying for Harry to join them inside. He knew Harry could only be in the courtyard to see him and it must be important or he wouldn't have bothered.

Once inside, Jack, who was already beginning to make himself at home, cleared a spot on which to off-load his edible booty. Then he lit a lantern, flooding the room with soft yellow lighting.

"I saw you earlier," Harry began, "pushing a cart up from the docks." He paused, but no comment either confirming or denying his statement was forthcoming. "So," he continued, "I thought maybe I could borrow your cart."

"What for?" Jack immediately wanted to know. 'What's the angle?' he was thinking. 'What could possibly be in it for me, well us?' He wondered.

"Well, I'd rather not say," Harry began.

"Yeah, I ain't surprised. Nice little earner is it?" Jack sneered.

Harry reddened and looked sheepish. Something not unnoticed by his audience.

Billy liked the way Jack was first in with the accusations. He appreciated having those few extra moments to weigh up a situation through Jack. He would remain silent, aloof, only adding a comment when he had reached a decision. It was useful having Jack around and now they had Tommy on their team, as well. Now, Harry? He had to admit Harry was always going to be useful in a fight and he had enough disrespect for authority that Billy felt he could work with. Not too much, just enough to enter every new situation, first and foremost, extremely warily.

Tommy stayed silent. This didn't really concern him but he stayed standing, only a pace or two behind Billy. He wasn't to know how this encounter may develop and if it turned nasty he wanted Billy to be in no doubt that he, Tommy, wanted to be part of the team.

Billy shot Jack a sideways glance.

"Well?" Jack demanded, "Tell us then." He had instantly picked up the authority Billy was conveying to him.

It was obvious Harry was only going to get use of the cart if he told them something.

"It's my bitch, Clara. She's 'ad puppies."

The boys all knew Clara. She was a mongrel terrier that was famous from Bethnal Green to Shoreditch, as the best little rat-killing machine on four legs.

"My Ma wants me to get rid o' the pups." All the boys knew this was a euphemism for, 'she wants me to drown them'. "But, with a cart I could run 'em all over to my cousins 'ouse down at Vauxhall. He said Clara can stay with 'im. It's only three more weeks an' they'll be old enough to go to new 'omes. See, my sister's just 'ad a new baby and Ma says the pups 'ave got to go."

Jack had made the case for the prosecution, now it was time for a verdict to be delivered. He gave Billy a look that said over to you.

"Do you reckon they'll be good ratters like their Ma?" was Billy's first question.

Harry nodded. A light was shining through the door behind him and it played up the grimy wall as he moved to scratch his neck.

Billy crossed the room towards him, smiling broadly.

"Give 'Arry some of that food, mind," he called to Jack over his shoulder.

He grabbed the big fellow by the elbow and looking him straight in the eye asked, "Where are you livin' now 'Arry?"

It had been a while since anyone had offered Harry fresh food or enquired after him. He was touched, but was unable to recognise the emotion for what it was.

"Kind o' at my Ma's, but well, with the new baby an' all."

Billy had asked the question but hadn't really needed a reply. One look at the boy, even by the weak gaslight in the room, showed it was obvious he was sleeping rough.

Billy, still grasping him by the elbow, said calmly, "Right, this is what we'll do. We will eat first, then go and get your pups and take 'em in the cart over the river to Vauxhall. We'll all go. We got to go over that way, anyhow."

This was the first Tommy or Jack had heard of it, although they would have been fully prepared to swear the complete opposite under oath in the highest court in the land.

"And," Billy smiled again, "I get one of the pups."

Harry frowned slightly but Billy pressed on.

"The one of my choice," he finished.

Jack thrust a cold sausage sandwich into the kid's hand, as if on cue.

Harry looked down at the sandwich, up at Jack, down again, then up at Billy and nodded agreement.

"Good boy, 'Arry. Eat up then."

Over the next two weeks London was bombed every day. Sometimes they would come in the daytime, sometimes at night, but always they would come.

The boys had all more or less moved into Billy's room on a permanent basis. Pops would turn up occasionally and want to know when they were going to leave, but he didn't mean anything by it. Most of their peers were making a healthy living, supporting numerous mothers and siblings on their nocturnal ill-gotten gains, but Billy considered his gang to be a cut above the rest. They were rescuers; heroes. Reggie Lawson was leaving the situation as it was and waiting to see how things developed. In truth he had so much going on and there was an endless source of evacuee kids who could run the errands Billy would normally do. As long as they paid the rent, he didn't care how many kids the old man moved in. He would leave them to their own devices for now.

One night the boys were making their way home from the docks. There was the usual multi warehouse inferno lighting up the path for them. The constant sound of anti-aircraft fire and bombs, both exploding and just crashing into the ground, was their background music.

"I'm tellin' you *we* are the bloody heroes 'round here," Billy declared for the hundredth time. "Tell Johnny Williams we rescue more people an' we do it quicker."

"An' we ain't lost anyone, yet," Jack added.

Billy's Dead-End Kids were building quite a reputation for themselves in a place containing so many large, extended families. It wasn't long before almost everyone they met was grateful for some relative the boys had risked life and limb to save. Within a few weeks some of the other neighbourhood kids were organising themselves into rival outfits, desperately trying to set themselves up as equally brave and daring as Billy's boys. The East End kids had invented a new game and they all wanted to play. Of these, Johnny Williams' lot were pulling off some rather impressive missions until, on one particular night, five weeks into the initial bombs-every-day period, one of Johnny's crew had slipped and fallen sixty feet to his death.

The push for top 'dead-enders' had then lost momentum. A lot of the teams started dropping out, so Billy's crew were quickly the undisputed number one outfit. Everywhere they went they were treated with respect from the housewives to the regular fire crews. Food seemed plentiful for the first time in their lives. With no obligation to attend school, even the truant officers left them to their own devices. War suited them and they were thriving.

"'Ave you 'eard of the Trade Unions?" Billy asked loudly one rainy morning. They all had, as Mr. Cooper, the rag and bone man, had made sure all the kids in his patch knew about the trade unions.

"Cooper says that after the war we will be recognised by the King for what we've done. 'E says we are bloomin' 'eroes. I should get a real job an' join the trade unions, 'e says. So, 'e's going to fix it so I can learn to write an' read a bit better."

"A bit better," repeated Tommy, snorting with derision.

"Yeah," Billy shot him a withering glance.

"Yes, when the war is over," Harry repeated the phrase, mentally adding 'whenever that might be'.

"'Ere boy!" Billy called and a black and white terrier pup shot through the doorway of a bombed out house, racing towards them. Bizarrely, the door was still hanging, only by one hinge, but it was still hanging. The roof and the top floor bedrooms had been blown to oblivion but the front door was still hanging in there. To the dog it was just a place to mark his territory; to the boys it was a part of their ever-changing playground.

The four of them, with their handcart and terrier in tow, were a regular feature of the East End now. Everybody knew about them and all the lives they had saved. They had transformed into quite the unique morale-raising unit. Obviously, Billy was the brains and the organiser. Then Jack was his loyal right-hand man, the acquirer of materials, the go-to guy and cheeky chappy. You had to be aware of his sticky fingers nearly as much as his way of getting you to agree to something you hadn't intended to. Jacky boy had the ability to charm the birds out of the trees.

Then there was Tommy. It was incredible how he could read a fire. Somehow understanding what was making each individual fire live and breathe. Realising at a glance precisely how each blaze should be tackled to achieve whatever it was they wanted to do. Tommy loved it; he already wanted to work for the Greater London Fire Department when the war was over. Mr. Cooper was going to fix it for him to get a job actually driving the big red engines.

Finally, there was Harry who was brave and strong. On more than one occasion his brute strength had proved to be vital when somebody had to be hauled out of a dangerous situation on a rope, but his real talent lay in the calm way he dealt with broken bones, deep lacerations or any other injury. Injuries that would make grown men reach for the sick bag, were tended and dressed by Harry with a minimum of fuss and a surprisingly gentle touch for such a big, gangly chap. Harry said he would like to be a doctor after the war was over and Mr. Cooper was going to fix it for him.

Everyone in the area knew, liked and respected them these days.

One evening the boys were heading back home, Jack pulling the cart, Billy trudging along beside him and Tommy and Harry bringing up the rear. It had been an exciting day, but a long one and they were all exhausted. They had spent nearly nine hours helping rescue people from a public air-raid shelter that had taken a direct hit. It had been absolute pandemonium for the whole morning until, at last, the bomb disposal truck had arrived and their officer had taken control of the situation.

He had set the boys to work dismantling what was left of a wall that was in danger of collapsing and they had attacked the task with their usual enthusiasm and good cheer.

"You 'eard 'im, didn't you, Billy?" Jack repeated for the umpteenth time, his face glowing with pride.

"Yes, I 'eard 'im." Billy smiled.

He was genuinely pleased for his pal. Jack had taken the bull by the horns and strolled straight up to the bomb disposal boss, Captain Wilks or Willis. Yes, that was it, Captain Willis. Jack had gone right up to him as bold as brass and told Captain Willis who he was and about some of the better known rescues they had pulled off since this crazy war had started. Then, to cap it all, he had finished by asking the captain for a job in the bomb disposal unit. Billy was jaw-droppingly amazed when the captain looked Jack right in the eye and replied to his cheeky request.

"You sir, are exactly the sort of chap the unit is always on the lookout for. I see no reason at all why you shouldn't be welcomed with open arms." Like all illiterates the boys had a talent for memorising things that they needed or wanted to remember. The captain's instant agreement had shocked the boys, as it was so out of keeping with their normal encounters with the officer class, that they all remembered it verbatim. Jack must have repeated it fifty times since then. If they had missed the exact wording originally they certainly knew what the captain had promised by now.

"Pops, we're back!"

I heard Billy and his pals coming down the alley. It was always a relief to hear them; it meant they had survived another day. I pushed open the door and prepared to welcome them home.

"Hey, Pops, I'm gonna be in the bomb disposal unit," Jack called as soon as he caught sight of me.

He was positively glowing; they all were. Clearly, they were exhausted and no doubt starving, but something had definitely given them all a lift. If Jack's incredible statement was true, that would be why.

"You what?" I replied, "'ave you gone soft?"

Then they were in, laughing and jostling and jumping without mercy on each other's faux pas, no matter how miniscule. I smiled. Oh, the joy of youth! I vaguely remembered it.

They made themselves comfortable scattered about the room and told me all about the day's adventures. I had to admit it did sound as though Jack had been promised a leg up. I knew some good was coming on account of all the rescues and good deeds these boys had been carrying out, but this just seemed unbelievable. Obviously, I was delighted for the lad. The next week, at 10am on the Thursday, Jack and Tommy were to present themselves at Bethnal Green Fire Station and ask for Sergeant Potter. We would have to wait until then and just keep our fingers crossed.

Jack spent the week getting more and more excited. Tommy kept his excitement well hidden. Mr. Cooper rehearsed them through what would be asked and what answers they should give. The women of the court managed to find a clean shirt and a pair of boots for them both. They had haircuts and on Wednesday night even had a bath in preparation for the big day. Thursday came and they were as ready as they would ever be, boosted further by the knowledge that they came highly recommended by a serving captain, no less.

Jack and Tommy arrived at the huge building with a few minutes to spare and joined a group of other lads near the main entrance. The other boys all seemed older and decidedly taller than Jack and Tommy but, no matter, they were experienced and came highly recommended. So, they joined the back of the queue and kept their opinions to themselves. Jack was not really used to queuing and after an hour he was on the verge of giving up the whole idea and just turning and running. Tommy encouraged him to stay calm, shuffle forward and wait his turn. Finally, he was motioned to the front and found himself entering the room and standing to attention, as Mr. Cooper had shown him, before three very distinguished looking bearded men in spotless navy blue uniforms and medals running right across their broad chests.

They looked Jack up and down and looked at their papers. After what seemed, almost a lifetime to Jack, the gentleman in the centre spoke.

"Step forward, young man." They waited whilst Jack did so.

"Where are you from?" enquired the same gentleman.

"Whitechapel, sir," he replied in a good, clear tone.

"And why are you here?" asked the same man.

Jack felt he must be in charge, as he was asking all the questions, so he decided to address his response primarily to him.

"Well, sir," he began and proceeded to inform the panel as to why he was here and what had led him on this path. He delivered his monologue clearly and politely. Jack had never seen a building or indeed a room remotely as intimidating as the sprawling Gothic fire station. His whole life he had experienced only negative encounters with anyone in uniform. Yet he had turned up, taken it all in his stride and delivered his speech as though he had been born to it.

He ended by emphasising again the words of Captain Willis of the bomb disposal unit, thanked the good gentlemen for hearing him out, bowed to the waist and stood there to await their verdict.

Again, it was the middle gentleman of the three who spoke.

"You are too young and we are not in the habit of offering employment to those from Whitechapel. That is all."

Jack searched their faces one after the other; he was confused. This wasn't right.

"That is all," repeated the dignitary, "we have others to see, young man."

Jack left as fast as he could with his head held low.

"Next!"

Tommy fared no better than Jack had done.

Chapter Twelve

October 1940

I HAD grown used to making allowances for the new danger that was now a factor of everyday living. Constant bombing raids interspersed with the imminent threat of more bombs on the way were the norm. It was getting rather tiresome. However, it was so easy to maintain my state of drunkenness that I almost preferred this to the way things were before the war. I just needed to shelter for a bit, to recharge my batteries.

One evening, after it had been raining all day, I had bedded down on the platform of St. Mary's tube station in Whitechapel Road. I had first been down here as a nipper in 1884 when the station had opened. I had known this station my whole life. It was the only one I felt comfortable in as it had always been my 'home' station. Then, a year before the war started they had closed it completely. Rather inconveniently Aldgate East became the closest station to beg outside of.

It was only when the Luftwaffe started their bombing that the authorities opened up St. Mary's as a shelter. It felt strangely reassuring to be back.

Over the previous few nights it had been unusually difficult for me to ignore the constant whine of falling bombs. They were giving me headaches and I couldn't sleep. I even missed my usual tossing and turning. I was exhausted, but tonight I had finished a bottle of whisky and was certain I was due a good night's rest. I gratefully accepted some dry toast from the Sally Army girl before bedding down.

Just as I was about to mercifully drift off to sleep a thunderous crashing noise rocked the station to its very core. First slabs of plaster, then whole bricks fell from the walls and ceiling. There was a loud whoosh and the air filled with dust. People began to scream and run about in panic. I pulled my legs closer in, shuffled as tightly against the wall as I could and I slept, fitfully.

St. Mary's underground station had taken a direct hit. The entrance was completely clogged with tons and tons of rubble. Many hands, working long hours, managed to clear a way through the rubble so by the time I woke in the morning the route was clear and I bumbled through the hole. It was a sobering thought to discover I had been trapped below ground all night. At ground level a warden was positioned at a pile of bricks that used to be the main gate. He was telling people that the air-raid shelter would not be opening tonight and we had best be advised that the nearest public shelter was either Bow to the east or Whitechapel to the west. I considered that the fellow was wasting his time standing there. Even a fool wouldn't want to risk going down there now.

I didn't bother with bomb shelters after that as I simply didn't want to end my life trapped in a hole. I decided that from now on I would just go home and take my chances. I knew that Billy and all his friends seemed to be living back at the room these days, but I didn't mind. I had grown used to their presence and there was safety in numbers. I sighed; Reggie had been collecting the rent from Billy for months, anyway. Nobody cared that a group of young kids were, to all intents and purposes, fending for themselves in one of London's most dangerous areas. Nobody in authority had cared when I was a kid and they still didn't care now. So long as the landlords got their rent that was all that anyone ever cared about.

"Good boy, 'e is," I mumbled repeatedly as I shuffled down the damaged road. I did it for luck, trying to keep the boy safe. I knew people thought I was a mad old tramp talking to myself but if my mantra helped keep the boy safe for another day that was all I cared about. 'Good boy, 'e is.'

Screaming bombs and shrapnel kept whizzing and flying about me in all directions. Vast fires were engulfing rows of houses at a time, raging uncontrollably at practically every turn. I was not afraid and ignored it all. I was not afraid because I hadn't cared if I lived or died for years so why should it start to bother me now. If anything, the war, the bombing, seemed to have improved my luck. I would pick up a bottle somewhere along the way and head back to the damp, old court. Back to where I belonged.

Chapter Thirteen

"WELL." From the tone of his voice it was safe to assume that Billy was pretty indifferent.

"Billy 'old on, it's good news. No, it's great news." Mr. Cooper tried to explain.

"Mr. Charrington is on the council an' he wants to meet you and thank you himself for what you did down Sidney Street, savin' that ol' lady."

"An' 'er cat," sniggered Jack from the shadows.

Mr. Cooper frowned at him. "Yes, and 'er cat."

"Will you be there?" Billy asked.

"Yes, if you want me to come with you. That will be fine, I'm sure."

So, it was arranged then. It seemed as though word of Billy's daring deeds had reached the ear of the local dignitaries. He was to be presented at the town hall to be held up as a shining example of how little boys might not be allowed to go to the front line but they can certainly do their bit for the war effort.

"An' it'll be a good way to get you used to dealing with the nobs. You're goin' to 'ave to if you want to 'elp the unions, you know."

"Yeah, alright! I'll go. How bad could it be?" he said.

"Good lad, it'll be alright, you'll see. I'll tell 'em to arrange it, then. What about the rest of you? Everythin' alright boys?" He looked at them scattered around the room.

"Jack, do you still want to be in the bomb disposal unit?"

"Not any more, Mr. Cooper."

Mr. Cooper's expression registered surprise. "Why not, I thought you was set on it?"

"Not no more, Mr. Cooper." Jack didn't even look up as he spoke.

'These boys would only go far,' he thought, 'if the East End's temptations didn't get them first.' Cooper glanced at his watch.

"Now, I've got to go to a meeting down the town 'all." Mr. Cooper neglected to mention the meeting was regarding the vast amounts of pilfering going on. The thieves were operating during the blackout; under complete darkness and getting away with some major hauls. The bosses were not happy.

"Maybe next time you may want to come along Billy, to see a bit of union business close up."

"Yeah, maybe," Billy replied. He had spotted Reggie Lawson loitering at the entrance to their little dead-end courtyard. Billy motioned his head slightly which gave an acknowledgment that could be easily missed and just as easily denied. Jack picked up on it and distracted Mr. Cooper with a question. Billy slipped out of the meeting.

Mr. Cooper watched him side up to Reggie and knew it was touch and go. To his eyes these boys were all good kids at heart and they just needed to be shown there was another life beyond the law of the jungle that took precedence around here. Having gangsters like Reggie Lawson hanging around was not really helping them, he thought. The things that impressed Mr. Cooper so much about Billy would not have gone unnoticed by the mobster. Here he was, ten or eleven years old and already running a household and head of a little fire and rescue team. This kid had potential to spare and there could be no other reason for that spiv Lawson to be hanging around.

"What does 'e want then?" Reggie Lawson asked Billy, rather directly.

Billy shrugged. "Nothin' really."

The boy was becoming an expert at keeping his cards close to his chest; telling only what needed to be told.

The door opened beside them and Mr. Cooper slipped out of the poky, little room. He doffed his cap at Reggie as he made his way towards the alley and away. Reggie glared at him in reply until he disappeared completely from sight.

"Billy!" he called.

Billy stopped walking away and turned to face the gangster.

"Yes, Reg?" he asked quietly.

"What does 'e want, the rag 'n' bone man?" Billy could tell when Reggie was in the mood to take out his frustration on some innocent party. He didn't want to say the wrong thing and risk it being him or Mr. Cooper.

"Just some rubbish about meetin' the councillor, that's all. 'Course I ain't interested in going."

Billy knew only too well the pathological hatred Reggie Lawson had for any members of the great and the good. He saw them all as the enemy and believed they were only in it for themselves and their cronies. He longed for the day of the revolution like the one in France. He would not think much of Billy getting involved in any morale boosting propaganda. As Reggie repeatedly said, 'this is their war, not ours'. Thinking was not really a healthy way to pass your time when you lived in the slums. Men like Reggie did the thinking for the masses. It seemed irrelevant that he was also only looking out for himself.

Billy returned to join his friends.

"'E's comin' over," Jack revealed quietly as Billy re-took his position. With his back against the greasy wall, his eyes watching all who passed in the yard outside, Jack watched Reggie Lawson as he worked his way towards them. Finally, he came in and was standing directly in front of Billy again; unaware he was standing directly above the Ripper's knife. He drew circles in the dirt with the tip of his walking stick. They all joined in watching it go round and round. Finally, he stopped the mesmerising movement, lowered down on his haunches, so as to be on the same eye level as Billy and declared, "I've been 'earing good things about you boys."

Billy looked down modestly; the gangster raised his chin with the tip of his stick.

"Good things," he paused for effect, "an' it's nice," he paused again, "nice that you go round 'elping so many people. So, I want to show our gratitude an' by us I mean, of course, all us that live round 'ere."

A crisp five pound had appeared somehow in the palm of his hand and he held it out to Billy. The boy looked down again. There were a few uncomfortable seconds, then Reggie slipped the note discretely back to wherever it had come from.

"Don't want it, Billy?" Reggie's tone of voice was neutral.

"I don't mean to offend. It's just that we don't need no charity."

Behind him the boys kept quiet. None of them would have done what their leader had just done. They were, to a man, shocked at the refusal of what, to them, was as much money as they would see in a whole year, but mainly they were shocked at the lack of respect shown to Reggie. The man was a killer and they all knew it.

Reggie stood up, well aware his posture was intimidating them. The kid should have been scared to death, but Billy wasn't and Reggie admired his guts. As far as Reggie was concerned Billy had passed a very important test and passed it with flying colours.

Reggie chuckled, a little forced, but he laughed.

"'ear that boys? He don't want no charity. You kids must be doin' well, eh? Well, if you find your luck changing you know where to find me. We," he gestured to include every single inhabitant of the East End, "are real proud o' you boys. None of us want anythin' to 'appen to any one of yous."

He winked theatrically and was gone. From the far end of the court Cooper, the rag and bone man, caught Billy's eye through the open door and was mightily reassured when the boy nodded at him before closing the door on his team inside their headquarters.

As soon as they were behind the safety of the closed door Jack spoke up for the remaining three kids.

"Bloody 'ell Billy, a five pound note!"

Billy gave him a glance as he sat heavily down on the filthy chair.

"Yeah, but it ain't about that is it? An' you know it."

Billy had read the situation correctly and they all realised it now. If he had taken the money they would, once again, belong to Reggie Lawson.

"Right now," Billy reminded them, "we makes our own rules. Ain't it best like that? Ain't it the best it's ever been?"

They all nodded their agreement; he had a particularly valid point there.

"Reggie can't touch us 'cos we're heroes. Ain't that right?"

The others nodded agreement again.

"If I 'ad took that money, he owns us again. Can't you see we are getting respectable boys?"

They smirked uneasily, glancing around at each other. Respectable? Them? From these streets? Strangely they all quite liked the idea.

All, except one. Jack smiled and pretended to crave this new found respectability as much as the rest of them, but the interview had made him realise they were never going to be accepted in society. As soon as they were born their cards were marked. He wasn't a fireman, he was a thief. He wasn't respectable and neither were they. They just didn't see it yet. They still wanted to believe in childish happy endings.

"An' what about Cooper?" Billy asked. "You know what 'e says. 'We're bleedin' 'eroes. After the war is over 'e's goin' to 'elp us get out of 'ere. Total heroes that's what we are, eh?"

Their nods were firmer this time and the agreement stronger.

"We ain't like the mob an' all them others, are we?"

"No," Tommy said, "we ain't."

"So that's that then." Billy was winding the conversation to its conclusion. "We don't need Reggie Lawson or no-one else. Agreed?"

They roared their agreement loudly with much laughter and excitement at the golden future they had been assured was theirs for the taking, just as soon as the war was over. Jack smiled along with them, hiding the effort it was taking him to do so.

Inside and out the shadows were starting to lengthen. Dusk would soon be upon them. Suddenly, the warning sirens started up again. This would be the fortieth day in a row that the German bombers would drop their loads over London. For the thirtieth consecutive night the London docks would be high up on their list of targets. Chaos and pandemonium would again reign supreme for all who lived in or found themselves on, the streets of the East End.

"Want me to put some oil in the lamp?" asked Jack, as the light started to die in unison with the drone of engines above them.

"Nah, let's go out boys."

They rose up as one, grabbing their things, itching to get outside and join the action. Billy clutched a heavy coil of rope, Tommy wielded an iron bar and a shovel and Harry carried a bucket of sand in each hand. These they took outside and deposited in Jack's cart. Jack took responsibility for the cart because it was predominantly he who added contraband, diluting the good deeds of his comrades every time he did so.

Jack didn't mind helping the community, but they still had to eat. They also had to hand over a shilling a week for the pleasure of having a tiny stinking pit, with no lock, that they could call home.

They left the room in darkness and followed Billy out of the court into Commercial Street. Once on the main thoroughfare he led them straight as the crow flies, through a bomb crater that had appeared three nights before. He led them around another bomb that had skidded into a row of shops and destroyed the frontages, but not exploded.

The boys had been there last night when the man from City Hall had visited and declared all four shops as unsafe to live in. Of course, the families had nowhere else to go, because if they had they would have already left. So the council representative had given each family a piece of paper declaring their homes unsafe, but giving them special permission to remain living in them. Billy had heard the story with his own ears, but had offered no opinion on it. Now he skidded down the steep edge of a crater with his men behind him. Silently, they crossed the ground and climbed out of the crater back up to the street. All of them had serious expressions. They were known round here now for something other than trouble and trouble-making. People were pointing and whispering to their neighbours. They were on public display and they knew it.

'That's them, those brave little soldiers,' 'God's speed, lads' and 'They saved my nanny's neighbour las' week, you know'. This was no longer a game, it was a serious operation and the boys were serious participants.

Billy headed north on Commercial Street until he came to the junction with Bethnal Green Road. Here he turned right, heading east, into Bethnal Green itself, away from the docks, but towards where most of the bombs seemed to be falling tonight. Billy didn't lead his little team of firemen away from the slaughter and danger. What would be the point? They were needed where the damage was being done, their place was in the thick of the action and this was what had become expected of them and what they expected of themselves. Clouds of smoke rolled across the sky. Dust was entering their mouths with each breath. All around them a layer of ash covered everything that wasn't on fire and still they went forward, on into the desolate landscape. The sky above them was filled with the smoke of anti-aircraft guns, huge barrage balloons, heavy bombers and thousands of bombs being unloaded. To the left and right of them fires raged and parts of buildings, sections of houses and lengths of solid brick walls collapsed into piles of dust and rubble. Beneath their feet dust, glass, pieces of metal, pit-holes and massive craters slowed their progress, but did nothing to halt their determination.

Fire engines also negotiated their way forwards, their bells jangling furiously as they inched towards thick plumes of smoke rising into the darkened sky, their progress being slowed to a snail's pace by the rough terrain. Small boys pulling a cart were making better speed.

"Billy, listen. What's that?" Harry had been the first to hear the cries for help they had all been listening out for.

Billy stopped, listened and then pointed, indicating they should detour more to the left. They should head towards the screams, find out what was going on and see if there was anything the dead-end kids could do.

Bethnal Green that night was taking a massive pounding. Incendiary bombs were falling at the rate of dozens per second. Firemen and wardens were throwing sand on those they could and spraying water over anything else that came into range, but they were fatigued and their ranks depleted. After weeks of continual bombardment cracks were beginning to show in more than just the buildings. Londoners were taking a perverse satisfaction in the knowledge that they were holding up the Nazis from total domination of Europe. They were prepared to do without things and struggle by, but they were collectively feeling the strain.

A month ago back in September, at the start of the Blitz, Bethnal Green tube station had been designated as an air-raid shelter. It had successfully sheltered thousands of civilians for two weeks before water mains had been hit by bombs. Bethnal Green tube station had flooded and was closed to the public.

The volunteers had done a magnificent job pumping out water and reinforcing walls. Their efforts had meant the shelter could be reopened on the 5th of October.

This meant that by 7th October ten thousand Bethnal Green residents had somewhere to go on the same night as 30,000 bombs rained down on them. Billy had no idea the bombardment was quite as many explosives as that, he just saw a lot of fire to head towards. He chose to lead his men towards the chaos. Many more with no such option were forced to spend that night underground wide awake and terrified.

Bethnal Green on that fateful night lost nearly three thousand men, women and children. Many others suffered horrific injuries and a far greater number simply lost everything they owned. It would certainly have been far worse without the tube station to help take the strain.

Billy wasn't interested in facts or statistics he was interested in looking like a hero in the eyes of his peers. Maybe picking up some food along the way, perhaps a pawnable thing or two to help with the rent and coming out of it with whatever else proceedings may offer, but mainly he was interested in coming out of it as nothing less than a hero.

"Tommy, which way is that fire goin' to go?"

Tommy still took his position as the fire expert very seriously. He hadn't expected to be admitted into an organisation as grand as the fire service anyway, so hadn't been particularly disappointed when he and Jack had been so casually turned away. He still liked fires, with or without official approval. He watched the flames licking around the edge of the house. His eyes took in the woman waving frantically from an upstairs window. He registered that the roof still looked solid, but the downstairs of the property was already burning ferociously.

The fire engine they had passed was now arriving at the scene. Men in smart uniforms and shiny metal helmets poured off it and began unravelling their industrial hose. The engine was soon joined by three others. More firemen were streaming off the vehicles as gallons of water began pouring into the damaged house but there was definitely room for more help.

Billy spotted the officer on the scene talking to a pair of wardens at the rear of the truck parked furthest from him.

"Wait 'ere lads. I'll go see if 'e wants us anywhere special."

"Alright," Jack answered sullenly, "if you must." He lowered himself down to sit on his cart. Tommy nodded agreement and squeezed in beside Jack. Harry ignored the comments, standing mesmerised by the giant dancing flames.

Billy sauntered across to the man in charge. A few people he passed offered greetings. Those that knew him were becoming rather fond of the lad. He and his team had taken on a sort of good luck status from some within the fire brigade. The men on the scene generally allowed him access and consideration whilst they were working, not afforded to many and very rarely afforded to East End kids.

The fire officer saw Billy approaching.

"Back again, Billy? You can't keep away can you?"

Billy smiled at him, "Oh, you know!"

"Yeah, I know. I know that a lad died last night trying to save somebody 'e shouldn't have been savin' an' I know that you boys don't take enough care."

Billy sniffed, wiping his nose. "'Im down Wapping, you mean?"

The officer shook his head in wonder at the sheer determination of these kids to get stuck in. He hoped, once again, when the war was over the bravery of Billy and his tiny team did not go unrewarded.

"We've got this one Billy. Why don't you take your boys over to Whitechapel? I 'eard there was a lot of damaged 'ouses over that way."

Billy studied the fire chief's face. He could detect the tiredness and the worry. But he could also spot the tell-tale signs of a man with plenty left in the tank.

"Yeah, we'll 'ead back that way." He glanced up to momentarily lock eyes, adding, "You should get some rest." Then Billy turned on his heel, calling to his little band, "Come on, lads." The chief smiled as he watched the children informally fall in behind their leader.

He shook his head at the absurdity of life. 'A ten-year-old kid who owns little more than the rags he stands up in, is leading a force of his own making, armed with little more than a bucket of sand and one tin helmet between four of them, into the most dangerous of nightmare situations and he still finds time to raise concerns about my welfare.' The chief smiled again and watched the motley crew departing.

"That boy will go far," he said to himself.

The chief had been born and raised in Surbiton, a small, picturesque town in Surrey, south of the river. Surbiton was only ten miles from the East End but it could have been on a different planet. Growing up in his cosy family home, situated in its leafy surroundings, he had always been warned about the dirty, dishonest illiterates that roamed the inner slums of London. It had been easy to believe the horror stories, but when he had been drafted here he began to think that these people, the children in particular, were nothing like the creatures they were portrayed as and even more so since the bombing had started. It seemed to Chief Nathaniel Forbes that the truth of the matter might indeed be connected to the fact that these kids were written off by society almost from the moment they were born. He was aware that some were using the bombing raids as little more than cover for pretty major pilfering, but he fully understood why they felt the need. Billy and his lot seemed different though. They stood apart from the others and they certainly deserved a little luck in their lives. The Chief looked towards where the lads had headed, but they had disappeared, hidden by the thick, acrid smoke.

Chapter Fourteen

IT had been a terrible night for me. It seemed like there was a bomb going off in every street I tried to settle in. I had a lovely pair of malt whisky bottles, but I couldn't settle down and get a proper taste of them. There seemed to be crying women and dead children scattered everywhere. It was a blessed relief when the dawn finally started to show through the blackness and the bombers returned to their bases, but as my eyes adjusted to the first rays of light I could see the devastation was terrible. I couldn't bear to look at the corpses in the streets any more. I just wanted to get back home and sleep until the moon rose again.

As I stepped from Commercial Street, into the mud of the courtyard I called home, I nearly fell into Reggie Lawson. He saw me coming and attempted to smile in greeting. He clearly wanted to talk. He certainly chose his moments; I couldn't feel any less willing. Oh well! Best smile back and see what he wants. Reggie looked every inch the mobster. His long camel hair coat was turned up at the collar. His trilby was tipped at a jaunty angle and despite the muddy alleys of the East End he wore white spats over his shoes, just like the ones he had seen Jimmy Cagney wearing in the film 'The Public Enemy'. He even favoured redheads purely on Jean Harlow's performance as Cagney's girlfriend in the same film.

"'Ello there," Reg greeted me.

I nodded and tried to squeeze past him, but in such a narrow alley it was easy for the mobster to block an old man's path.

"'Ow's that boy of yours? Alright is 'e?"

I nodded, still not looking up into the younger man's face.

"Tell 'im I said 'Hello', won't you?" He smiled cruelly at me and wandered away.

I waited motionless with my head bowed and my back stooped. I listened until I was sure that Reggie had gone. I had my opinions on why Reggie should show any interest in the welfare of a ten year old.

Everybody knew that Billy showed promise, that he was a cut above most of the boys around here, so it was only logical that the mob would be headhunting the lad. Around here Reg Lawson and his friends represented a step up the corporate ladder. They were, more often than not, the only employers in the area. Legitimate businesses did not often come to this part of the capital looking to swell their ranks of employees.

With a heavy heart I shuffled down the dark, narrow, muddy passage. I knew I had let the boy down and let his mother down. I also knew I was weak, not strong enough to take on the system or to try and mess with the way things worked. As a young man I had been a tearaway, as a middle-aged man a violent nuisance and now I was a nervous drunk. My life had gone rather well, though, when I compared myself to most of my old mates. Most of them were long gone or crippled from years of heavy work at the docks. No, I didn't consider myself hard done by, I was still here.

Of course, that wasn't to say that I had no regrets, but most of my regrets lay in other areas.

Chapter Fifteen

Two nights later, once again, the boys were listening to the sound of high explosives falling all around them. Smoke was wafting across the street, the smell of it thick in their nostrils. Jack was on the roof monitoring exactly where the bombs were falling. He could see people scurrying about in total confusion. Mentally, the damage was unseen, but ever present, besides, there was nothing could be done about that. Physical damage, however, the Dead-End Kids could help with and Jack focused on deciding where their services would be most in need. He liked it up here and was still happy to fulfil his role. Far below him, Billy was in the doorway sharpening a wooden pole with his pocket knife.

A shadow fell across him and he looked up to see Reg Lawson. He quickly looked back down but the shadow remained in place.

"All right boy?"

"Yeah," he glanced up briefly, sullenly, "all right, Mr. Lawson."

Lawson lifted his foot, resting a highly polished shoe on the edge of Billy's seat and rubbing at an imaginary speck of dust. He said, "Need any work, son?"

Billy's sullen expression caught the gangster's gaze briefly, "No thanks, Mr. Lawson."

Lawson chuckled, removing his shoe from the boy's chair. As Reg moved away Billy lifted his head, watched him go, his expression still sullen, his eyes burning into the man's back.

Tommy and Harry were playing snap on the bed, slamming cards down on top of each other with gusto. I slumped in the chair, my back to them and my eyes closed, as I pretended to sleep. Visions of a caped man pressed against a dark wall as a horse reared up, played over and over behind my eyes. Over the years the scenes I saw when I closed my eyes would change, fluidly moving from one segment of that horrible night to another. I had learnt that tonight's particular re-run was the equivalent of getting off lightly. Experience had also taught me that were I to open my eyes and close them again, the segment of proceedings playing over and over would probably be worse, much worse.

Finally, I was in that beautiful place of the insomniac. I was drifting, practically asleep, yet just awake enough to know it.

Then the air-raid warning sirens started again. They put an end to my chance of sleep and wakened many thousands of others in the streets and alleys all around. Whitechapel had been targeted for four consecutive days and nights. The bombers seemed to be directing most of their fury towards the electricity substation, which they must have known was vitally important. Unfortunately, it was very near where we lived. Perhaps the bombers also knew that we were unimportant.

I heard Jack's voice boom out, "Billy, I'm comin' down!" That boy really had the lungs of a market trader.

"It's the substation, innit?" Harry guessed.

Billy smoked the roll-up to its absolute limit and flicked it away.

"Least we ain't got far to go, eh?" he replied, nodding.

They laughed, rather too loudly, at the gallows humour.

That night the boys did not have far to go. They lived on the east side of Commercial Street. On the west side was Spitalfields Market. The market was a one minute walk from their room, less for healthy young boys. That night it took a direct hit. A thousand pound bomb had crashed to earth, right in the centre of a cluster of stalls. Seven people were killed instantly, lethal shrapnel flew in all directions, resulting in much blood and screaming. Crowds of people lurched and elbowed from one side of the market square to the other, their panic rising as one exit after another proved to be blocked by either huge flames or mountainous piles of shattered buildings.

Billy had cocked an ear as the screaming missile grew louder and louder. He jumped slightly the split second it landed. It was so close that the ground shook under his feet and dust fell from the ceiling. The boys fidgeted eager to be out there.

"Right boys, that's us, I reckon." Billy rose up and they fell into line behind him. I kept my eyes shut, feigning sleep or indifference. I listened to them go and once again had to admit the boy put me to shame.

'If only I had been one tenth as brave at his age,' I shook my head wistfully. The lines around my eyes betrayed a whole lifetime of bitter treatment, what Americans call 'unresolved issues'. That poor girl would still be alive if I was as brave as Billy. I shook my head sadly. She should still be alive. An image of her, lying on the wet cobbles with her throat ripped open, jumped into my mind. In my experience there were occasions when time did not prove to heal.

The room seemed empty once the boys had left me to my own devices. I opened my eyes and turned around, making sure I was indeed alone. A truly rare occurrence for me now that the boys had all moved in permanently. My melancholy mood was intruded upon by what sounded like absolute pandemonium breaking out in all directions, but right here, as long as I didn't move, at this precise moment, I was alone. I risked closing my eyes. The memories came flooding back.

I slumped forward, my head in my hands, rocking slightly, as wave after bitter wave rolled over me. I glanced down at the step where the Ripper's knife still lay and my crooked body rocked some more at the memory of that terrible night 52 years ago. I had known who had done those poor girls. I was aware exactly who was committing these atrocities, causing such fear amongst my neighbours, yet I had done nothing until it was too late for poor Mary Kelly. I see now, that was the day I became withdrawn and started to keep myself to myself more. Such behaviour was common amongst the kids of the East End. Nobody paid particular attention or noticed us as children that society was failing. We were left to fall apart alone and if we became bitter little street thugs, so be it.

I knew now, that straight after they had found Long Liz butchered in Dutfield's Yard was when I should have said something, but I didn't know it then. When they found Cathy that same night and three weeks later when the Ripper had struck again I was still unsure what I should or shouldn't do. I had started wetting myself after that incident and was beaten for behaving like a baby.

"It's 'cos I know!" I had wanted to scream, but I never did. Now, of course, it was too late, much too late. The Ripper had been stopped in his tracks by the juggernaut that had been Mickey Tippings. But Mickey had died before I had returned the knife. Therefore, I still had the knife and the nightmares that came with it.

Sometimes, during good spells, I would go three or four nights without waking up in a cold sweat. I would no longer expect to be confronted suddenly in my sleep by the man we had spied on. Then the torment would return as though I was being punished for my part in the murders that had haunted Whitechapel in that cursed autumn of 1888. I felt responsible in my own way and it was killing me. The secret I was cursed to carry to the grave was killing me.

From then on, I was a scared little boy carrying the weight of the world on my shoulders with no-one to turn to. So my formative years consisted of consciously bottling up any emotion, no matter how small and doing whatever it took to drink myself into oblivion every single night. Alcoholism was not a disease in the East End of the 1800s; it was the way we dealt with reality.

But here was Billy, the saviour of us all. Billy wasn't going to turn out like me, like all the rest. The boy was going to make something of himself and get out of this slum. I knew the lad wouldn't be taking this old man with him. I knew I was destined to end my days on these filthy streets that had caused me a lifetime of misery but I considered it a price worth paying if it meant Billy would do better, would at least get a chance in life. This war and the way those boys treated it as one massive game could actually turn out to be a blessing in disguise. Billy was getting noticed all right by wardens and fire chiefs, no less. Men with real influence who could help him get a step up the ladder. To me these truly were men in high places. These men were actual living, breathing pillars of society that I could see with my own eyes. Those in Whitehall and Westminster never ventured down here and they meant very little to us, to me. I was using my grandson's bravery to fight the self-recriminations that haunted me so.

'I may not 'ave been much use but look at my boy now,' I mumbled, rocking pathetically in the darkness. Hoping the boys made it back to the safety of this flea-infested slum.

Chapter Sixteen

"WOULD you look at that?" Jack was truly awestruck by the sheer scale of desecration that the bombers had wreaked on London once again. The 'ack ack' of the anti-aircraft guns was a constant noise and the bombs screamed relentlessly. A child close by shrieked in terror, a noise that made every hair on your body stand on end. On the periphery of the smoke, people that could ran from exposed ground.

A gas pipe at the Aldgate end of Whitechapel High Street had taken a hit. The blue flames of burning gas were shooting twenty feet up into the night sky. Billy glanced at it cautiously and kept moving towards the market. A large crowd were obstructing his view at ground level, but above their heads, as the crowd ebbed and flowed, he could see a fallen wall right across the main entrance. Access to the market square was blocked before them. Totally blocked. Impassable. Billy could hear the screams from the other side of the rubble pile. They needed to get into the market square; he could see flames leaping high in there and knew that this was the place where they would be needed tonight.

"Jack, get up on that roof an' see what's what!"

"'Arry, go with 'im an' take the rope."

"Tommy, come with me." The two pairs of brave boys moved together along the row of burning shops and fallen walls.

Jack was barking encouragement at those they passed, Billy was thinking as he did so. They needed to get into the square. That much was obvious and the best way in would be through one of the damaged buildings, but they all seemed to be ablaze. Incendiary bombs falling in batches of a dozen per second were flashing terrifyingly all around them, burning white hot and causing yet more fires to start, more buildings to catch alight, far quicker than the milling firemen could smother them with sand.

Billy needed an overall picture; he needed a way into a building that would allow Jack access upwards. He needed to find a route through the burning rooms.

"'Ere, 'ere!" Harry called across to them. He was standing in front of a warehouse that, although burning quite merrily all down its left side, seemed perfectly intact along the right side, where there was an alley. They raced through the black smoke following Harry's back as he darted down the lane.

Jack waited in the shadows a short distance before them, but his excited voice carried through the gloom.

"It's a side door. Look, I can get in through 'ere."

"All right, let's give it a try." Billy tried the door but it was locked. "Harry, open this door," he exclaimed, stepping back as he did so.

Harry swung his axe at the door and it flew inwards. Jack chuckled in delight as Harry entered the dark room and then fell in behind him.

"Come on 'Arry, let's go. We're 'olding things up." Jack pushed his friend in the back. At the same moment Harry had found, and was turning, a door handle. Then they were gone. They had disappeared into the burning building hopefully to re-appear on the roof far above.

Billy and Tommy retraced their steps back down the alley and stood on the pavement nervously craning their necks skywards.

"Where the 'ell are they?" Tommy muttered for the hundredth time.

"They're comin', they're comin'," Billy exclaimed just loudly enough for his friend to hear.

Suddenly, the terrible grind of a wall collapsing could be heard above the roar of the 'ack ack' guns and the crackling flames. The boys glanced at each other and nodded. Both establishing that, yes, they had heard the wall collapse and yes, it definitely was a wall. Now it had fallen normal audio service had been resumed.

Billy raised his eyes skywards once more. He was in his element and he allowed a smile to cross his face. He struggled to see through the thick smoke.

"Where the 'ell are...," Tommy never finished the question.

"There they are," Billy declared and he was absolutely correct. There they both were craning their necks and leaning over, way too far.

First Harry's head, then Jack's, appeared over the jagged edge of the roof far above. Harry's beaming face framed with the pink smoke and massive red glow of the anti-aircraft shells bursting all around him.

He had tied a yellow rag to one end of the rope and he dropped it over the side, aiming to hit Tommy with the weighted end. They all laughed as Tommy was forced to avoid it slamming into the top of his head. Then he hauled it back up until the dirty, once yellow rag hung halfway down the front walls of the terraced row. The plan was for Billy and Tommy to follow the rag as the other two made their way across the rooftops which joined in a big circle of buildings around the market area. When they found a house they considered was not a flaming death trap or a pile of loose bricks just waiting to collapse, they would tug frantically, as was the pre-arranged signal.

Harry set off along the roofs and the yellow marker danced from house to house as he moved, its progress easily followed by his comrades at ground level.

Tommy and Billy followed the yellow marker as it worked its way around the houses. At first it made good, steady progress from one property to the next in a measured, orderly fashion but now, just a few minutes into the operation its movements were rather more erratic. First to the left, then right, then back again. They knew Jack was making sure which was the safest route. They had come to trust his judgement but there was no need for him to play them this way.

"What's 'e bleedin' doin'?" Tommy demanded to know.

"'E's 'avin' a laff," Billy agreed.

What they didn't appreciate was that Jack was manoeuvring backwards and forwards across extremely treacherous brickwork. It crumbled away as he tried to proceed. Long cracks were visible up here that seemed to permeate across whole sections of the gantries, with scant respect for the boundaries between one property and another. It was hard to make out the cracks until he stepped on them and they opened up unexpectedly, sending bricks bouncing downwards into the darkness. He worked only by the low pinkish light of the raging fires and he worked as fast as he could but the boys only possessed one tin hat between them and he was wearing it. He didn't want to send too much rubble downwards as it could potentially fall on his two friends. He proceeded as best he could, checking and double checking, then leaping across widening gaps that had been solid bricks just moments before.

Behind him Harry hung back a few paces and kept silent. He trusted Jack to work things out and knew he would do so, much more quickly, without constant interruptions. He had been snapped at by his pal enough times to know which way the land lay on that one. He didn't take offence. Jack found it easier to concentrate with no advice being shouted at him and that was fair enough in Harry's book.

Only when he was absolutely certain that he had uncovered the safest possible entry for his pals, would Jack tug furiously at his rope. He would make the yellow marker dance frantically against the side of whichever building he felt was the best one for his pals to use to get right through and into the vast square of Spitalfields Market.

Jack had raced up a burning staircase in order to get to the roofs. The staircase no longer existed. He was becoming rather good at accessing attics and shinning up drainpipes and even better at judging which fires were too dangerous and which, with a good dollop of luck, they should be able to fight their way through.

The collapse of the wooden staircase meant the two kids were effectively trapped. Jack ignored the thick smoke that was stinging his lungs and leapt to a neighbouring cornice. Close behind him Harry landed with a thud and rolled into his partner. They jumped to their feet without complaint and ran at full pace along a ledge only two bricks wide. The boys were running blind, their surroundings coming and going through the smoke. Jack barely seemed to be looking where he placed his feet as he ran. He scanned each building that presented itself through the smoke until his eyes fell on what he had been looking for, a chink of light from a doorway. He raced through a burning hole and slowed immediately to a walking pace. They were inside the roof space now, the smoke was thicker and the light almost non-existent. He groped his way through the dark, feeling for the loose tiles which would enable them to get back on the rooftops. Harry was tight up behind him, matching him step for step. It was Harry's way of telling him to move faster.

His left palm made contact with a wooden handrail. Instantly, he quickened the pace again and started to climb. Both boys had pulled their ragged shirts up to use as a filter against the smoke, but Jack considered the best way to be able to breathe without it stinging was to burst out of a top floor window back onto a roof, back outside. He would rather take his chances with the height, the fire and the crumbling masonry than be trapped inside to be smoked to death. They reached the attic room and Harry smashed through the roof tiles breaking out into the slightly improved air that filled the London sky. They lifted themselves through the hole and slid on their backsides down the v-shaped roof, using their feet as brakes as they reached the edge. Then skilfully slowing down, just before they shot into the smoke clouds and landed eighty feet below. In a controlled manner, that can only be achieved with extreme confidence, Jack was up and running along another narrow ledge in one fluid movement. With Harry's breath hot on his collar he ran high above the streets just one slip from oblivion.

Jack's chest pounded with adrenaline. He felt invincible, literally on top of the world and having the time of his short life. In Jack's book this was truly living. He leapt, extending his leap like an Olympic athlete, as his chosen landing spot disappeared in a heap of tumbling bricks and he was forced to re-adjust in mid-air. For that split second he was only a heartbeat away from death and he had laughed out loud in the very face of absolute danger.

Back at ground level Billy was leading Tommy by the hand. They were fighting their way through smoke filled darkness, each wearing their shirts as filters and using their free hands to grope around for the feel of something wooden, preferably a door. Billy had no choice but to press ahead. Conditions such as these made him feel claustrophobic and vulnerable; feelings he felt obliged to face head-on and something he would never admit to his pals.

Tommy made a sound. The actual words were unimportant, he had made a sound and that was enough. Their modus operandi at such times was to remain silent until you found a way out, then be noisy until feeling the touch of whoever else was with you. This, they had discovered, was the best and only way to avoid confusion. It worked well and none of these dead-end kids had the slightest inclination to mess with this particular system.

Billy shuffled as silently as he could towards Tommy's voice. He saw a beam of light through the smoke. Tommy was forcing a door open and light was rushing in. Billy grinned in the darkness. Once again, they had looked death in the eye and would live to fight another day.

Tommy's wiry frame filled the light that he had created. Instantly, Billy knew he had hesitated and was waiting for instructions.

"Let me go first," Billy called. He was already squeezing past his friend as he completed the sentence.

"Come on Tommy, let's 'ave it," he added.

Way above Jack and Harry were back in the night air once more, illuminated by the pink glow of a thousand fires. A pair of tiny insignificant creatures with a bird's-eye-view of a terrible sight. It seemed like hell, as if the world would never be right again and they wouldn't have missed it for anything. From their vantage point it really looked as though, finally, the lunatics had taken over the asylum and all should abandon hope. However, like the birds and bats who shared their lofty position, the boys were far from despondent. They hadn't given up all hope of things ever being good again. They were whooping loud curses at the bombers soaring above them and wearing the broadest grins their faces could cope with. They were alive. They were in the centre of their known universe and no adults were on hand to rein them in. To this pair of ten-year-old sons of Whitechapel the war was the best thing that had ever happened.

They had done their bit to identify a route into the market square. Flames crackled loudly and Jack knew it was time to leave.

"Go on, 'Arry!" he called to his partner and Harry threw one end of his rope eighty feet to the ground below. He tied the other end to a chimney stack and both boys flew down it at a speed only achieved with loads of experience.

Below them a group of firemen marvelled at the agility and daring of such young boys. Chief Forbes sent his men in through the identified route and following behind was just in time to see Jack and Harry make good their landing.

Chapter Seventeen

REGGIE Lawson flicked the butt of his cigarette into the street and pulled his collar tighter around his neck. He had been waiting for nearly ten minutes now and to his mind he had waited long enough. A pair of busy-body wardens had already told him that he should be heading for his shelter and he had no business being outdoors on such a night. They hadn't been overly convinced by his story about searching for his mother's cat, either. Fortunately, they had been in too much of a hurry to check his papers or question him closely, but it was an unnecessary hassle that wouldn't have come about if he hadn't been hanging around. Reggie did not take very kindly to being kept waiting.

A vehicle pulled up at the kerb beside him and the passenger door of an army Land Rover was pushed open for him.

"Alright, Reg?" a man asked from the driver's seat. He wore the cap of a military policeman but with the door open and his clothing visible, he was clearly not a member of the British Military, despite the vehicle he was driving.

"Never mind 'Alright, Reg', you're bleedin' late."

"We 'ad a problem wi..."

"I ain't interested in your stupid problems. You're 'ere now. Let's just get on with it."

Reggie hopped into the passenger seat and they raced away accompanied by the scream of an untidy gear change.

"I told you to be 'ere at eight thirty sharp."

"All right Reg, only there was a bloody big crater blocking Bethnal Green 'igh Street an' we 'ad to take a massive great detour," the driver offered up.

Reggie glanced across. He privately had to admit that was a reasonable excuse.

"I ain't interested, park closer next time." He was scowling, making a big deal of such a trivial matter.

Dennis Cummings, the driver, kept his eye on the road. Reggie would be unbearable if anything else went wrong. He drove as fast as the conditions would let him. The roads were littered with huge, deep craters that appeared suddenly out of the blackness. He skidded from one side of the road to the other to avoid them and the potholes. Either side of them buildings were blazing high into the sky but Dennis was glad of the light they offered. Small groups of people and single individuals roamed aimlessly or stood dumbstruck watching their lives go up in flames before them.

Dennis kept driving west. They were headed for Bond Street and he was treading that fine line between maintaining enough speed to make them difficult to identify or stop whilst going slow enough to ensure they didn't end up in a crater.

As they raced along Fleet Street the sounds of the night fell quiet and the licking of flames ceased. As Fleet Street became the Strand, once again all was ablaze, cries went up into the night all around and bombs screamed through the sky. This had become what they were used to and it was strangely reassuring. They glanced at each other, pure adrenaline pumping through their bodies. Reggie almost smiled as their eyes met and Dennis was glad to see he had calmed down.

'We've come a long way since this war started,' was Dennis's thought and he knew his boss was thinking along the same lines. They felt no loyalty to anyone outside their circle of friends. If power crazy statesmen wanted to slaughter thousands of innocents over some trivial matter, that was no concern of Reggie, but the scale of it, the total annihilation. Men like Dennis and Reggie would never kill so indiscriminately or in such large numbers, but it wasn't his war. Besides, he had done some bad stuff of his own, so probably wasn't best placed to cast stones. Reggie had to admire their front, though. He knew from personal experience that going to war was about as expensive as it got. He couldn't begin to imagine what destruction on this scale cost, but he had no doubt it was an impressive amount. That alone had to be admired, he thought.

"Look at it Reg, it's a bloody wasteland." Dennis had to say something. Despite the great tragedy, the immeasurable losses, the sight of a major City being reduced to rubble, truly it was daunting.

"Makes our aggro look like playground spats, dunnit?" replied the biggest mobster in the whole of England.

"An' who's gonna pay for it all, eh?" Reggie said.

"I'll tell you who. The little people, Dennis. It's always the little people that pays the piper," he said, as they sped past a sixty foot wall of flame.

A family sat on the roadside amongst a pile of rubble, shell shocked residents sitting in the open space that yesterday was their front parlour. These were not East Enders; they were wealthy folk who lived in the exclusive heart of London. They were used to life following a carefully constructed plan and were not equipped to deal with sudden, unexpected disasters. So they gathered in the space they still thought of as home and stared into space.

Dennis raced down through the gears to take the sharp right hand corner at Trafalgar Square. He increased speed up the incline and changed noisily down again as the Land Rover screeched to the left, straightened out and flew along the smooth tarmac of Piccadilly, Dennis pretending that he was Al Capone.

"Easy, Dennis," Reggie offered as they turned into Oxford Street. "Slow down a bit now; try not to get us noticed by everyone, eh?"

Dennis raised his foot slightly from the accelerator, allowing the Land Rover to slow down as he neared the turning into Bond Street.

"All right, Reggie, 'ere we are. 'Ow far down is the one we want?"

"Pull over there." Reggie pointed to their left.

Dennis did as he was told, killing the engine and lights as he rolled the vehicle quietly and gently up to the kerb.

They sat in the darkness, listening. The sounds of the bombs were clearly heard but they were not close. This part of the capital was not on the bombers' list of targets tonight and no stray incendiaries had fallen nearby, so far.

They sat in silence for a few moments longer, Dennis patiently awaiting the plan. He knew his boss was thinking and would reveal what needed to be revealed when he was ready and not a moment sooner.

Ever since he had been a child playing in the streets Reggie had been the same way and he hadn't let many down yet. Dennis waited and listened.

Finally Reggie turned to face him. "'Ere's what we'll do."

Whilst outlining what was about to happen, he pulled a pair of hammers from underneath his seat and handed one to Dennis.

They sat still for a few seconds, Dennis checking in his rear-view mirror, Reggie looking straight ahead, between them scanning the area for signs of life.

"Seems quiet enough, eh, Reg?"

"Yeah, I reckon so. Let's go. Nice an' easy now."

Dennis pulled the key from the ignition as they climbed out. They shut the doors as quietly as possible and Dennis followed his partner in crime across the street.

Reggie carefully opened a gate and led the way down a side lane; he then jumped over a back gate and landed in a courtyard at the back of a jeweller's shop.

Reggie knew where he was going and what he was doing. Without a pause he had strolled nonchalantly up to a back door and hit one of the small, square glass panes with his hammer. He thrust his gloved hand through the hole and was soon turning a key and opening up. With a cursory glance around to ensure they weren't being observed, they were in. Reggie headed for the front of the building, towards the shop front. As they went into the hall, he paused, listening for a few heart stopping moments. Dennis wasn't sure if Reggie was simply being cautious or if he had actually heard something. He stood motionless as his heart pounded, his hammer raised, ready to strike. Reggie nodded towards the front door. 'Oh God, surely they weren't coming from that way! That was the way back to the car.' Dennis held his breath.

"See that bar across the door?" Reggie hissed, motioning at the front door. A solid looking piece of timber lay across two custom-made brackets to ensure any burglar defeating the lock would still be unable to enter the premises. Dennis began to breathe again.

"Move that piece o' wood, in case we need to make a quick getaway."

Dennis nodded and moved forward to carry out his boss's request.

Simultaneously, Reggie headed towards the shop front and the glass-topped display cabinets, shaking a hessian bag from his pocket as he did so.

Dennis not only removed the piece of wood but also opened the door and left it on the latch. Soon, they were both in the front room of the shop, hidden from the street by heavy blackout drapes, with their getaway car no more than a hundred paces from the door. They filled their bags in silence as bombs dropped on London in the distance and as soon as they had filled them with loot it would be a quiet exit out of the place.

"Ready?" Reggie half-whispered, half-hissed across the shop.

Dennis looked up at him, nodding and pulled the drawstring to close his bag.

They slipped quietly out through the door, took a quick look around and seeing no-one else about, walked briskly back to the vehicle. Dennis started the engine and headed south into Chelsea, hoping not to meet any tin hats or police on the quiet suburban roads. He intended to cross the river, drive through the quieter roads of Lambeth and then on into Southwark. They would approach the East End from a totally different direction, just in case it mattered in the future. Reggie believed that you could never be too careful when it came to deceiving the police.

Chapter Eighteen

I SAT hunched over in my chair as the dawn crept into the eastern sky. The embers in the fireplace had turned cold many hours ago and the bombs had kept falling, incessantly. Large sections of East End property had disappeared overnight. Areas totally flattened, to such an extent that lifelong inhabitants of the area were finding it impossible to get their bearings. Fires were leaping hundreds of feet into the sky, blazing furiously and many lives were being lost. I had been miraculously untroubled. I had listened in fear some time in the early hours as I heard the whine of one particular bomb falling and thought to myself, 'this one's real close, it's gonna land on my bleeding 'ead for sure,' but somehow it never did and then dawn had arrived and I was still alive. Now the droning noise of the bombers was starting to fade. They were heading back to France or wherever they came from and I was still here. It had felt as though Hitler's boys had pounded London with all their might yet, somehow, I was still here.

I had become an old man racked with guilt, not really caring if I lived or died, while others, far more worthy, would never see another day. Guilt became my constant companion and nothing seemed to ease its terrible burden. I genuinely preferred it when I was racked with regret and hunger. Guilt was an emotion I didn't much care for.

Somewhere nearby came the searing whoosh of a section of wall that had suffered a structural hit and was falling noisily to the ground. As it did so the floorboards creaked beneath my feet and I couldn't help glancing guiltily towards my secret hiding place.

Instantly, I recalled the all-engulfing feeling of mass insecurity in that autumn of 1888. That feeling was as nothing compared to this. I listened as outside an adult tried in vain to explain to a child why we were being attacked so viciously, night after night. De-mobbed soldiers with limbs missing or heads still full of gunfire, were out begging for food and I could hear them from here. They were now an embarrassment to the

Empire; it was inevitable that they would find the roads that lead to Whitechapel.

I leant forward and poked at the dead fire, confirming what the chill had already told my aching bones and rose unsteadily to my feet.

'The boys will be back soon,' I told myself. It was time to burn the last few pieces of coal I had been saving.

"They are bloody 'eroes an' they deserve to come back to a bit of warmth," I muttered as I skilfully produced flames from the bare minimum of kindling.

"Bloody 'eroes," I repeated. I placed the first lump of coal carefully in the grate whilst listening to the engines of the last planes as they faded into the distance.

Chapter Nineteen

DENNIS gunned the engine, pushing the vehicle hard across London Bridge. The tyres screeched as he took a sharp right-hand turn, swerving in and out of the multitude of obstacles blocking what used to be the main road to and from the East End. Beside him Reggie was starting to relax. Within a few short minutes they would be back and safe.

"Bloody 'ell!" he said in a shocked tone, "Been some damage round 'ere last night, wouldn't ya say?"

Dennis nodded, his eyes struggling to fully comprehend the damage to streets he thought he knew like the back of his hand, but he was now driving through, more or less on instinct in places.

"The 'ole world 'as gone mad," he declared as way of reply.

Reggie's features hardened as he nodded agreement, "Too true my ol' mate, an' that is why we 'ave to make our own luck."

They glanced at each other as Dennis raced on squealing tyres into Commercial Street; they both knew home was practically within touching distance now.

"Well, we certainly made ourselves plenty of luck last night, eh?" They both howled with glee and raced ever closer to the slum where they felt safe.

Dennis jabbed a chubby finger at a group of kids huddling round a cart they were pushing up the busy pavement, "Ain't that those kids from the court?"

"Yeah," Reggie replied, "it's that Billy an' his mates. Smart kid that one," he added as an afterthought and they both glanced at the ragged group of boys.

Dennis shrugged. If his friend had a particular interest in the boy, well, it was none of his concern.

They were just about home now. Dennis slowed the Land Rover as they came level with Dorset Street. He nodded at a thug standing on the corner, but he didn't stop. He allowed the vehicle to carry on further, both of them scanning the crowded pavements for police or tin hats, as they slowed to a halt.

"This'll do," Reggie declared shortly.

At his command Dennis stopped the car completely and applied the handbrake. They climbed out and quietly walked away without a backward glance.

He had left the keys in the ignition and the engine was running. They knew this area intimately and they both knew with total certainty the army vehicle would be gone before they had covered the two minute walk back to their base.

They strolled at an easy pace through the early morning crowds on Commercial Street. Most of those they passed recognised them and wisely avoided eye contact. On the corner of their street Reggie's man watched them approach. He smiled without humour and spat tobacco juice onto the pavement.

"Oi!" came a high pitched voice.

He had narrowly avoided spitting onto the shoulder of that young kid who lived at the other end of the court with the drunken old man.

He motioned as if to strike out at the four boys pushing past him.

"Don't you 'oi' me, you cheeky little..."

The end of his sentence was drowned out by Jack repeating "Oi!" in a far louder voice. Immediately, all four of them were shouting 'Oi!' loudly and in direct defiance of the gangster's orders. His measured threat had accomplished the exact opposite reaction to the one he had hoped for. The boys were laughing as they disappeared from view.

Just then Reg and Dennis were with him.

"'aving problems with the kids, are ya?" Reggie sneered.

"Want me to sort 'em out for ya?" Dennis added.

The look-out scowled, but said nothing.

"Stay there Alf, we don't wanna be disturbed unexpectedly, all right?"

Alf nodded, "Right, Reg."

Billy led his band of junior fire-fighters into the narrow alley that was the only way in and out of their court. When the alley opened up into the space that made up the six addresses the boys turned right and there was Pops and he had the fire burning. They were home.

They had rescued three people from the market blaze and made it back intact. They felt they could take on the world and so had been just in the right mood to backchat a gangster.

Moments later Reggie and Dennis passed through the same alley. Once in the court they turned left past the oil drum and the men loitering there, to the end of the muddy yard and to the room they called their base. Reggie had a lucrative enterprise which he ran with an iron hand. His boys were the toughest, smartest villains in the East End and this was turning into a real growth period in their business ventures.

The two men climbed the old wooden staircase to the upper rooms and once inside, sank gratefully into padded armchairs that had recently been acquired from a West End gentlemen's club. Reggie loosened his tie and demanded someone bring him a scotch. He removed the sack from his inside pocket and glanced over at Dennis to do likewise. They tipped the contents onto the glass topped table and as their eyes locked on each other, burst into laughter. On the table a variety of jewels and diamonds glittered in the dim candle light. "Drinks, where's our drinks?" Reggie demanded in a loud voice.

"'Ere you are, Reg." A thick cut crystal tumbler was placed into his hand.

"Dennis." A glass of the same finest scotch was handed to him respectfully.

Dennis may not be the cruel sadist that Reggie was capable of being, but Dennis' star was rising and everyone in the room knew it.

Chapter Twenty

JACK had acquired a loaf of flat bread and a side of mutton from his cart and the old man was sharing out the food as they relived the evening's adventures.

"It was amazing standin' up there lookin' down on all you little people," Jack sneered towards Tommy.

Tommy took the insult in good faith. "Took your time gettin' up there though, didn't ya?" he shot back.

"Yeah, well, it ain't always that quick fightin' through burnin' buildings, ya know," Jack replied.

The boys were smiling as they played their game of verbal macho posturing. These bombing raids, night after night, gave them a real chance to shine in the neighbourhood. To them the war was a huge adventure, full of excitement. Tonight, at the market, they had all been there. They had attracted the attention of not only Mr. Cooper, the union man, but even the fire chief had said he hoped they would apply to join the London Fire Brigade. Them? Four urchins from the slums of Whitechapel had practically been told they could be firemen after the war ended. It really was too good to be true. The Blitz was bringing them into contact with those from other walks of life. Connections were being made that would have been impossible without the backdrop of the worst atrocity to hit London since 1888. These urchins clearly had a bit of gumption about them. They were saving lives on a daily basis under extremely dangerous conditions and their efforts were very much appreciated. They were well on their way to joining the ranks of that rare breed, people who had escaped the East End and improved their lot. They knew it and the prospect thrilled them, each and every one.

Pops knew why the lads were so excited. When he had been their age he had sat in this very same courtyard with his pals as they had rejoiced in selling a few matchbooks down the market. They had laughed and joked and planned to take over first Whitechapel Market, then the whole world. Three months later the murders had begun. Six months later Stan Wilson, his closest friend, was dead and the fallout of what they had witnessed together effectively broke up the little gang. They had dared to dream and all of them had crashed and burned. Now Percy was the only one still alive.

He listened to the boys as each offered up in turn their analysis of the not too distant future.

"We're all gonna live in big houses up West," Tommy pronounced dreamily.

As always, Billy took on the task of keeping their feet firmly planted in the real world.

"'E said 'e will 'ave a word an' we might be able to take reading an' writin' tests", he declared, "an' that was it."

"I ain't interested," Jack said sullenly.

"Yeah, an' I reckon those sticky fingers are with you 'til the day you die," Harry replied, sniggering.

They all howled at the memory of the firemen trying to locate a side of mutton that Jack had already safely tucked away on the back of their cart.

"Bet they're still wondering where their food went?" Jack ventured.

I listened to their banter with considerable pride but with a deep foreboding for the future. I was only too aware that dreams, around here, had a habit of dying on the vine.

'If they do get out of 'ere there won't be no room for this ol' dog,' I reasoned to myself, but if it meant my Billy getting a real chance in life it would be cheap at half the price. I knew that gang of villains at the other end of the court were slowly indoctrinating the boys into the way things worked round here. I knew that they would get sucked in deeper and deeper until, before they knew it, they would be criminal class for the rest of their lives.

I glanced around the room at their happy faces. These four children that I had known since they were babies were on the crossroads that would determine the route their lives would follow. They didn't know it, of course, but the time for childish games was drawing to a close. Soon all manner of temptations would be coming their way. Once again I prayed to God for Mr. Cooper to come good and show them a way out of this rat infested hovel.

"I'm goin' for a wee," Billy announced as he rose up and headed for the door, "An' I'm 'aving the chair when I come back," he shot a warning glance at Jack.

Jack smiled, "All right, all right, keep your 'air on."

Billy emerged into the courtyard just as Reggie was coming from the opposite way. They glanced up and caught each other's eye. Billy nodded acknowledgement and quickly averted his gaze in deference. He tried to keep moving but Reggie had stopped in his tracks. He veered left to intercept the boy. Three other large men in double-breasted suits fidgeted behind him.

"Wait 'ere lads, won't be a minute," Reggie said, as he detoured towards the boy.

Billy looked up in response to his voice.

"Saw you earlier, out with your boys, pushin' that cart," Reggie leant in close and muttered quietly.

Billy glanced up to look into his eyes, then quickly down again. He shrugged. "So?" he hissed. Reggie smiled at the implied defiance.

"So, I saw yer, that's all." He turned with a big grin on his face and headed towards the alley, towards the street, out into the East End, out into London and out into the whole wide world. "Come on boys, let's go." His gang followed.

Behind the door of the tiny hovel we called home, I had eavesdropped on Reggie's words holding my breath. Through the slit of the half-open door I watched as the mobsters swaggered down the alley.

'Yep', I told myself, 'those temptations will be coming thick and fast for these boys now.'

Billy relieved himself against a fence. He was just finished when he heard the air-raid warning sirens start up and automatically he raised his eyes to the sky, searching for the bombers, his ears straining for the first exciting sound of their droning engines.

'Really,' he mused, smiling to himself, 'really, again, so soon?'

His smile became a grin of anticipation as he tucked himself away and the bombers droned ever louder.

"Hey, Billy!" Jack was calling him from the doorway. "Seems like ol' Fritz is at it again, eh?"

Billy walked back towards his pal, nodding his head in agreement and grinning broadly.

"It's a war out there," he replied and both excited boys laughed far too loudly. People would lose their lives in the coming hours, but to these boys the sirens had the same effect as the end of day school bell. It was a signal for them to go out and play.

"Get the cart, Jack. Let's hit it!" He had heard U.S. Marines use that phrase and he liked the ring of it.

Jack turned on his heels, practically running with the excitement of getting out there once again. Yeah, rescuing people was a blast, but air raids to him were a time for making a living. Reggie had told him a number of things he needed and that he would pay good money for, if Jack could deliver. Say what you like about Reggie Lawson but he always paid cash on delivery. Jack and Billy often listened as other kids talked excitedly about shrapnel finds. To Jack, scrabbling for bits of shrapnel to swop with your pals was a complete waste of time. He set his sights much higher than that, unaware that he was an entrepreneur, full of the business acumen of generations of big-city survivors. Billy turned a blind eye to Jack's excesses, brutally aware that he was responsible for paying the rent and feeding a family of five. Jack loved the air raids in a more innocent way. He wasn't responsible for paying the bills. He thought in terms of treasure. As Jack rolled the cart out from beneath its tarpaulin cover, he whistled a happy tune.

Tommy and Harry fell out of the door together. The boys had rested, albeit rather briefly and they had eaten rather too much, but they were young, they recovered quickly and each of them was raring to go. However, Billy was in charge, so they hovered at the alley entrance and waited watchfully as their leader headed back into the dark little room they called home.

"All right, Pops?" he asked, with just his head and shoulders poking through the door.

I had lain out on the bed and pulled an old blanket over myself.

"All right, son, you go on now. Don't you worry about me."

We stared at each other briefly.

"Billy, be careful out there," I added.

"Sure Pops. See you later."

"All right, son," I replied and he was gone.

I admonished myself the moment they had all left.

'Be careful out there.' Is that it? Is that the best advice you've got for him?

I was still mumbling to myself as I threw the blanket aside and rose gingerly to my feet.

I would try not to drink too much today, try to have a word with Billy when the boys came back. I knew I owed it to him to steer him towards a better life but I didn't know how to achieve such a thing without upsetting Reggie. I felt trapped, helpless. I reached for my bottle and realised it was empty, as soon as I lifted it. Wasn't that just typical? I would have to get up and go out now.

I pulled the door shut behind me and headed out into Commercial Street.

The air raid was already in full flow. The sky full of sound, planes, bombs, heavy guns, screams, smashing glass, falling masonry; just the normal cacophony of an average day in London. Enough to strike terror into the biggest of men, but nowhere near enough to deter me in my quest to drink myself to oblivion and generally go about my day as though the war wasn't really happening.

To add to the misery heavy rain was starting to fall. Any right-minded person would have turned back to get a raincoat or an umbrella before setting out on a journey that had no distance or time limits to it. But I owned neither a raincoat nor an umbrella. If I wasn't deterred by the fury of a high explosive aerial bombardment I was hardly going to be put off by a little bit of inclement weather. I headed deeper into Whitechapel.

Chapter Twenty-One

19th March 1941

LONDON had been under attack for six months. This very day a 500 bomber raid on the docks killed 750 men. All over London decent, law-abiding people, deprived of sleep and nourishment, tried to carry on and do their bit for the war effort. They tried to observe the advice and attempted to pull together for the good of the nation but the strain was starting to show. Lips were chapped, skin tone was beginning to show slightly grey around the eyes, tempers were beginning to get a little frayed and people were hungry, really hungry, every waking hour. In Whitechapel the general populace couldn't put that one down to Hitler. Empty, rattling stomachs were the norm for as far back as anyone could remember.

Reggie Lawson stood on a street corner by the docks. He was dressed in a three-piece suit tailored in Savile Row and he was smoking an American cigarette. He glanced impatiently at his gold Rolex watch again and then looked upwards as wave after wave of German bombers drifted noisily across the sky. Heavy smoke was drifting along the river and on the opposite bank he could see large swathes of Southwark burning furiously. To his left, 400 yards down the street, firemen aimed their hoses at a burning warehouse. Flames were leaping hundreds of feet above their heads. To Reggie they resembled children tackling an angry fire-breathing dragon, their efforts seemed irrelevant, almost pointless. In Reggie's mind they might as well let it burn and come back in the morning. It seemed to him as though the whole world was on fire, so what was the point of risking life and limb to save a building when the bombers would, he reasoned, be back tomorrow to try again.

A large explosion caused him to glance suddenly at the source of the bang.

'Blimey, that sounded like something big just got hit.' Away in the distance, through the gaps in the devastated landscape, he could see the glow of a massive fireball.

He strolled to his left to try and get a better view. It looked to him as though one could have landed somewhere in Whitechapel and he became instantly concerned, not about people but about the rolls of Chinese silk he had stashed in a warehouse. It was a bit different when it was his goods that might be going up in flames.

"All right, Reg?" An approaching figure broke his chain of thought.

"No, I am not all right! I told you to be 'ere at 'alf past. It's nearly quarter to."

The anger etched across his face negated the need for any response.

"If you let me down again..." he glared at the man and let the unfinished sentence hang uncomfortably between them.

"Sorry, Reg, it's just that..."

"I ain't interested in your pathetic excuses. 'Ave you brought the motor?"

"Yeah, it's over there, facin' towards Mile End Road, like you said."

Reggie started moving in the direction of the car. "All right, let's go."

The other man fell into step beside him. He was a heavy-set individual of an age where he should have been on active service.

"You wanna drive, Reg?" asked the younger man.

"No you drive, an' go through Wapping. That looked like a big blast over Whitechapel way an' we don't want no more delays."

Dennis kept his thoughts to himself. He took pride in being the best getaway driver in the whole of London. Yet even he kept having to stop and get his bearings. Trusted landmarks were no longer in the familiar positions they had always held; whole areas could be shut to traffic at the drop of a bomb. He had been only ten minutes late for the meet. Surely, he reasoned, he should be cut a little slack if the whole of east London was up in flames. Surely he should have been praised for making the meet at all, but that was not Reggie's way and he paid the young man's wages. He would have to leave a bit earlier next time, that was all.

Now he was in the passenger seat and they were moving, Reggie felt a little less tense.

He glanced across at the young man driving. Should he say he had just snapped and he knew it wasn't easy getting around these days?

"Go left 'ere. Up the hill an' pull in. I wanna see where that big one landed."

The driver's face lit up like a grateful child.

"Sure, Reg." He gunned the engine up Shadwell Hill and expertly pulled over at the top to give a clear view of Whitechapel below. Reggie looked down at the mass of flames and smoke in awe. It was easy to see the huge fire, not so easy to tell exactly what had been hit.

"Where do you think that is?" he asked the young man. "That big fire, there," he pointed for clarity.

"I reckon that's the electricity sub-station right next to Aldgate East underground station," the driver replied with some confidence, "They got 'it, at last."

Reggie looked again. 'Yeah,' he thought, 'I reckon he could be right.' His Chinese silk was a long way from Aldgate. He could relax, the booty was safe.

He turned to face the keen young driver. "So, you do know London then," he said, his comment loaded with sarcasm.

"Yeah, I'm sorry Reg. It's just that it's getting more an' more hard to find decent roads that ain't full of Bobbies or tin hats."

Reggie nodded in attempted sympathy; he was feeling much calmer all round now.

"Yeah, I know son. You ain't doin' too bad." He punched the man's forearm as he returned to his seat in the car. A beaming driver got in beside him, the words, 'you ain't doin' too bad,' ringing in his ears. Praise, praise, indeed.

"So, where to Reg?" he asked, enthusiastically.

"Go through Hackney an' make your way towards Islington. I'll tell you exactly when we get closer, alright?"

"Yeah sure, no problem," Dennis Cummings replied happily. He was young, excited and raring to prove himself.

The car sped through the decimated landscape that was looking less and less like the city they knew with each passing day. The further they got from the East End the fewer people they saw out on the streets. And those souls who were prepared to brave the aerial onslaught were of a different breed. They dressed differently, they behaved differently and they were generally suspicious of people like Reggie and Dennis. People they would regard as spivs, mobsters or draught dodgers and they would be right on all counts. Reggie was indeed a spiv and the young man a genuine draught dodger and they were both mobsters. However, they were no more or less than products of their environment. As they passed the underground station at the Angel crossroads and turned right into Essex Road, into

Islington, Reggie reached into the glove box and pulled out a revolver.

"Next left, 'alf way down on the left 'and side, all right?"

The driver nodded and did as instructed.

"There," Reg nodded to a tree a few hundred yards in front of them, "There, pull in there."

They were now parked on a side street just off the busy Essex Road. They sat in silence for a while, scanning the area for any signs of unexpected or suspicious movement.

"Right, this is what we are going to do," Reggie whispered. "You are goin' to sit 'ere and wait," he stared him in the eye, "all right?"

"Yeah, sure," Dennis replied.

Reggie kept staring at him a moment too long. "Good," he said and got out of the car without a backward glance.

The young man sat in the driver's seat and watched him disappear from view down an alley between two blocks of offices. He sat in silence, his heart pounding, his mind racing. 'What is he up to?' he wondered. They all wondered why Reggie still went out on jobs himself, but nobody as yet had deemed it wise to ask Reggie outright. Perhaps he likes the thrill, mused some. Maybe he's looking for something suggested others.

In less than five minutes Reggie came back into sight. He appeared out of the same alley he had gone down and walked calmly to the car. He was holding a bag. He climbed back into the passenger seat.

"Drive," he commanded and the young man started the engine and pulled away from the kerb.

"Where to, Reg?" he asked as they pulled into Upper Street.

"Soho!"

They laughed in unison and London burned as they drove through it.

Despite the falling bombs, despite the lateness of the hour, Soho, when they pulled into Dean Street, was a hive of activity. The pavements were filled with off-duty servicemen. On their arms females in fancy clothes strutted on high heels. Police officers and military police stood at regular intervals, scanning the crowds for deserters or outbreaks of trouble. Despite their presence there was a real party atmosphere in every street and alley.

"Right, come on," Reggie said, "let's go. You grab the bag an' follow me. Leave the keys in the ignition; we ain't goin' to be needin' this car no more."

The young man did as instructed and followed Reggie to a building a few yards down the street. They entered through a narrow doorway and headed in darkness down a steep, narrow staircase to the basement.

At the foot of the stairs a gorilla in a tuxedo nodded at Reggie and stepped aside, allowing the two men to enter what was clearly an after-hours jazz den.

Reggie nodded back at the gorilla and skirting the busy dance floor, he made his way towards a door in the far corner of the room. This door was also guarded, but they were allowed to pass into the inner sanctum. Reggie opened the door, pushed aside a plush velvet curtain and they were no longer in the club. They were now in the presence of 'the buyer'.

The room was full of smoke emanating from the cigar of its only occupant. He was dressed in a starched, white shirt, loosened at the collar. A tartan waistcoat struggled to contain his ample stomach and he sat behind the desk checking columns of figures on a sheet before him.

He lent back in his chair as the two men entered his private space.

"'Ello, Reggie, 'ow you doin'?" He glanced at the young driver loitering behind, briefly acknowledging him with a movement of his head then he fixed his gaze firmly back on Reggie, smiled broadly and took a long pull on his cigar.

"So, what can I do for you, Reggie?" he asked.

"I got some diamonds, thought you might be interested," Reg replied.

The man smiled broadly. "I might be. You got 'em with you, I see." He eyed up the bag in Dennis's grasp.

"That's right. We thought it might save a bit of time."

Reggie nodded him forward and Dennis hoisted the bag up onto the desk; then unzipped it to reveal a diamond necklace and matching earrings.

The man sat back in his chair, the broadest of smiles playing across his face. "You're always in such a hurry, Reg, I like that about you. No point hanging about, eh?"

Reggie didn't find the interchange so amusing.

"No!" he spat out.

The buyer, still smiling, sat forward again, his elbows resting on the desk in front of him. He had barely bothered to glance at the jewels before him.

"I'll take 'em", he hissed. "Why don't you come back tomorrow evening and pick up the payment?"

"'Ow much?" Reggie wanted to know.

The buyer lent back again and allowed himself another little bout of laughter.

"There you go again, straight to the point as always." He motioned vaguely towards the diamond jewellery sparkling even in such dim light.

"How much do yer want?" he addressed Reggie's assistant for the first time.

The young man shrugged, looking towards his boss for guidance.

Reggie said nothing.

"Then I need to have them looked at and I will see you tomorrow," he lent back, "all right?"

The buyer, smiling coldly, with total insincerity waved his fingertips in the manner of one giving something tremendous consideration.

"Because I like you, Reggie, I can promise my best price, but not a penny more." He smirked at his own witticism, brought his hands together and waited for a response.

Reggie also allowed the beginnings of an awkward silence to develop before he spoke.

"All right," he said.

The two men shook hands across the table.

"Now, you are my guests. Why not go upstairs, have a drink and watch the show? They are all very beautiful girls in my clubs."

They stayed in Soho until sunrise.

Chapter Twenty-Two

THE walls were six stories high on all sides of the courtyard, yet still Billy could see the pink glow illuminating the night sky. Behind him two boys slept soundly in the room they called home. Jack was still out, somewhere. Pops hadn't been seen since the boys had returned many hours ago, but Billy wasn't worried about the old man. He knew he was out drinking, trying to block out his personal demons, as always.

Chapter Twenty-Three

JACK scurried through the crowds on Commercial Street, weaving first into the road then back onto the pavement, as he avoided a succession of feet and wheels. He saw Pops falling out of a pub and crossed the road so that the old man wouldn't spot him and try to tap him for coins. As he approached the turning into their yard he spotted Peter, Reggie Lawson's boy, standing guard duty.

"All right, Jack? You got our parcel safe did you?" Peter asked.

Jack nodded as he shot down the black alleyway.

"Yep, all taken care of you can tell 'im."

He spotted Billy lying on the ground and went to join him.

"What you doin' Billy?" he asked, sitting down on the mud beside his pal.

"What parcel?" Billy had heard him coming down the alley and caught the brief exchange.

"It's nothin'. I took a parcel to that old tailor down the High Street. He looks after things, you know that."

Jack lay back beside his pal; as far as he was concerned that topic of conversation was over. "What you doin'?" he asked.

"Just lookin' at the sky. Look it's red with all the fire. Ain't it crazy?" Billy shook his head at the craziness of it all. "Do you remember before?" Billy looked at his pal quizzically.

"You mean before the bombers started comin'?" Jack asked.

"Yeah," Billy turned, genuinely interested in what his pal would say in reply.

"Not really," Jack had a faraway look in his eye. "It feels like it's always been this way," he muttered.

"I know!" Billy rose to his feet, "Crazy innit?"

Jack sat in silence entranced by the bright red sky.

"What you got under your coat?" Billy was curious; he knew that Jack would only be concealing something of interest.

Jack scanned the empty courtyard surreptitiously before pulling an envelope from under his coat. He carefully peeled it open and showed Billy a glimpse of white cotton, before hurriedly covering it up again.

Billy looked at him quizzically, "What was that?"

"Arm bands, Billy, ARP armbands," Jack revealed proudly. "I'm goin' on a job tonight, wiv Peter."

Billy shook his head as a little smile played across his lips. His friend was full of surprises.

"You will 'ave to stop all that when we're firemen, you know."

"Yeah, right," Jack replied, his reply heavy with sarcasm.

"I'm serious, though," Billy prodded gently.

"Yeah, yeah I know," Jack smiled dismissively.

"Put 'em away for now, Jack." Billy didn't realise he was frowning.

"Yeah, I know. Don't worry I'll keep 'em safe."

They sat in silence for a few moments before Jack added, "Hey, I saw Pops just now, down Commercial Street. Fallin' out of a boozer he was. Do you want to go get 'im?"

Billy could hear that the incendiaries were falling all around. There was no way he was going to be able to sleep under such noisy conditions.

"Yeah, let's get the cart; go give the old man a ride home."

Chapter Twenty-Four

I SAT slumped on a stool in the corner of the Ten Bells pub. I had been drinking since first light and was now at the point where my mere presence was annoying the other patrons. Inevitably, I was ejected. Rather than go home I slumped into a shop front and carried on drinking from the bottle at my side.

"Lizzie, Lizzie," I mumbled, feeling as though I was right back in 1888, "I won't let nothin' 'appen to yer. I won't fail yer."

My head slumped forward and my voice trailed to barely a whisper. It was untrue. I had failed her. I had let something happen to her.

"I'll go to the police an' tell 'em everything." I knew I was drooling, could feel the spittle at the corners of my mouth, but I didn't care how I looked to others. I knew it was way too long after the event to inform anyone about what I knew. I hadn't let anyone in on the secret at the time and with hindsight it was just another decision I regretted. Hindsight is a terrible thing. Turning back the clock and doing things differently wasn't an option.

An incendiary bomb whistled close by. I barely noticed it. It smashed through a glass shop-front causing a fire to start barely twenty yards from where I rested my feet. Oblivious to the danger, I sat rocking, wallowing in self-recrimination and cursing the helplessness that had dogged me from that day to this.

At least I was managing to do better for the lad. Billy was going to grow up to be a fireman now and that was a good thing. Better than turning out like those mobsters at the end of the court.

Chapter Twenty-Five

As usual the Soho district of London was absolutely heaving with people. Military personnel of all ranks swarmed from one drinking den to the next, raucously determined to spend every penny in their pockets as quickly as was humanly possible. Piccadilly's infamous 'ladies of the night' strutted from the statue of Eros at the roundabout, all the way to the top of Wardour Street and back again. They skilfully searched the crowds for anyone with the time and the inclination to do business. Military police took up vantage positions on the roofs of their vehicles, scanning the sea of faces for anyone of the vast legions of deserters who always seemed to make their way here eventually. Young boys pushed through the crowds offering up for sale a wide range of items that were supposed to be in short supply. The rationed beer and gin flowed freely in the vast number of public houses. Despite the sound of heavy bombs, regardless of the incendiary devices that fell like heavy rain on nearly all streets leading to Soho, people continued to come in their thousands, day and night, to party as hard as their wallets would allow, looking for some much needed respite from the constant stress and worry that always accompanied civilians caught up in squabbles between armies and their leaders. The area had always enjoyed a reputation for loose women and even looser morals but the Blitz seemed to have cranked up the carnival atmosphere by many degrees. These crowds were acting as though tonight may well be their last and, of course, in some cases it would be, if not their last, then very close to it.

Reggie waited in a car ignoring the legions of faces that passed by his window. He had already collected his money for the diamonds and now he was working again. Like any businessman, Reggie didn't rest on his laurels. He also hated to be kept waiting, especially here, where the police were thick on the ground. He glanced at his wristwatch again and cursed under his breath.

"Where the hell is he then, eh?"

Beside him in the driver's seat Dennis shrugged. He kept his opinions to himself, just kept smoking an American cigarette and looking at the procession of girls that seemed to be flooding past them. Some strutting up the pavements, others half way in the road, but all of them, it seemed to him, young and attractive. There were off-duty nurses, dancers from the numerous theatres in the area and an abundance of waitresses. He marvelled that even with Hitler's bombs falling all around, there were still plenty of beautiful girls walking the streets of Soho. He watched a spiv on the corner make a sale to a gaggle of giggling young women and resisted the urge to steal the man's takings.

A car pulled in behind them and its headlights flickered. The young driver started his engine and nosed the vehicle gingerly into the road. The crowds were strolling haphazardly from road to pavement and back again, most of them totally oblivious to the moving cars and too drunk to move aside even when the car was almost on top of them.

They carefully cleared Soho and entered Oxford Street. Here, the shop fronts were boarded up, the number of people walking about could be counted on the fingers of one hand and the car behind could finally overtake and lead the way.

They drove in convoy along Oxford Street, around Marble Arch and turned into Edgware Road. Within a few minutes the car they were following slowed and finally disappeared into a garage and the young driver followed suit. Once safely away from prying eyes they got out of their vehicle. Ahead of them the occupants of the first car had also got out and now they were busily putting on tin helmets and rolling ARP Warden armbands up the sleeves of their coats.

"Right Reg, 'ere's yours." A gruff man, with the smell of nicotine, handed Reggie a pair of white tin helmets and a pair of matching armbands.

"Put these on an' climb aboard."

Already the man's partner was kitted out and climbing into the back of an ambulance that was parked in the garage.

The gruff man glanced up at Reggie's assistant, "This is your driver, then?"

"Yeah, this is Dennis."

"Driven an ambulance before, 'ave you Dennis?" The gruff man stopped, awaiting an answer. A shadow of light caught the serious expression on his face.

Dennis sensed this was not a man who appreciated sarcasm or glib remarks; he nodded and tried to portray gravitas.

After studying his face for slightly longer than was necessary the gruff man turned on his heel, "Right, let's go, shall we?"

Dennis gunned the ambulance out of the garage and up the slight ramp to street level. He turned left, then left again and back onto the Edgware Road. He cut through the maze of backstreets that made up Mayfair and in less than four minutes they were coming out onto Regent Street. They had not been observed and still there was no sign of any wardens or police. Dennis rolled to a halt outside the door of a high-end jeweller and before he had applied the handbrake his three passengers were all out, running up to the shop and caving in the windows with hammers. With the glass gone, it was a simple matter to grab as many items as they could reach and then hightail it back to the waiting ambulance. In less time than it took for a bomb to smash through a building they were all back inside the ambulance and Dennis was racing through Mayfair, taking a winding route back to Soho. Here they dropped off their two passengers and with the ambulance bells ringing on an uninterrupted path, headed back to the East End.

Chapter Twenty-Six

BILLY and Jack found me slumped outside the Ten Bells.

"Come on Pops let's get you 'ome." Billy grabbed me by the forearm and tried to help this old man to stand up.

I resisted. "No, no, no!" I mumbled, before launching into a tirade of irate mumbling, containing only two distinguishable words.

"Liz, Lizzie," I had said somewhere in the middle.

Those two words were all the boys needed. Pops was having his nightmares again.

"Get round his other side, Jack, come on, let's lift him together." The old man emphasised a point, sending alcoholic fumes up Billy's nostrils.

"I was only your age, far too young to witness death." He stopped dead in his tracks, causing Billy to stumble and Jack to bump into a lady passing them on the pavement. She had given them a wide berth, but hadn't allowed for the sudden lurch. She scowled at us as she passed; Jack made a face back at her.

"What you lookin' at?" he wanted to know, but she was gone, swallowed up by the crowds.

The boys eventually managed to put Pops on the cart for the ride home. They smiled at each other as they realised they were pushing the 'hand cart' making them part of a well-known phrase.

Three of Reggie Lawson's men loitered at the alley leading to our yard.

"Been on the sauce again, 'ave we, Percy?" one of them enquired.

The sound of mocking laughter stung Billy as they pushed his granddad through the muddy passage.

"What's the matter Billy?" Jack wanted to know. Even in the poor light he could see his friend's face had gone noticeably red.

"I hate it when they laugh at us, that's all," Billy spat out.

Both boys seemed touchy as they helped me off the cart. Held up between them I stumbled again and they both gripped me a little tighter, perhaps a little too tightly. They seemed irritable, which wasn't like them, but bombs dropping from the sky day after day, night after night, tended to make people touchy.

We reached the door to our room. Jack flicked the latch and kicked the door open.

"'Ere we are Pops, let's get you on the bed."

I fell in a heap, sending a thick cloud of dust up into the air.

The boys stood watching me as bombs whistled through the sky.

Billy saw Tommy and Harry outside as he glanced back through the open door.

When they saw Billy they called out, "We're off out again."

Billy nodded, but said nothing. He looked at Pops a while then cast his eyes around the dingy room and turned to Jack. "Pops is all right now. No point 'anging about 'ere is there. Let's go out too, shall we, eh?"

Jack smiled back, he agreed, he liked it on the street, bombs or no bombs and it didn't smell as bad. They left the room, closing the door behind them and noticed the cart had gone.

"They've taken it," Billy observed.

"Feels a bit odd not 'aving the cart, eh?" Jack felt almost naked without it.

"It won't slow us down then, will it?" Billy didn't seem perturbed. "We can go a lot faster without it."

Chapter Twenty-Seven

DENNIS drove the ambulance into Whitechapel High Street. He had turned off the bells but they were still wearing the tin hats so, at a glance, they appeared to be on official business and a fleeting glance was all anyone was likely to get at the speed they were still travelling.

"There's the boys on the corner. Good, all must be well at 'ome. Slow down 'n' let me 'ave a quick word."

Dennis slowed the ambulance to a crawl and pulled into the side of the road. One of the men came over to it as Reggie wound down his window.

"'Ere, take this." He passed a heavy cotton bag surreptitiously through the window. It disappeared beneath the man's long overcoat before any prying eyes would have a chance to register the skilful handover.

"Put that somewhere safe. We are just gonna dump this thing an' we'll be back." The serious expression on his leader's face stopped the man from making any quips about how ridiculous they looked in the ill-fitting tin hats and too-tight white coats.

"All right, Reg." He stepped away from the vehicle and they pulled back into the road. The gangster watched them go. Then he scanned the faces of the crowds, looking for someone who might be paying him too much attention or might be a little too interested. All seemed normal, well, what passed for normal these days. A mule pulling a flat-back cart laden with beer barrels was refusing to move and the owner was trying to whip it to go forwards. He was being enthusiastically assisted by a bunch of urchins using the palms of their hands as makeshift whips. The donkey brayed constantly yet was barely heard above the din of frantic buying and selling. The gangster sauntered back to the corner where his friends loitered menacingly.

One of his fellows raised a quizzical eyebrow. 'What were their orders?' that one raised eyebrow asked.

"Reggie gave me a bag, 'e said to keep it safe 'til they come back." He pre-empted the obvious question that was sure to follow. "They've gone to dump the ambulance an' they'll be back, so they ain't gonna be long."

"That's true," Peter shot out the corner of his mouth, "plenty of places to catch a vehicle afire round 'ere." He chuckled at his own joke. The others ignored him.

They waited until he came closer to the burning barrel they were standing around.

"So, what's in the bag?" Peter whispered.

He received withering stares from all sides. Suitably admonished he returned to staring blankly into the flames.

This was Alf's corner; he was expected to give the orders when Reggie was not around. He didn't disappoint.

"Come round 'ere." He motioned for the man holding Reggie's bag to join him with his back against the wall, with a clear view of the busy junction and all who may be coming their way.

The man casually made his way to Alf's side.

"That's it son, you just stand 'ere next to me. 'Ere take a little drink while we wait." He produced a hip flask and they scanned the crowds for police or wardens as they drank.

Chapter Twenty-Eight

I WOKE up in an empty room. I was lying on the bed covered in an old blanket. Billy or one of the boys must have covered me. I reached out to touch the fireplace and my fingers touched the cold metal grate. It was obvious the fire had gone out some time ago. I lay back and considered my next move. It wasn't often I was in here alone and now twice in a few days. With my ears pricked for the sound of any approaching feet I peeled back my secret floorboard. I stretched out my fingers to the absolute limit of their reach and felt the panic of not grasping what I was expecting to feel. Groping a little more frantically, pushing my hand so far in it was hurting, yes, there it was. My fingers felt the remnants of the hessian sack. I paused briefly to listen out for company, but heard nothing untoward. I pulled out the tatty sack. It now lay open by my side and I had the dagger in my hand. The phrase 'if only they knew, if only they knew' playing over and over in my mind. It had been a long time since I had taken the dagger out of the secret hiding place and now I was reluctant to put it back.

Chapter Twenty-Nine

REGGIE woke up to the sound of coughing. He half-opened his eyes and slowly turned his head in the direction of the noise.

"What?" he demanded, none too politely.

"It's the gruff man, 'e's downstairs, Reg."

Reggie was awake now. What was he doing here and at this hour?

"What time is it?"

"It's nearly mid-day, Reg," came the eager reply.

"What the 'ell is 'e doin' 'ere so early?"

"Dunno Reg. 'E wants to talk to you." He lowered his voice, "'bout last night, is it?"

Reggie answered the question with one of his own.

"What you waiting for? 'oping to see me naked are you?"

"No, Reg, course not," he blushed slightly.

"Well get out an' let me get dressed then."

Reggie came down the stairs a few minutes later. He didn't appreciate being woken unexpectedly.

The gruff man stood at the foot of the staircase, smoking a large cigar. He looked every inch the theatre impresario. His coat was lined with astrakhan from the back of the neck all the way down both lapels. His trilby was a rather unusual light sand colour, its brim wider than the norm that most conformed to. He wore spats over white calfskin shoes. Yes, this man was in the theatre world and it was obvious. What was less obvious was that his girls worked on their backs more than they worked in any chorus line and he would have a man killed if he found him objectionable.

He looked up as the top stair creaked under Reggie's movement and smiled. Not bothering to inject any warmth into his face, he spoke as Reggie descended.

"Sleep well, did you?"

Reggie forced a smile onto his face to match his visitor's. "Well you know, it's 'ard to get a good kip with all this noise." He reduced the Blitz of London to nothing more than a noisy inconvenience. "But me, I slept like a baby, was 'ere all night an' I've got fifty witnesses to prove it."

They both roared with laughter out of all proportion to the joke.

As Reggie stepped from the staircase and extended his hand to shake, he was trying to read the situation. The gruff man was nervous that much was blatantly obvious. 'What with all the laughter, and me just woken up as well,' thought Reg.

Reggie guided him towards the back of the room by the shoulder and keeping his voice low, asked "So what you doin' 'ere at this time o' day then?"

He chose not to mention the fact that it better be a hell of a good reason to risk them being seen together the morning after the robbery.

The visitor flicked ash distastefully on the bare floorboards.

"Why do you live down 'ere Reg? I can fix you up a nice place in Dean Street, right in the thick of it."

Reg smiled to show he wasn't offended. "I like it 'ere, it's nice and close to keep an eye on things."

"Yeah, I 'eard you was running out o' girls last week."

Again they laughed in unison; again there was no humour in the gesture, no comradeship, no relaxing of any guard.

"Anyway," Reg turned to face his unexpected visitor, "why're you 'ere?"

The visitor smiled, unable to completely conceal his slight pleasure that Reggie had allowed his annoyance to show, no matter how slightly or how briefly.

"Straight to business, eh? All right, Reg, 'ere's the thing. You seem to 'ave ended up with a pair of cufflinks las' night an', well, the thing is..." he paused slightly, "we need 'em back."

Reggie studied the man's face for any signs. He was getting on, he thought, coming down here, waking me up and demanding bloody cufflinks. Reggie had had enough.

"To tell you the truth, I ain't even looked through it yet." He scowled openly now. "When I do, I'll 'ave a look for some cufflinks an' maybe..." he moved in closer, "maybe I'll sell 'em to you."

Reggie was starting to turn red as anger rose up in him. The gruff man had heard about the snotty little robber and his legendary temper but he certainly hadn't expected to be on the receiving end of it. He regretted leaving his minders out by the fire but Dennis had insisted.

Now he found himself at the mercy of this East End psychopath and he didn't much care for his chances against *the* Reggie Lawson.

"All right, Reggie, easy now. It ain't me. They're Masonic, that's all an' the bloody Masons 'ave asked for 'em back, but they'll pay, don't worry."

Reggie allowed his temper to abate. He had him now and that was enough. He smiled coldly.

"If, an' I say 'if', I 'ave got these bleedin' cufflinks, 'ow much are these Masons willin' to pay?"

"I dunno, Reg. I just know they once belonged to Prince Albert himself."

"So, they're royal cufflinks now, are they?" There was amusement in his eyes. "Maybe I will be needin' that little place up West, after all."

The gruff man nodded his head. "Sure, Reg. I got a nice little place tucked in behind Wardour Street."

Reggie frowned. "I thought we agreed Dean Street, right in the thick of it. I'll pass by tonight an' pick up the key, shall I?"

"Yeah, sure, whatever you prefer Reg an' you'll bring the cufflinks?"

"We'll see." Reggie opened the door and stood back making room for the other man to leave. He watched him walk up the courtyard with a scowl now firmly on his face. This signified displeasure to his men watching from the far end of the court. The scowl on Reggie's face revealed that the departing visitor was not one of them and should not be made to feel welcome here, so they took a little too long clearing a path for the gruff man. They muttered oaths about 'ponces from up West' and laughed en masse, with rather too much gusto, when he stumbled slightly on something lying in the darkness. In short, they showed him no respect at all.

As the gruff man moved from the courtyard into the alley out of sight of Reggie and with his minders at his back he felt emboldened enough to mutter a reply to their taunts. Instantly, hackles raised on all sides. The taunts grew louder and nastier. Like a pack of wolves they sensed weakness in an instant. Men strategically positioned to block the way stepped into view and stopped the gruff man from leaving. Voices grew louder. Someone came running from the courtyard and threw a punch. From nowhere coshes were drawn and used without mercy. The free-for-all was too one-sided to last long. The gruff man and his two minders were chased from the alley and forced to limp away into the crowds.

Reggie listened with amusement until the last shouts faded then, as if without a care in the world, he strolled to where his men still blocked the passage.

"Alf!" he shouted towards the crowd of large, dark figures and the din faded instantly. "Come 'ere." He turned on his heel, heading back to his dwelling while Alf scurried to catch up.

Reggie waited until they were both inside and the door was closed. The noise had died down at his intervention and he had no wish to be overheard.

"Bit much, weren't it?" The words Reggie used were accusatory, but the smile on his lips said so much more than the mere words ever could.

Alf returned the smile, letting it flicker briefly across his lips, but his wasn't a face used to the exertion of those particular facial muscles and he soon gave up the pretence. "What d'ya want us to do, Reg?"

Reggie allowed the question to hang in the air, letting the silence assert itself, making sure no floorboards were creaking that shouldn't be or no rats scurried as though disturbed by humans. There was nothing, just the distant whine of sirens and the ever present hum of the East End.

"Well, the thing is, he's gonna let me 'ave a flat in Soho."

"What do we need a place up West for?" Alf interrupted. Reg scowled at the disrespect and his lieutenant lowered his gaze and allowed his boss to continue.

"I like it up West an' we've got somethin' they want." He spoke so low the words seemed to disappear into the air, but Alf had remained submissive. The balance was restored and Reggie continued talking in a more relevant tone.

"This is what I want you to do. Go to the stash, find some cuff links, flashiest ones in there an' bring 'em to the pub. I'll meet you there in an hour, all right?"

The question was a rhetorical one and Alf just nodded for the sake of good manners. He picked up his hat, placed it on his head and went out into the courtyard.

"Peter, come with me!" He paused by the oil drum to address the other two men in quieter tones. "You boys stay 'ere 'til Reg comes out. Then, I want you to go with 'im to the pub an' make sure that 'e stays out o' trouble."

They rubbed their hands together over the fire and nodded. They understood and they knew their role in the proceedings. It was work they were used to; work they had done a hundred times before. They could sense that the gruff man's unexpected visit seemed to have given another level to whatever was going on, but they were Reggie's men and they trusted their leader to do the right thing. Without him they would all still be hustling for small change.

Tommy sat on the doorstep watching the mobsters' comings and goings. It had amused him greatly when it had suddenly kicked off with the spivs from up West. He had tried to share the fun with his pal, "Oh, will you look at 'em now, Harry. I swear that Alf's just punched one of 'em into the fire. Come quick, see for yourself." Harry had declined, preferring instead to lie on the bed. Maybe he was sick, mused Tommy. The room shuddered and dust fell all around them as a bomb landed close by. Still, it seems like the whole world is sick, so why shouldn't Harry be having an off day.

It was obvious to Tommy that something was afoot with Reggie Lawson's gang. There seemed to be an awful lot more activity than normal and then the fight. Tommy wished he had all the things that they seemed to enjoy, but he reminded himself, as Pops kept saying, those spivs ended up behind bars, eventually. Still, Tommy watched and wished he had what they had.

Pretty soon they had all left except one man, Dennis Cummings. Tommy knew that Dennis was generally more approachable than some of the others and as Harry was fast asleep now, he decided to venture over and say 'hello'. Maybe Dennis would have something tasty to eat; he often did.

Dennis Cummings was a career criminal. He had first come to the attention of the authorities at the age of five. His mother had been arrested yet again for soliciting and this time the magistrate had no option but to sentence her to a short spell in Holloway. Dennis had become an issue at that point because, as there was no father present, the boy would have to go into care whilst his mother served her sentence. Dennis had been no match for the manpower and resources of the State so he celebrated his fifth birthday behind bars in the children's home, while his mother served her three months at Holloway prison. On her release, against all the odds, she managed to get him back and the two of them returned to Whitechapel. They were instantly accepted by the friends and neighbours they had left behind.

The next time they came for him under very similar circumstances he was nowhere to be found. By then he was seven years old, practically a man and he had easily managed to avoid being rounded up like a stray dog. He had lived under the watchful care of his neighbours. Since then he had spent his life avoiding the law. Locally he was known for his quick temper, his right hook and his tolerance of children and old ladies. He watched as Tommy approached. Reg was adamant that these kids would be useful one day and constantly told his men to be nice to them. He caught the boy's eye and nodded in greeting, before turning back to the fire.

"'Ello, Dennis." The kid hovered uncertainly standing slightly back. Dennis looked up again.

"It's all right. You can come closer and warm up a little if you want."

Chapter Thirty

BILLY and Jack had ventured far indeed. They were sitting on a wall halfway down Fleet Street, deep in the heart of the City of London. On the opposite side of the street a bank burned ferociously. The two boys kicked scuff marks into the wall as they watched a fire-fighting team attempt to gain some semblance of control. Their fire fighting seemed futile but as the building was a bank and it was out of office hours at least there was nobody trapped inside. There was no reason for the boys to offer assistance and besides, they didn't have their cart or any of the tools of their trade. They were enjoying a day off, killing time until this afternoon when Billy had his meeting with some very important people who should be able to get him a job with a council department.

Mr. Cooper had explained to him that he wouldn't go straight into a seat on the council, that these things could take years and it was necessary to follow a carefully mapped out path before he would get there. It would take years of study and hard work, Mr. Cooper kept stressing, but he wasn't giving Billy any time for second thoughts. The lad grasped the reasoning of the trade union movement and he wanted in. It was as simple as that. He was smart, resourceful and a natural born leader. Given a few breaks he would be perfect for a life in public office.

Jack turned to face his pal saying "I bet there's loads of cash in there." He continued to stare at the side of Billy's face, waiting for a response.

Finally, Billy relented, "Yes, I bet there is."

He hadn't said much but he had delivered those few words with a cheeky grin and Jack knew his pal was tempted.

"So, let's go for a little walk around the place," Jack said, as he dropped off the wall to the pavement below, "shall we?"

Billy dropped down beside him. "Might as well, seeing as we're 'ere. I gotta meet Cooper later, though. I don't want to be late," Billy reminded his pal.

"Don't worry about that." Jack remembered his meeting and wondered if Billy would receive the same treatment.

Thick smoke was pouring from the upper windows of the bank. It caught the wind coming off the River Thames and headed west towards the general direction of Trafalgar Square. The boys took a wide circular walk until they made contact with the edges of the smoke, then they disappeared into it so they could use it to hide their discreet change of direction. Quickly they could see glimpses of the burning building as the smoke ebbed and flowed.

They edged their way to the back of the burning bank.

"There ain't nobody guardin' I . . ." Jack put into words what his brain had registered.

"Cover me, Billy," and he was gone, through a shattered door and out of sight, inside the bank.

Billy cupped his hands together, blowing on them as though he were trying to keep warm. He hopped a little from leg to leg, trying to ward off the sudden need to relieve himself.

'That bleedin' Jack, always doin' stupid things on a spur.' He looked around him, noting that he seemed to be alone, but hardly daring to wonder how long it might be before the firemen realised that the doors at the back had been blown off their hinges by the blast and would get it in their heads to call the police.

Billy took a few steps back and crouched down low, trying to blend into the shadows and doing rather a good job. He could hear sirens and bells in all directions. It looked as though the police would be having a busy night and maybe Jack wouldn't be too much longer. Maybe he would even find some cash.

Suddenly, Billy heard the sound of voices and a rustling in the overgrown buddleia and brambles. Someone was coming. He abandoned his crouching position and lay against the mud. He pulled his legs up beneath him and snapped off a clump of long couch grass to hold across his face. The voices grew louder, it sounded like two men, Billy decided. He was right and suddenly they were there, pushing through the vegetation and coming into view. Two wardens in their white tin hats and white armbands had arrived. Billy knew that Reggie's men used the ARP uniforms as cover for their criminal activities, but these two looked like the real deal and now Billy could hear their every word.

"Look Ken, that bloody bomb 'as only gone an' blown the bleedin' doors off."

Billy lay face down as he heard the second man do a passable impression of a 500 pound bomb screaming earthwards, which he followed with the words, "an' boom, doors, windows, the lot. Best we call the Bobbies then, don't want no villains gettin' their sticky little fingers in there tonight, do we?"

"Good idea. I'll go an' fetch the ol' bill, an' you wait 'ere. Make sure nobody gets inside, all right?"

The man must have nodded because Billy didn't hear him respond, but he did hear one set of footsteps forcing a path back through the vegetation.

He lay still, trying to clear the pounding of blood that dominated his mind. He was going to have to take a look, see where the remaining warden had positioned himself and then decide what best to do. He knew that if he was desperately unlucky and the warden was looking his way, his face would beam as white as any flashlight and, as a last resort, he would have to make a run for it, leaving Jack to take his chances. Billy may not have been given a say on whether he wanted to get involved, but the moment his pal had darted inside the broken door he was involved and he wouldn't dream of deserting his friend now, unless he had to.

He cursed Jack one more time and rubbed some mud on his face. He then began slowly lifting his head, hoping for a glimpse of the man's ankle.

Billy lifted his head as much as he dare and then stopped. It felt like he was going too fast and was bound to be discovered at this rate, yet he couldn't see a thing. He scanned to the very limits of what could be seen by moving only his eyes. First with the unhurried pace of a hunting python he rolled his eyes as far left as they would go. Nothing. Then, in the same deliberate way, he scanned his limited horizons as far right as he could. Nothing moved and nothing seemed out of the ordinary. He decided to risk lifting his head a little higher, this time shuffling onto his forearms at the same time. Now he was on his knees and forearms and he held the thick clump of long grass in front of him, hoping to camouflage any shine that might come from patches on his face that he missed with the mud camouflage job. This time he spotted the warden almost straightaway. The man was slumped against a wall, looking directly away from Billy and towards where his colleague had gone for assistance. When Jack came out through the door he would run away from the man and towards where he had left Billy. The man would not be expecting a foot race with two fit young boys, well versed in the art of escaping clutches and even if he did, Billy fancied their chances. Yet still he wanted to shift the odds slightly more in favour of him and his pal. He crept backwards until his heel made contact with a pile of rubble, the remains of a previous air raid. Using his foot as a hook he quietly pulled a variety of half-bricks and pieces of masonry towards him. When he was satisfied with what he had collected he started to lay them out in front of him. Many times he had followed a similar pattern, when there was to be a gang brawl with the Blind Beggar boys or kids from Bethnal Green or years before, in the winter time, when the snow fell and snowball fights was the only game in town. This time Billy was a little bigger, a little stronger and his aim had been honed to perfection by years of childish warfare.

He never did have time to organise his ammo to his complete satisfaction. He could hear footsteps coming at speed, slipping on uneven surfaces and definitely coming from within the bank. Billy stood up slowly, correctly assuming that the warden would be so preoccupied with the sound that he would have his back to him. He picked up three half bricks and prepared to fire. Jack's clambering steps grew clearer, closer, until suddenly, his head appeared around the door frame.

"Hold still, young man!" ordered the warden, shining a torch at Jack.

"Leg it!" screamed Billy, simultaneously releasing a torrent of three well aimed bricks that ensured his pal could race free of the approaching figure of authority and run with practised speed towards his escape. Billy had aimed well. The first shot had hit the warden squarely in the back, causing him to fall and no doubt causing considerable pain, the second whistled through the exact spot his head would have been if he hadn't fallen and the third flew slightly wide and to the warden's right side. He had taken enough punishment and disappeared into the dark cover of the brambles, shouting "ouch", as he landed heavily. The second volley of bricks fell into the brambles around him.

Billy turned on his heel, laughing at the man's misfortune, laughing to be young and free and laughing because his pal had got clean away. He made no attempt to catch up with Jack. He had no idea which direction his pal had taken and he knew Jack would not be waiting for him anywhere close by. That was simply not how they operated. No, he would see Jack back at home, so Billy ran as fast as he could.

Chapter Thirty-One

I AWOKE in a cold sweat. I scratched my nose and watched a rat as it scurried away at the sudden movement I had made. My perspiration soaked the tatty old mattress. It had obviously been a hell of a nightmare. Fortunately, I had been drunk enough to block out the whole thing. Although I didn't really need to remember, I had experienced it enough times to know every last detail. Long Liz, queen of the restless spirits would make sure I never rested comfortably. She came to me while I slept. First she loomed over me smiling, then in a heartbeat her facial expression transformed into the exact same look of shock and horror she had worn as the Ripper had grabbed her throat. Then somehow, Billy would appear and she smiled at him through her strangled expression. I drank in order to sleep, in order not to remember my dreams any more, but they still haunted me all the hours that God sent. A lifetime of regret garnished with the childhood memory of a vicious murder in progress. My torment was personal to me but the emotions I struggled with were the normal state of affairs to those who lived around here. We are all human after all and humans run on emotion.

I lifted myself onto one elbow and surveyed the room. I had the place to myself again and I didn't enjoy it any more. Only ghosts for company haunting my every word, every gesture, and every thought. 'Where were those boys?' I hated waking up sober and left to my own devices.

'When will this bleedin' war ever end?'

'God, I need a drink. If it ain't the voices in my 'ead, it's the sound of those bleedin' bombs.' I slumped back down and a cloud of dust puffed up around me. I had to admit the drink was a lot easier to come by these days. Sometimes, I reminded myself, before the War, before the bombing had started, it was a real struggle to get drunk enough to block out all the memories, but now, now I could pretty much just walk in and help myself whenever the mood took me. The mood took me constantly and the demons lurking in the shadows knew it and mocked my weakness.

'Sod You!' I screamed at the walls, a thousand memories floating past my eyes, each and every one of them laughing and mocking my weakness. At their head the unmistakable figure of Long Liz, floating at waist height around and around the small enclosed space, the look of terror firmly etched on her face, her eyes locked onto mine.

I thought my mind was playing tricks on me. Before the bombing had started I would have been sure it was my mind playing tricks, but now I merely thought it was. I had to get out. It was the confined space and I needed some air. That would do the trick. I scurried out, not even bothering to grab the rag I grandly referred to as my new overcoat. I pulled the door closed, unable to resist a last worried glance, just in case the demons were real after all.

This sudden emergence into the courtyard had naturally been seen by Reggie's men.

"'Ave a wash, Pops," one of them called out. They all referred to me that way. The old boy who had lived here since before Reggie Lawson was a nipper, since Jack the Ripper had been a resident.

"Look how white 'e is", laughed one. "Seen a ghost, 'ave ya, Pops?" Oh, how they laughed at their witty banter.

"Seen the Ripper again, 'ave ya?"

Their laughter followed me down the passageway. I kept my head bowed and avoided eye contact. I knew they meant no harm and had no idea what they were doing to my fragile, stressed mind.

'Yes, I've seen the Ripper,' I wanted to tell them, 'and he was a lot scarier than all you lot put together.' Instead, I said nothing and scurried away down the alley, not slowing, not answering, not playing their game and trying to make myself a boring target. As I hit the street their half-hearted taunts were quickly drowned out by the noise of more planes above.

German bombers were passing overhead in their hundreds. The drone of their engines in the night sky was, as always, causing panic on the streets below. All around me people were hurrying to the air-raid shelters; mother's rounding up small boys to get below ground, struggling to make themselves heard above the sirens that now added to the pandemonium. Hundreds of fighter planes escorted the bombers, too high and fast to pick out, but their higher pitched engines declaring their undoubted presence. The thump of anti-aircraft guns added further to the deafening noise of war. Despite the late hour, Commercial Street had been awash with people buying, drinking, talking and living. The planes were driving most away. I trudged eastwards ignoring the bloody Germans; I was sick of them.

A solitary figure shuffling through the debris caught the sharp eye of young Tommy heading home with Harry.

"Look, there's Pops." The shorter boy raised slightly on to his tiptoes, just in time to see the old man lurch dangerously close to a pair of soldiers drinking outside a pub. They saw the soldiers berate him slightly, then laughed as the squaddies realised they were wasting their breath.

"Come on," Harry upped the pace and headed towards the old man, Tommy following close behind.

"Hey, Pops!" Harry grabbed Percy by the sleeve, and repeated, "Hey, Pops!"

Somebody was grabbing my sleeve, shaking me from my daydreams. I stopped at the obstruction and only when I heard, "It's us, Harry an' Tommy," did I tear my gaze away from the world at my feet.

I tried to smile at them, but it came out all wrong. Still, they were good boys.

"You're good boys," I said, trying to envelop them both in a tangle of arms, they playfully batted away my attempts at bonding.

"Is Billy 'ome?" Harry asked.

They waited for what seemed an age before I managed to shake my head in the negative.

"Did you get 'im a present, then?" They both giggled loudly at the absurdity of that. Imagine Pops buying someone a present; pigs would fly first.

I shook my head again, "Why would I buy 'im a present?"

"Cos it's 'is birthday, maybe."

For some reason this produced howls of laughter, but that was all right, I wasn't about to rain on their youthful attitude. There would be plenty of time for cynicism and bitter regret soon enough in their lives. Let them enjoy the small bites of pleasure life still offered up. Heaven knew, it wouldn't keep coming forever.

"'E's a good boy, too." I was mumbling again but they had both understood. I turned away from them hiding my expression, the haunted look of a man who had forgotten the most important birthday in the calendar year. I knew I would never get the opportunity to put back the clock and right this particular wrong. No, it would have to be yet another one chalked up in the column of regrets.

"You comin' 'ome, Pops?"

"Nah, I'm 'eading out. What's it to you?" Nosy little sod, I thought.

"All right, easy, see yer later," Tommy shouted to my departing back.

"His mood changes so quick, dunnit?" Tommy said.

Harry shrugged, and the two boys started moving towards the alley they now called home.

As they closed in on the alley Alf called quietly towards them, "All right, Tommy?"

Tommy replied, "Yeah, all good Alf."

"Done that thing Reggie asked, 'ave ya?"

"Yeah, no sweat Alf, all taken care of."

Alf nodded his satisfaction and gave the boys respectful clearance as they passed down the alley.

Tommy put the cart back under its tatty piece of tarpaulin and followed Harry into their room.

Only when the door was closed did Harry ask, "Are we going to tell Billy 'bout that?"

"I ain't sure, what do you think?"

"I think we should." Harry's tone suggested he was sure it was the right thing to do.

"All right, I'll tell 'im when they get back."

They smiled at each other, fellow conspirators, who had pulled off a successful caper. Running errands made them feel grown up, part of the adult world to which they so desperately wanted to belong. Reading between the lines they both thought life would be easier if they did more of Reggie's bidding. Both felt better now that the decision had been made and they were sure that Billy would understand.

The boys looked up together towards the door. They could hear the sound of footsteps getting closer. Tommy pulled the door open just as Jack was about to push on it.

Jack came into the room red in the face and sweating profusely, he scanned the space quickly then asked, "Billy been back yet?"

Harry sat quietly in the chair studying his friend's face. Clearly something had happened but Jack didn't seem too perturbed. He would let Tommy ask the questions, it would mean getting the story quicker. Tommy knew the drill; they all did. He inclined his head slightly and raised an eyebrow. He was saying, 'well, what happened?' and Jack knew it.

"We was down in the City, just lookin' about 'cos you 'ad the cart." They ignored his attempt to deflect blame onto them.

"An' all of a sudden, we see's that this bank has 'ad all its doors blown off in a blast." He paused but there were no interruptions. "So, anyway, we goes round the back an' I'm in there, you know!"

Oh, they knew all right, a bank with its doors blown off. It would have been impossible to resist. They both nodded to show they understood, and Jack continued, "Well, Billy, 'e waited outside. Anyway, its pitch black in there, I can't see nothin', but I can see there ain't that much damage so I starts upstairs to see if maybe there's something in the offices or whatever, you know?" He paused again but this time for dramatic effect. "An' I found this in one of the desks." He pulled a black, leather wallet from within his jacket and held it out for them to see. It looked official but neither boy was overly impressed.

"So, where's Billy?" asked Tommy.

"Yeah, so I came back down an' as I'm goin' back outside this warden shouts for me to stop, just as Billy nearly takes 'is 'ead off with some rocks so we both legged it out of there."

At this point they all glanced nervously towards the door. They all knew the drill, so where was he now?

"Did 'e get away?" Tommy wanted to know.

"I think so…" he paused, "yeah, he got away," he added and they all knew it was far from certain.

The uneasy silence that settled was broken by Harry's first input. "What's in the wallet, then?"

Those few words lightened the mood. Jack broke into a broad grin and looked at the wallet. He opened it slowly and pulled out with a theatrical flourish, what to the boys was a small fortune, four large, crisp five pound notes.

"Ah, look at that, will you?" Jack was milking the moment for all it was worth. He didn't have to milk very hard; his two pals were mightily impressed.

"Wow, look 'ow new they are."

The boys did not come across many fivers on their travels and the few they had seen or, even less often, held, were generally tatty and well-thumbed. These looked as though they were straight off the presses.

"Let's 'ave a look," Tommy held out his hand.

Jack quickly put the money back, closed the wallet and pushed it into the recesses of his pocket.

"Let's wait for Billy." Again they glanced in unison towards the door, willing their leader to return.

Chapter Thirty-Two

REGGIE sat with his back to the wall nursing a tumbler of Scotch. He was facing the door and glanced intermittently between it and the clock on the wall. The pub was busy, but most of the male drinkers were part of his gang or wanted to be. All the women worked for him in that oldest of traditions. He was safe here, yet he hated to be kept waiting. The door opened for the umpteenth time and finally it was Alf coming in from the night. He headed straight across and slid in at the table beside Reggie.

"'Ave you got 'em?" Reg wanted to know before he had even sat down.

"Yeah, I got 'em." He patted his breast pocket.

The stress vanished from Reggie's face and he was transformed. A wide smile broke out across his face and the clientele, as one, took that rare occurrence as a signal that all was well in their world. Smiles were breaking out all around the bar on faces that usually felt right only when they were wearing a grim expression.

"Peter, get Alfie a drink," Reg shouted to the bar.

Simultaneously, beneath the table, Reggie opened his hand and a little velvet bag was dropped discreetly into his palm.

He opened the drawstring and tipped the cufflinks out into his other hand.

He raised and lowered them a couple of times, as though judging their weight. Then he slid them back into the bag, tied the drawstring tight and placed it in his inside pocket.

"That's definitely the ones?" he queried quietly.

"They were the only bleedin' cufflinks in the whole haul. I checked it myself."

Reggie glanced at his friend and nodded.

"Well done, Alf." He raised his glass in salute, and finished half a tumbler of neat Scotch in one easy mouthful.

"Looks like another night up West again, eh?" A smile of sorts accompanied the comment.

"I quite like it up there an' it would be simple to ease out Old Gruff. Don'tcha think, Reg?"

Reggie shrugged noncommittally and flicked ash onto the floor.

Dennis came across to their table with a drink for Alf. "Do you want another, Boss?" he asked.

"Yeah, get me a scotch. Get yourself one an' all but drink it quick, you're goin' out."

Dennis nodded and returned to the bar, feeling so self-satisfied he would burst if he tried to stick his chest out any further. Reggie trusted him with more and more these days and he knew he was proving himself to be a worthy member of the mob.

Another bomb landed in the East End as he stood waiting at the packed bar. The candles that were deployed because of the blackout flickered at the nearby blast. Dennis stood there waiting to be served. He passed the time trying to look like Cagney, unaware he was frightening the prostitutes with what he considered a winning smile.

Dennis returned to the table with his boss's drink and Reggie motioned for him to take a seat opposite, so that they could lean towards each other across the table and their conversation would not be easily overheard.

Reggie was not known for his polite chat, so Dennis wasn't surprised when he beckoned him to come closer and launched straight into the heart of the matter.

"I want you to get up to Soho. Go see that gruff git an' get 'im to show you the little flat 'e's got lined up for us." He leaned in closer and grabbed Dennis's forearm to emphasise his point, "An' whatever 'e shows you, you tell 'im that it ain't good enough. Tell 'im what a fussy bastard I am. I want him sweatin' by the time we turn up, all right?"

Dennis held Reggie's eye, "No problem, Boss. What if 'e shows me a few gaffs? None of 'em is any good, right?"

Reggie smiled coldly, "That's right, you got it."

He released the younger man's forearm and sat back in his chair. He studied Dennis as he knocked back a mouthful of the Scotch whisky, then he added, "So, go on then, drink up."

Dennis drained the last of his whisky and stood up to leave. At the bar a large-set man watched proceedings. When he saw Dennis making good to leave he also drained his glass, placed his trilby on his head, nodded farewell to those drinkers either side of him and followed Dennis out onto Commercial Street. Fires raged all about them, such a common occurrence these days that they barely noticed.

"Where're we goin'?" Dennis's companion wanted to know.

"Get the motor, my old son, 'cos we are going for a night up West."

They smiled broadly at each other. The boys in the Mob were all speculating as to whether Reggie was going to get a club of his own up there.

They took the most direct route from east to west, straight along Fleet Street, then the Strand, all the way to Trafalgar Square. They drove through the burning, ruined landscape, barely giving the shocking devastation a sideways glance. Unstable buildings, leaking pipes, it was nothing new to them anymore. Dennis actually liked the war and he was not alone in that stance. Before hostilities had begun East End spivs were despised the length and breadth of London Town, but now, now everybody wanted to be their friend. They even had vicars and gentlemen on their list of clientele. The whole city was being asked to do without and the whole city seemed unwilling to do so. Soho had been allowed to thrive as a place for our hard-working boys to unwind away from the pressures of the frontlines that now criss-crossed the whole world. Clubs and theatres catered for our boys on leave. With every third man in the country enlisted, that was a lot of spending. Soho was becoming a source of big money. No wonder Reggie wanted a piece of the action.

Chapter Thirty-Three

BILLY had been out-running the warden with ease, skipping from one pile of bricks to the next with all the dexterity of youth. Then, just as he was about to dash out of the rubble-filled alley onto Fleet Street, he hopped at high speed onto a pile of house bricks that shifted suddenly under his weight. He adjusted instantly but not quite quickly enough. The noise of the bricks collapsing suddenly had given his position away and his ankle had turned as he fell. Although it didn't feel broken or twisted, it was certainly not taking any weight. Billy, hopping furiously, had only just evaded the whistle-blowing wardens. His position was becoming less and less comfortable with each moment. They had passed him once. He had been holding his breath in the middle of a clump of stinging nettles, but they must have gone as far as the perimeter wall and now they were returning, re-tracing their steps. He could hear them getting closer and closer; hear their voices clearly above the more distant sounds of aerial warfare.

"I'm sure that little bastard is in 'ere somewhere, Jim."

They were almost on top of him again. Billy held his breath as they passed by. Then the two figures rounded the corner and he took advantage of the brief moment of solitude. He had no option, it was now or never. Using his one good leg he flung himself headfirst into an open doorway directly opposite his clump of nettles.

Billy forced himself to breathe shallow and dragged himself deep into the shadows. He had no idea whose house he was in, but it didn't appear to be bomb damaged. It smelt a little musty perhaps, but much nicer than he was accustomed to. He used the wall for support, his injured leg trailing behind him and pain shooting through his injured ankle. He could still hear the whistles blowing, but they were moving further away. He felt safe. Those tin hats wouldn't be searching for him in here, he felt certain of that. The incoherent shouting of the exasperated wardens grew closer again; close enough for him to pick out individual words. He shuffled backwards into the dark, dragging his near useless foot. Back he moved as quietly as he could, methodically one pull of his weak leg at a time until he gently thudded into a chest of drawers. It was creating a dark recess at the back of the room and Billy crouched down into the shadow it caused and pulled his legs up under his body. As he huddled into the recess the light of a torch illuminated the area around the shattered doorway.

"What about in 'ere?" he heard a man's voice ask.

Footsteps could be heard slipping across the rubble and the light beam swept further into the room.

Billy was impressed they had come to look for him in here. It showed real commitment and he could appreciate that. In the darkness he smiled to himself at their tenacity.

Then another figure appeared, a silhouette in the doorway also shining a torch in.

"Nah, 'e won't be in 'ere. 'E was only young. I bet 'e kept running. Come on!"

The first man played his light across the room. Billy pulled his legs tightly under him and the recess he was tucked behind kept him from being discovered by the shadow cast at the angle the man shone his light from. Another few steps in and a further sweep of the walls and he would have been caught in the torch light, like a rabbit in the headlights, but the man turned his back and crunched his way unsteadily back towards the door. He had done enough clambering across bricks in the dark.

"Wait up, Pete. 'old up." Then he was gone.

Billy exhaled deeply as the smile on his lips became a broad grin spreading across his face. He bent forward, reaching out to gently check his ankle. He instantly realised it had swollen up horribly and the grin fell away as he cursed himself for being so stupid. He was angry at himself, at Jack and at the war.

Billy had not eaten properly for many days. His head was aching, his ankle was throbbing and his stomach was rumbling. He was going to have to brazen it out though; there was no other way for it. He was in no condition to get home under his own steam. He would have to become an innocent passer-by. That was the story and he was going to stick to it, no matter what. The tin hats had gone by now for sure, but he would give them a little while longer. Then he would make his way as best as he could, down to Fleet Street, the main artery, from east to west across London and more importantly for Billy from west to east. Surely, he could make his way home from there.

With a plan he felt better. He took a handful of deep breaths, pulled himself to his one good foot and hopped noisily out of the house. It took considerable effort and concentration, but he somehow struggled the thirty yards to the main road. Now he was on Fleet Street, just a poor child caught up in the Blitz and in need of some human compassion. An ambulance raced towards him and it was heading east. It was going his way. Billy watched it pass with its bells ringing. He made no attempt to stop them; that was not what he had in mind. Then another vehicle appeared. It was a shiny sedan car that looked as though it belonged to some toff or other, not the sort of vehicle Billy would ever consider approaching for compassion. He watched it pass, staring defiantly at the elderly man in the back seat who stared back at the scruffy urchin as he glided by.

Then another vehicle came into sight, approaching from the west. It was a beer cart, pulled by a pair of magnificent dray horses. This was the sort of thing Billy had in mind, he watched with interest as the horses slowly came closer. After what seemed like eternity to him, but only a few minutes in real time, the horses hit a slight bend in Fleet Street and slowly, letter by letter, Billy could see the signwriting down the side of the cart. 'The Old Truman Brewery' was painted in bright red letters. He had no idea what the letters actually were but he knew those bright red symbols with their intricate black and gold edging. The cart was from the Truman Brewery in Brick Lane and it would be bound to go down Commercial Street. If he could hitch a ride he was as good as home.

He pushed himself away from the wall he had been half perched on and hopped pathetically into the road. He attracted the attention of the drayman, who flicked his reins lazily, just to warn the horses that he might be forced to stop, depending on the lad in the road that they would soon be on top of. The horses plodded along at the same easy pace, they too had seen the lad. They did not consider him a threat in even the remotest of scenarios, but they accepted the signal from the drayman and started to slow their pace.

"Hey, Mister!" Billy called as the large cart drew nearer. "Where you 'eaded, Mister?"

The man looked down at him; Billy had his undivided attention now. He pressed home this slight advantage.

"Only I slipped an' my Ma will be worried sick an' I gotta get back 'ome." The man was frowning slightly as he began to understand the gist of what the lad was hollering. Billy pressed on. "See, I knows you, well, I knows your wagon an' I thought, well, I 'oped, that if you was 'eading back east, back to Brick Lane, then maybe, you could see your way to givin' this boy a lift." Billy winced dramatically, adding in as weak a voice as he could muster, "Only I'm worried sick about me poor Ma, you know."

The cart had been slowing as it approached him and now Billy was alongside it. He decided to take the bull by the horns and push his luck that final bit. He reached out for the cart, then grunted as though in considerable pain and pulled his hands away, letting his shoulder fall against the cart and allowing another noise of pain to escape through his lips. The man flicked his reins, ordering the horses to stop. They did so without any fuss and once the cart was stationary, Billy fell gratefully against its side again. Profusely offering thanks to the stranger for his kindness and in order to ensure that the deal was done, he pulled himself up on to the bench seat beside the drayman, who now studied this cheeky little lad with amused interest on his face.

"Climb up 'ere, if you like. Oh, you already 'ave, I see." They smiled at each other and the driver flicked his reins over the backs of the horses as a police car raced past them, its bells jangling. They watched it tear down the road as though clearing a path so they and the magnificent shires could simply plod along behind it.

"Not after you, I 'ope," the drayman said, a smile playing across his lips.

"Not after me, I'm good, I am," Billy protested.

The man threw his head back and roared with laughter.

Billy looked up at the huge brute of a man with his laughter lines, testament to years of a happy disposition. He decided that he liked the fellow. He relaxed and laughed along at the sheer joy of his clean getaway.

"Where you want me to drop you, little man?"

"Commercial Street on the corner of Dorset Street, that's where I'm 'eading please, Mister."

The smile slipped from the drayman's face as he looked down at the scruffy boy beside him. "Dorset Street, that's where you live, is it?"

"Near there, yeah. Do you know it?" Billy asked brightly.

"Yeah, I know it," the man replied, the smile now gone from his face.

The two shire horses made their way solemnly down the left-hand side of Fleet Street. Hundreds of bombers passed over them, explosions boomed out all around. Spitfires chased Stukas across the early evening sky and fire and bullets crashed, whizzed and spluttered to a hundred sounds of death and mayhem.

The horses ignored it all, steadfast creatures with a genuine ability to live firmly within the moment and this precise moment they were still gloriously alive. Above their shoulders the drayman and Billy both went to great pains to ignore the carnage that London had experienced. They both sat with their own private concerns, plodding slowly eastwards. Neither could ignore that most of the bombs tonight seemed to be landing in the place to which they were heading. They were human; of course they worried about the future and what it might bring. The horses took them ever closer enjoying each step of the journey. Billy resolved to be strong and to be a man. The drayman assumed his wife would be gone to the shelter by the time he returned.

They made it back without incident. Finally, Billy was able to say, "Over there, where those blokes are standin' on that corner. Drop me there."

The drayman lazily flicked his whip and smiled down at the confident little boy. Full of East End bravado and prepared for whatever hand life dealt him.

The drayman knew Dorset Street by reputation, knew it was where a band of thugs operated from. He even had a few colleagues that had come across the gang for the wrong reasons. No wonder the kid acted tough if he had to deal with that type.

"'Ere all right?" He slowed the cart to the side of the road and brought it skilfully to a halt directly alongside Dorset Street.

"Perfec'. Ta very much for the ride, it's much appreciated, Mister."

He lowered himself gingerly to the ground as one of Reggie's men came over to see why the cart had stopped.

It was Alf and he was in no mood to deal with thick, lumbering draymen. He couldn't park those bleeedin' horses there, that was for damn sure. He was blocking their view up the main road and he was just about to be moved on, but look who's climbing down out of the cart. So this beer guy, he must be a good guy. Still, it never hurts to check and Reggie always wanted to know the ins and outs of everything. It was always better to ask a few questions.

"Hey kid, where've you bin?" He attempted a smile at Billy; fortunately the boy knew what the facial gesture was supposed to be, so it didn't frighten him. Billy mused 'Kid', 'who did 'e think 'e was, Jimmy Cagney?'

Billy nodded a greeting then swiftly followed it with a grimace as his painful foot made contact with the road. Alf was on it in a flash. He glared at the drayman now but spoke to Billy as he did so.

"Did 'e do this to you, kid?"

"No. No, 'e 'elped me, Alf, 'e brought me 'ome. 'e's all right, Alf." Billy grabbed Alf's shoulder, "Lead me down to the alley, will ya?"

"No, I will bleedin' not. Get one o' your little pals to do it, I'm busy". He shook the boy off.

Billy smiled again at the drayman who was already pulling back out into the traffic, waved his hand and gave the man a wide smile.

"Thanks, Mister!" he shouted and the man nodded at him as his cart joined the throng of other carts and motor vehicles going about their business.

Billy hobbled for home stopping every few steps to holler as loudly as his lungs would allow.

"JACK! 'ARRY! TOMMY!" Then he would wait for a reply before shuffling a little nearer before repeating his loud calls.

Inside the court Jack was the first to prick up an ear.

"Ssssh," using the age-old fingers on the lips signal Jack cut Harry off in mid-sentence. The three of them held their breath and listened. The whine of bombs, the shouts of the market traders, a child wailing in abject terror, a dog barking and the crackle of flames were all there. They continued listening, but heard nothing of any significance. Finally, Jack broke the silence in the room.

"Maybe it was nothin'," he said, but they all knew it most certainly was not. It was something. Jack didn't make too many mistakes and Billy was still out there somewhere.

When the call came again they all heard it and raced each other out into the courtyard, whooping and hollering with youthful exuberance. One minute they had been right down at the bottom of their spirits and the next instant they were flying again and every little thing is going to be all right.

Of course, Jack had reached Billy first. "What 'appened?" He glanced down at Billy's twisted shape and moved closer so he could support his friend's weight.

"What 'appened?" he repeated as Harry and Tommy closed in and Billy used them as crutches to quicken his pace.

"Let's get inside first, then I'll tell you."

Halfway down the alley Alf's ears pricked up at that last telling sentence. 'Let's get inside first' can only mean one thing. Those kids are up to something and he was going to find out whether it was some childish nonsense or not. As Reggie kept insisting, 'those kids are going to surprise us all one day' and perhaps that day had finally arrived.

The boys went into their room and shut the door.

"Where's Pops?" Billy wanted to know.

"Don't worry," Harry told him, "we seen 'im earlier, goin' out for a drink, 'e was."

Billy nodded and then turned to Jack. They held each other's eye before Billy smiled at his pal and asked,

"So? What was in that bank that made you come runnin' out so fast? Anythin' good?"

Jack rose to his feet and crossed the room. He commanded the room as though it were the stage at the Palladium itself.

With a bend of the hips, he reached deep into his jacket, produced the black wallet and with a flourish worthy of any magician he flashed the fivers at Billy.

"Wow." Billy was impressed. "'Ow much is there?" he wanted to know.

"There's four of 'em, twenty quid." The grin widened further, "Twenty bleedin' quid, Billy."

The boys joined arms and danced in a circle around Billy and around the threadbare, old room as Alf listened outside the broken window, smirking.

Finally, Billy interrupted their high jinks and brought them crashing back to earth.

"We can't 'ave crisp fivers like that. They'll think we nicked 'em." He paused to give them time for more hysterical laughter.

Billy looked down at the dirty floor and uttered the words they had all been desperate to hear. "We'll 'ave to take 'em to Reggie."

Outside Alf smirked to himself and crept away.

The mood in the room was not so merry now.

"'Ow much do you think 'e'll give us?" Tommy, ever the pragmatist, wanted to know.

"I don't know, but I know I can't go over there with this ankle." He slumped down into the chair. "You go, Jack. Get us a good deal."

Nobody had even mentioned that Billy had missed his council meeting with Mr. Cooper, his ticket out of the slums and, possibly, his route to a better life. It hadn't been mentioned but it was too late now. Billy had lined his rocks up in the bushes, ready to assist in a bank robbery. He had known that he was going to miss the appointment that could change his life and might take him away from all this. He wasn't really sure that was what he wanted. He wanted to stay with his pals in the East End, stay where they all said he belonged.

He was ready to do a deal with the devil.

"Here, Jack, take these to Reggie an' get what yer can."

Jack skipped across the courtyard and was soon admitted to the inner sanctum.

Reggie sat at his table with four crisp bank notes laid out in front of him and Jack hovering opposite him.

"So, Billy told you to come to me for 'elp, did 'e?" Reggie asked again.

"Yes, that's right, Mr. Lawson." Jack was clearly in awe of the man.

Reggie slid four sixpence pieces across the desk towards the boy.

"Take these, Jack. That's one each, mind an' tell Billy I'll see 'im later, all right?"

Jack nodded and made to pick up the coins.

"What about the rest of you?" Reggie asked, "'Appy to accept my 'elp again, are yous?"

"Oh yes, Mr. Lawson, we like it 'ere," Jack said with a nervous smile.

Reggie smiled back at him and sat back, watching the lad scoop up the coins and exit the room.

Chapter Thirty-Four

13th May 1941

BILLY and his boys sat around in their room. There had been a massive raid on 11th May but nothing for two days and two nights now and they were, if truth be told, a little bit bored. They had not taken the cart out since Sunday night, two days ago. Billy had been obliged to go to Reggie asking for more coins and now he had to do the same thing again.

"Come in, Billy, 'ave a seat." Reggie motioned to a chair and waited while Billy lowered himself into it.

"What can I do for yer, young man?" The mobster acted concerned, as though he wanted to help.

"Well, we was wondering if we could 'ave another sixpence each on the back of those fivers." Billy kept his gaze lowered. He needed food, they all did.

"Well, I would love to 'elp but I'm a bit strapped for cash at the moment." Reggie attempted another look of concern as he lent in closer to the boy. "I'll tell yer what I'll do. You boys can put all that rooftop skill to some use an' open a few windows for my boys tonight. Then, we will 'ave a whip round an' get some grub money together for yous all, all right?" Reggie wasn't smiling now or looking concerned.

"Because to be honest, Billy, all that rescuin' people, well, it looks like the Blitz is over. It looks like you boys is out of a job now, don't it?"

Billy nodded.

"So maybe it's time to put all that behind yer. Maybe it's time to let me do the thinkin' for you again, eh?"

Again, Billy nodded. He knew Reggie's words made sense.

It was time to put all those silly notions behind him. He had done his best to join the ranks of civilised society, he and his boys and they hadn't been wanted. Well, that was fine. Reggie wanted them and that was probably the best thing. At least they wouldn't have to learn anything new. This was what they knew and where they belonged.

"So go 'ome. Alf will let you know when, all right?"

"All right, Mr. Lawson," Billy agreed.

"Good boy, off you go then."

"Oh, 'ere, what's this?" Reggie fished a silver coin out of his pocket and flicked it across the room.

"Go an' get your boys somethin' to eat down the market."

Billy snatched the coin out of mid-air and secreted it about his person.

"'Cos you can't run an army on empty stomachs, remember that, boy!"

"All right, Mr. Lawson, I will."

Reggie waited until Billy had left the room then turned to face the stranger sitting patiently across the table.

"So, you used to be part of Mickey Tipping's mob, did yer?"

The old man across the table nodded.

"Yeah, until I had to leave one day in a bit of an 'urry. You know how it can be. Anyways, I ended up in Australia and it's taken a hell of a time to get back to good ol' London town."

Reggie nodded; he knew how it could be.

It was forty years or more since Mickey Tippings had been shot dead in a war with the Watney Street mob. Didn't they used to be the Blind Beggar mob back then? It was so long since Reggie had heard the old stories he wasn't sure. Anyway, it was a long time ago, back in Jack the Ripper's day, back in the last century. Reggie had not even been a babe in arms.

"Well," he told the old man, "the only person still around from those days would be ol' Percy. 'E lives in the far room from 'ere. Over near the alley."

"Ol' Percy, well, ain't that a turn up for the books. Didn't 'e live in that very same room when 'e was young Percy?"

Reggie Lawson snorted, "'ow the 'ell should I know? Anyways, 'e's the only one still around from those days. So, if you want to know what 'appened to your wife, if anyone knows, it's Percy."

"Well, Mr. Lawson I thank you very much for your time and your local knowledge an' I will leave you to your business."

The old man rose unsteadily to his feet and hobbled to the door.

Chapter Thirty-Five

WHEN I arrived back at the room there was nobody in. I slumped down on the bed and was so exhausted I fell asleep almost immediately. I was suffering from the nightmares worse than ever now that booze was no longer in such a plentiful supply. I heard someone knocking on the door at one point, but I ignored them and they went away.

It was only when the boys returned, many hours later, that I was woken by the smell of the fresh bread they carried in with them.

"Pops, Pops, you awake?"

I heard Billy calling me and rolled over to face him. He caught the slight opening of my eye and I heard him say, "'ave some bread, Pops, while it's still warm."

I raised myself on one elbow and ripped a hunk off the loaf he offered to me. I swung myself round into a sitting position and Jack immediately commandeered the space I had just vacated. He tipped an assortment of pocket watches out of a bag. I ate my bread in silence, ignoring his haul. What they got up to out there was really none of my business.

"Did you see that ol' fella?" Harry asked me, between mouthfuls of bread.

"What ol' fella?" I asked curiously.

"Just some ol' fella. Said 'e knew you from the ol' days, is all." He tore off another hunk and stuffed it into his mouth.

I was instantly suspicious. An old fellow! From the old days! Not once in fifty years had anybody shown up from the old days. They were all dead.

"What did 'e look like?" I asked.

"Old!" said Jack and they all laughed. All, except me, I frowned.

Chapter Thirty-Six

THE boys had stuffed the bread into their mouths as fast as they possibly could. Then in a whirlwind of laughing and mocking they had spilled outside and disappeared into the night. I was left alone in the room. I was awake now. 'An old fella, from the old days.' Nobody ever returned here. That statement was riddled with suspicion. I had more than enough reminders from the old days. I carried them around in my head. I certainly didn't need any more. I was tired of the old days. All that remained were these stinking old buildings, me and *that* knife. My eyes darted down to the secret step.

I lowered myself down onto my knees and for the first time in a while, teased the floorboards apart and fished around inside the cavity. I felt the sack touch my fingertips; I grabbed it and scraping my wrist, pulled it free. As I did so the old hessian wrapping fell apart.

I listened for any unfamiliar sounds before I opened what remained of the hessian wrap, then I slipped the knife into my pocket. I had kept it hidden for far too long. It was keeping me tied to those terrible days. I could see that now. Maybe if I got rid of the knife, the memories, the old man and things from the past would leave me to see out my days in peace. I lifted the latch and headed outside.

I ignored the familiar taunts from the men at the oil drum and shuffled down the alley with my eyes fixed on the ground. I paused only for a passing wagon, crossed Commercial Street and headed south, directly towards the river.

Billy and Jack were coming back from the market. They saw Pops crossing the busy road and they also saw the mysterious old man peeping from behind a cart and then following Pops. They set off in discreet pursuit.

"That's the old fella," Jack said.

"Let's follow 'em, Jack." Billy could spot suspicious behaviour from a mile off and he was highly suspicious of the stranger following his grandfather.

The two boys hugged the shadows of the dark walls that so enhanced the gloom of their surroundings. They were experts at moving through these filthy streets without being spotted and they did so now. The mist coming off the river hid them further.

I reached the river and pulled the knife from my pocket. I took a couple more steps closer to the edge. I wanted to make sure it flew into the water and didn't end up embedded in the muddy foreshore. The wet grass sucked at my feet and I slipped over. As I was hauling myself back up I heard my name being called and I looked around.

He was much older and he looked frail and worn out now but I knew him instantly. He held a pistol in the manner of one who was used to holding a weapon and he was pointing it right at me.

"'Allo Percy, 'ow are you, son?"

"You!" I wanted to scream, but I could not make a sound. The silence was broken by the click of a pistol being cocked ready to fire.

I threw myself back down on the grass just as I heard the shot ring out. A searing pain tore through my shoulder as I landed with a thud, knowing I was hit. A second shot, closely following the first, echoed through the gathering mist. Somewhere nearby a flock of pigeons exploded into the air. I heard the long grass being frantically pushed around and had no idea who was doing the pushing or how close they were. I reached around to feel my throbbing shoulder as a scream resounded through the mist. It was rolling off the river now and playing tricks with the acoustics. I had no idea if the scream had emanated in front of me or behind, I crouched low. Did I scream?

Heavy footsteps raced through the vegetation and thinking he was coming to finish me off I tried to roll over, tried to move. Instantly pain seared through my shoulder. I could do no more than cower face down in the dirt. It was pathetic; this was no way to die. I forced myself to roll the other way; if I was to take my last breath here, I wanted to at least see him coming at me. I lay shivering, my shoulder was throbbing in agony, and the warm sensation of blood was rolling down the neck of my shirt. I didn't have to look, I knew I was bleeding heavily. Maybe I was dying after all.

I lay panting, extremely aware that around me all was silent. It was a very brief respite. Suddenly someone was crashing through the grass, closely followed by a series of chaotic noises then, immediately, a second blood-chilling scream. A whimper escaped my lips, I covered my mouth with my one functioning hand and another bolt of pain ripped through my shoulder as I struggled for balance.

Again all went quiet, then the grass began to wave in front of me and once again someone was racing through it, causing it to sway and move. I shielded my eyes in anticipation of the shot or knife that was surely about to appear.

The grass in front of me suddenly swayed again with the force of somebody behind it. I braced myself, was this going to be it.

It was Billy, my Billy, crashing through the tall grass so fast he had to jump right across me to avoid stepping on me.

"It's 'im Billy, kill 'im son, kill 'im."

Billy landed like a cat and stood over me breathing hard with a face like thunder. As we locked eyes I heard two shots ring out. Their echo barely gone before Jack appeared at Billy's shoulder.

"He's dead now Pops, 'e's dead alright," Jack said coldly.

"Come on Jack we gotta get outta here. 'Elp me lift Pops, let's go, afore the Bobbies show up."

I let them haul me to my feet and drag me across the wet grass, away from the river's edge. The mist was lifting as quickly as it had fallen, we needed to move. The boys knew if they got me back to our little hotbed of lawlessness we would be safe.

As they guided me past the old man I couldn't resist glancing down. His head lolled at an impossible angle. A trail of dark red blood stuck thin wisps of hair across his face. At last I felt some degree of satisfaction.

"What's this?" Jack asked, bending down and scooping something shiny out of the grass.

I tore my satisfied eyes away from the dead shape and looked across at him.

"What's what, son?"

"This," he held up the knife in his right hand to show me, not wanting there to be any confusion. "This, what you was goin' to throw in the river."

I dragged my feet, looking down, his dead, cold eyes stared back at me. I turned my back on him, faced the boys and sighed heavily.

I glanced around to make sure that we were alone, and then told them straight. After fifty-three years the words danced easily off my tongue.

"That my boy, is Jack the Ripper's knife an' that…," I turned back around and faced him for one last time and leaning on Billy pointed at the body lying at our feet, "… and that is Jack the Ripper."

THE END

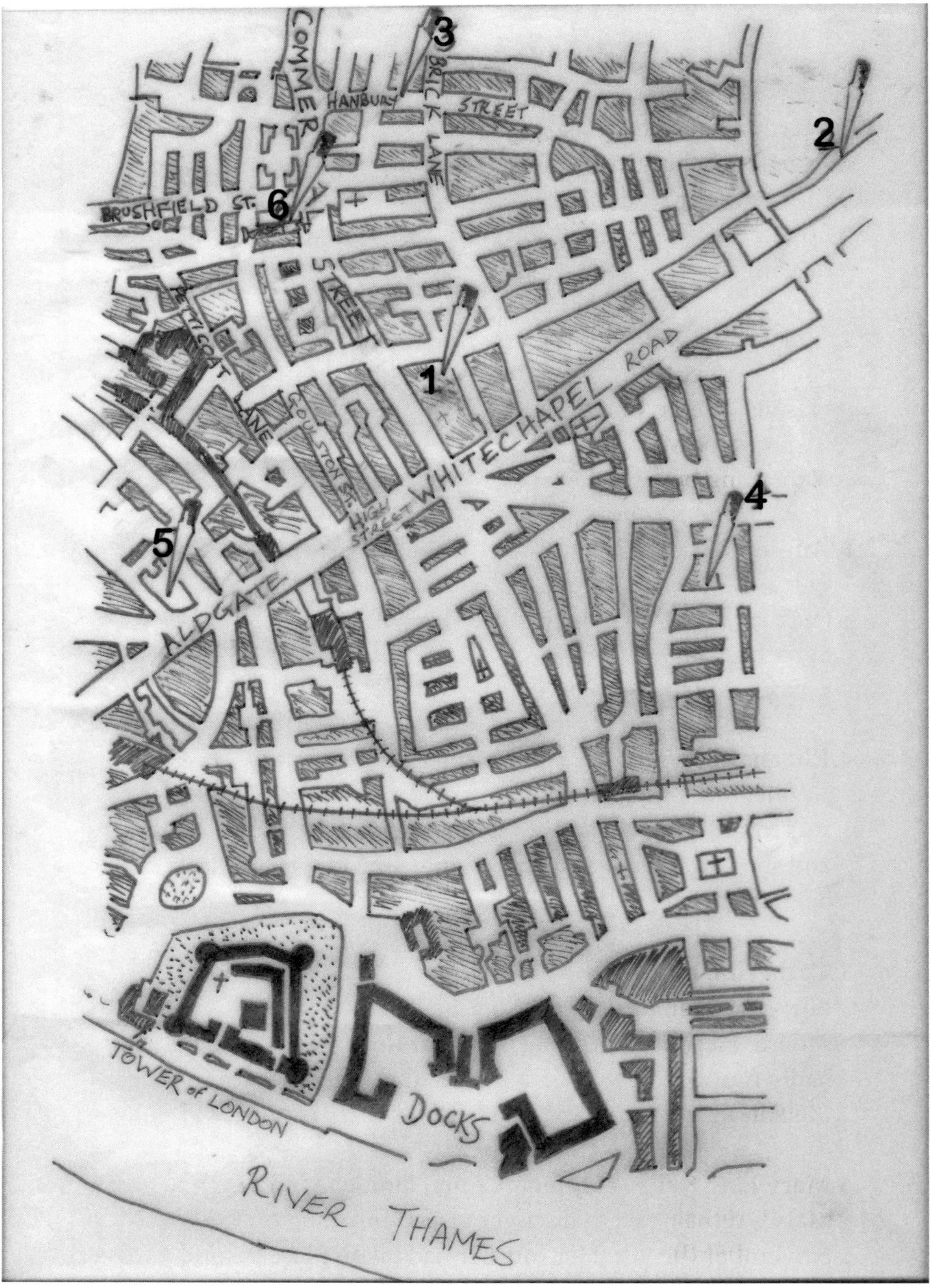

COMMER
HANBURY
BRICK LANE
STREET
BRUSHFIELD ST.
1
2
3
4
5
6
WHITECHAPEL ROAD
WHITECHAPEL
HIGH STREET
ALDGATE
TOWER of LONDON
DOCKS
RIVER THAMES